Hivemind: Utopia

Mackenzie Spenrath

Published by Mackenzie Spenrath, 2023.

This is a work of fiction. Similarities to real people, places, or events are entirely coincidental.

HIVEMIND: UTOPIA

First edition. December 15, 2023.

Copyright © 2023 Mackenzie Spenrath.

ISBN: 979-8223783503

Written by Mackenzie Spenrath.

"We live in capitalism, its power seems inescapable—but
then, so did the divine right of kings."
Ursula K. Le Guin

Chapter 1

I'm barely eighteen years old, how am I already fed up with adult life?

I've only been working for a few months now, since graduating high school, and that's long enough for me to dread the next, oh, fifty or so years of slaving under this oppressive system. I still live at home, of course, along with basically everyone else in my age group. People in this country used to leave home when they finished school and started working, or moved on to college. Not so much anymore.

I live in a world where housing is treated as a commodity instead of a human right. The idea of someone legally being able to extract wealth from the lower class by simply having enough capital to buy property or inherit it in the first place, and the fact that their wealth is nearly universally gained by unethical means, disgusts me. I find it unbelievably hypocritical for the general population to hate ticket show scalpers but approve of rent-seeking landlords. I don't see a difference. Neither provide value, they simply hoard something of value from those who need or want it by virtue of having the capital and ability to buy it first.

Despite growing up in reasonable comfort, financially at least, I've always felt an unwavering empathy for those struggling every day to live. The house me and my mother live in was purchased decades before housing prices became completely unsustainable. It's now worth at least ten times what my mother and father originally paid for it, but my mom refuses to realize those gains, considering she feels it would be wrong to capitalize off of the human need for shelter.

We have real estate agents knocking at our door weekly, desperate to get another listing and make tens of thousands of dollars for simply connecting a buyer and a seller. Both me and my mom know that any potential buyer will either be a trust fund kid or a corporate stooge looking for a new investment vehicle to extract wealth from the working class while having their mortgage paid by a worker toiling under another capitalist leech, unable to get approved for their own mortgage because of these scum-suckers. It's a vicious cycle of exploitation.

There's a knock at my bedroom door. I lift my head from the pillow it was resting on, comfortably in my bed, and call out, "Yeah?"

The door slowly opens, followed by my mother's face peering through the gap. She asks, "You decent?"

"Yes Mom, you can come in," I reply.

She enters the room, carefully stepping on the parts of the floor that aren't covered by dirty clothes, and makes her way toward the computer chair by my desk, opposite the bed. She pulls the chair out from under my desk and sits down on it, facing me. "Hi, honey. How are you feeling?" she asks.

"Oh, you know. Weird. Confused. Annoyed."

"Me too. I'm getting tired of all of this attention. We managed to avoid it for so long, luckily. But when someone as... uh... *controversial* as your father dies, it's kind of a big deal."

"I know, I know. I just want to forget he even existed, honestly. I was teased enough in school, just for being 'lucky' enough to be related to him and Grandpa. It doesn't help that you guys felt the need to pass on the family name, despite everything."

My legal name is Maximus Karlson, the same as my father, who was named after *his* father. Honestly, I've always secretly liked the name; at face value, it's badass. I refuse to respond to it though, instead going by 'Max' for my entire life. Whenever a new teacher or substitute did roll call in school, I could see the confusion on their face as they read my name aloud. It was typically followed by snickers and gasps from my classmates. I was always quick to correct them, explaining that I answered only to 'Max'.

"Like I've said a thousand times, your dad chose it, not me. He wanted to continue to honor his father. You seem to ignore that Maximus the First was an extremely accomplished scholar and engineer before defecting," my mother says.

"Yeah yeah, whatever. Don't you have to leave for work soon?" I reply.

"I'm about to leave. I just had to tell you something important first."

"Have at it, I'm all ears."

"So listen, I understand why you skipped the reading of your father's will this morning. I know you try to distance yourself from him, and because we've been divorced for almost your entire life and you haven't even seen or spoken to him in over a decade, I don't blame you. I mean, he essentially disappeared off the face of the Earth."

"Okay…"

"I'm getting to the point, don't worry. Your father left you something in his will. Uh, technically, it was your grandfather's. It's a vintage watch that was previously passed down from your grandfather to your father. They both wore it for their entire adult lives and now it's yours. If you want it."

"I wouldn't be caught dead wearing anything linked to Dad or Grandpa."

"I know, I know. But it was in your father's will. He wanted you to have it. Think about it, okay? Even if you just keep it stuffed away in a drawer somewhere. There's also a note. I didn't read it, so I can't tell you what to expect if anything. Anyway, it's in a box on the kitchen table downstairs. I have to go, love you." She leans over the bed to give me a quick hug and kiss.

"Love you too, bye," I say.

After she leaves the room and closes the door behind her, I stay in the same spot I'd been for most of the morning, unwilling to get up or do anything productive. I want to conserve my energy for work, I'll need all of it. I don't particularly appreciate her intruding on my relaxation time, especially not with that nonsense.

I don't want to think about my father anymore. I've been perfectly fine with how the last decade or so has gone. When I heard the news about his passing a few weeks ago, I didn't feel anything, positive or negative. I hardly knew the guy. Even before he disappeared, he was barely around enough to spend time with me as a child. My mother has had full custody of me for almost my entire life, since they divorced when I was very young.

When my grandfather defected to the Soviet Union in the seventies, my father, Maximus the Second, was faced with extreme scrutiny from the authorities. He and his ex-wife, my mother, were under constant surveillance. The FBI didn't even try to hide it. They had an unmarked black car sitting outside of their house twenty-four hours a day, with a black-suited occupant always sitting in the driver's seat, silently watching. The phone made a clicking noise every time my mother picked it up to make a call.

From what I've heard from my mother and what I learned in school about the Cold War, it was a pretty tense time between the Soviet Union and the US. When America's most esteemed scholar and engineer, Maximus the First, defected from his country of origin to join the other side, it almost resulted in a full escalation of nuclear war. It was colloquially referred to as the Second Missile Crisis, after what happened between Cuba and the US in the early sixties. For the second time in a decade, both world superpowers seemingly had their fingers on the trigger, ready to end the world as they knew it.

This was a massive slap in the face to America, especially considering it happened only a few months after they put a man on the moon. They went from declaring victory in the space race to losing one of their greatest assets and visionaries. But ultimately, the Soviet Union crumbled a couple of decades later, and the US won the Cold War. And five years after that, Maximus the First died.

Even though the defection of my grandfather didn't result in a Soviet victory, my family has still faced scorn and derision since then. It didn't help that my father not only refused to condemn Maximus the First, but he also went so far as to praise him and the Soviet Union every chance he got. He was vocal about his complete and utter disdain for America, the West, and Capitalism.

For this reason, among others, I detest my namesakes—both of them. I actively avoid political discussions because I am terrified of being potentially associated with my father and grandfather in any way, shape, or form. But secretly, and ashamedly, I didn't necessarily disagree with my father. I was forced into capitalism, I didn't have a choice. I hate nearly every aspect of this society. Since graduating high school and entering the workforce, I wake up every day furious to be laboring under capitalism. Quite frankly, I think America is a veritable shithole of a country.

Nearly every week I hear news of another mass shooting. Another bomb dropped on innocent brown kids in the Middle East. A new trillionaire popping up who built their wealth off the backs of the working class, most of whom couldn't even afford to see a doctor. Or pay for insulin. Or shelter.

But my self-suppressed leftist ideology probably comes more from my mom than my dad or grandpa. After all, the thing that drew my mom and dad to each other in the first place was their identical political leanings, considering they met in college at a Young Communist League event. Even though I barely knew my dad, I was raised by someone else with a complete and utter disdain for capitalism, and America specifically.

I grew up listening to commie punk with my mother, and to this day it is still my go-to genre almost every time I put on my headphones. My mom and I used to watch the local news during dinner every night, and scoff at how they misdirected from or downplayed the failings of capitalism. I've developed a firm yet completely justified distrust of Western liberal media. It's unbelievably obvious to me how desperate the media machine is to suppress anything that doesn't fit a positive narrative of late-stage capitalism.

Every puff piece I see on the latest cancer-stricken kid meeting their crowdfunding goal to pay for treatment leaves me with a bad taste in my mouth, despite the 'wholesome' spin the media puts on it. I don't even think charity should need to exist in a developed society, I think it should be baked into the system to help out the least fortunate. But alas, capitalism forces those marginalized people to beg for scraps, hoping to catch the attention of the local rich 'philanthropist'.

My phone emits a buzzing sound from the side table next to my bed, breaking me out of my daydream stupor. It's time to get ready for work.

Chapter 2

Stepping out of the steaming shower, I reach for a soft towel hanging on the metal rack attached to the bathroom wall. As I dry myself off, I can't help but run my fingers through my shaggy brown hair that falls just past my shoulders. I refuse to use a hairdryer; it always gives me too much volume, making me look like a reject from a Harlequin novel cover shoot. Definitely not as attractive as those 'Fabio' types, though, if anyone actually finds them appealing.

As I make my way towards the bathroom mirror, I nearly stumble over a heap of unwashed laundry on the floor. I consider myself fortunate to have my own bathroom separate from my mother's. It's conveniently located just down the hall from my bedroom. My mom has her own en suite in the master bedroom, and there's a powder room downstairs for guests to use. But this particular bathroom is mine and mine alone, and therefore it reflects the chaotic state of my bedroom.

I methodically wipe the condensation off of the mirror, taking a quick peek at my reflection. I don't know why I bother; I've always been average-looking in every way imaginable, and that's how I see myself as well. Just average. I gaze intently into the mirror, only to see my dull brown eyes staring back at me. I stretch up onto my tiptoes, hoping to appear taller, but I soon give up and return to my usual height of five feet and ten inches. I tightly grasp the skin on my stomach, attempting to find some trace of fat. No matter what I eat, I remain at a steady, average weight with no fluctuations in either direction. My body seems determined to stay at this completely unremarkable mass. I raise my arms above my head and try to flex my biceps. Not much muscle anywhere, either. I steer clear of the gym and was never interested in organized sports growing up.

After making sure I'm completely dry, I wrap the towel around my waist and head back to my bedroom to finish getting ready. My mom took off to toil at her boring desk job in an office downtown, so I have the house to myself. I know I don't need to cover up, since no one can possibly see my nude body, but I do anyway because it would be strange to roam around completely naked.

I'm too awkward to try to stand out, so I tend to dress in a nondescript manner, opting for blank, neutral-colored clothes without logos. I rarely step foot in a shopping mall, preferring instead to buy nearly everything I wear at local thrift stores. After all, it's much better for the environment to buy secondhand. I rummage through the laundry pile in the corner of my room, searching for the least wrinkled shirt and pants. Finally, I find a slightly creased button-up and a pair of black slacks. I quickly slip them on and grab my backpack, phone, and keys from the nightstand before heading downstairs to the kitchen.

As soon as I take the last step down the staircase, I come to a sudden halt. Right in front of me, perched on the table, as my mother had promised, is a box with my name clearly written on it. Well, my given name, Maximus. Amidst my usual daydreams and getting ready for work, it had completely slipped from my mind. Something stirring deep within me gives me the feeling that this is no normal hand-me-down. I feel inexplicably drawn towards this plain and unassuming box, like a drowning person desperately reaching for air. At first, I had no intentions of acknowledging this 'gift' left to me by my late father. But now, I feel an overwhelming urge to delve into its contents.

I grab the light gray shoebox-sized container that is beckoning to me, in both a literal and figurative sense, as my name is scrawled on the side. Upon further examination, I realize this *is* just a plain old shoebox. It's strange how such a mundane object can evoke such a strong desire within me to grab onto it and never let go. I carefully and slowly lift the cardboard lid from its base. I half expect a bright light to burst outwards like the briefcase in *Pulp Fiction*, but nothing like that happens. Somewhat disappointingly, the inside of the box contains only two simple items; a blank envelope, and a small green velvety box that almost certainly holds a watch. It was exactly as I was told, yet not quite what I had expected given the overwhelming emotions and sensations rushing through me at this moment.

But it will have to wait. If I linger any longer, I'll be late for work. I suppress the intense urge to inspect the watch and read what my late father wrote to me, close the shoebox tight, and hastily stuff it into my backpack. I no longer have time to grab a snack, I'll have to pay a visit to the cafeteria at work. I shuffle to the front door, slip into my employer-approved steel-toe shoes, and head out into the warm autumn Seattle afternoon.

The singular benefit of my place of work is its proximity to my house. It's only a fifteen-minute walk away. I don't even need to use public transit, let alone buy a car, which seems to be the norm for those unlucky souls with a long commute. I walk to work every day but typically take transit home at night. Not because I'm scared to walk at night, but because my feet are always sore after a long day at work. I don't mind transit, despite it currently being trendy for the general population to espouse their contempt for it due to the ongoing opioid and homeless epidemic.

I use transit fairly often to get around town and honestly don't understand why people are suddenly so adamant about it being unsafe. Sure, you occasionally share a train car or bus with an unfortunate soul who had to turn to hard drugs to dull the pain of living on the streets, but even then, I never feel unsafe. Although, I often forget to consider that it could be due to the privileges afforded to me as a white, able-bodied, cis-het man.

I can't possibly imagine what it would be like for a marginalized person, and I don't bother to try to compare my plight to theirs. However, the loudest voices I see complaining about safety issues on transit tend to come from other men who hold the same privileges as me. If their experience is anything like mine, they have nothing to complain about.

Despite potentially higher instances of addicts hitching rides on transit, there hasn't seemed to be any noticeable increase in muggings or violent attacks. It's nearly the same as it always has been, since the days when I would take a public bus to school five days a week. It's fairly obvious to me why certain people are suddenly starting to complain. I notice that right-leaning people love to take any potential opportunity to denigrate homeless people and drug addicts.

You know, the same kind of idiot that spews classist anecdotes about 'pulling yourself up by your bootstraps' or other such nonsense. 'I work hard for my money, these *lazy* homeless people need to just get a job' and the like.

I reach the end of my street and pivot North to continue towards my place of work. I'm now on a stretch of road that most privileged people tend to avoid. Even though I don't have to take transit to work, I still encounter plenty of homeless and drug-addicted people on my journey. The quickest route for me is straight through a dilapidated former industrial area, where the sidewalks are lined with tents and various piles of what most people consider trash.

I know it isn't trash, though. For some of these unfortunate souls, every earthly belonging they own has to be haphazardly contained in a pile on the street. Is it ugly? Sure. Of course. But I don't understand why people demonize the homeless over this. What are they supposed to do? Every time the cops come and raid these 'tent cities', they just end up moving somewhere else. That's how it is when you're homeless. You have no other option.

As I walk past tent after tent and pile after pile of belongings, I see a few familiar faces poke their heads out past tent zippers and from behind trash can fires or from deep inside scrap wood shanties. Most of the denizens of this street keep their heads, and eyes, down, but not all of them. I've chatted with a few of these people before. I occasionally bring some water bottles or snacks with me on my commute to help out as much as I reasonably can. I receive a few reassuring nods as I pass through, and return them in kind.

Then, I hear a familiar deep, scratchy voice from a ways down the street. "Hey *Maximus*," the voice calls out in sing song.

A figure emerges from behind the tent, a tall and lanky silhouette. His face is weathered and covered in a layer of dirt, giving him a weary and aged appearance. He is dressed in tattered black pants and a stained white shirt that hangs loosely on his frame. The coat draped over his shoulder looks nearly new, though, standing out among his worn and ragged clothing. "Hey, Joe. You know I don't like that name, bud. Nice jacket, is it new?"

"I know I know I know, just messing with you. Some kind soul handed it to me while I was begging out by Main Street. He said it didn't fit him."

"Score! Listen, I'm running late, wanna walk with me?" I ask, already continuing on my path towards the warehouse.

Joe has to break into a half-jog to catch up to me, matching my pace. He's spry for an old man. "Maybe if you're late enough, they'll fire you. Then you wouldn't have to work for those scum suckers," Joe says with a grin.

"I wish, unfortunately there's nothing else out there for me. But you know I hate them too. Maybe not as much as you. Believe me, I know what they've done to you and so many others, even from this very street. I've heard all the stories."

"What, you mean by demolishing my apartment and putting me here on the street? Or buying out the company I gave thirty years of my life to and then laying me off?"

"All of the above. They're soulless, life-sucking parasites. I know. I sold my soul and my back to the devil for a measly little paycheck."

The mega corporation I work for, Idolon, is known for abusing legal loopholes to 'renovict' people from subsidized housing so they can tear it all down and build luxury condos or townhouses in their place. They own nearly half of all real estate in the country. They also have a habit of 'merging' with other companies, laying off most of the existing employees in the process to streamline operations and reel in more profit. They truly are the worst of the worst.

Joe and I walk in tense silence for a few minutes. In the distance stands the colossal Idolon warehouse. With its black, nondescript facade, it towers over everything else in sight. It's by far the largest building I've ever laid my eyes on; you could probably fit a hundred football fields inside. Its presence consumes this part of the city, a menacing symbol of the corporation that operates within its walls, mocking all those who have been exploited or oppressed by its mere existence.

Idolon happens to be owned by a man who had, just a few short years before, become the world's first trillionaire. The first trillionaire, yes, but now not the only trillionaire. Four others have followed in his footsteps since. For decades, the disparity between the rich and the poor has been growing exponentially. Now, with a handful of trillionaires making their debut, it's just another indication of civilization's downfall. I know that from Joe's perspective, that wealth was stolen directly from him and every other person just like him.

I finally break the awkward silence, "Sorry I didn't bring you anything to eat this time, by the way. I had to run right out the door, I've been a bit distracted."

"What, because of your dad?" Joe says.

"Er, yeah, I guess. I just got my, uh, inheritance. It's complicated. But I promise to bring you something next time."

"I appreciate the help but don't feel any obligation. You don't owe me anything. Those assholes do," Joe points towards the black building, "but I'm thankful for it all the same."

"Well, like you said, I do work for those assholes."

Joe comes to a sudden stop as we reach the end of the street, which is the edge of the Idolon parking lot. "I can't go any further. Last time I did they sent a huge security guard out to rough me up. Good luck, Max. Give 'em hell."

I turn around and walk backward, giving a quick salute to my friend. "Catch you next time, Joe". I quickly turn around and jog across the street. After checking the time on my phone, I increase my speed as I weave through the massive parking lot filled with rows upon rows of vehicles. I can't afford to be late, or else I'll face consequences.

When I reach the main entry doors, I stop and turn back around to take one last look at the tent-lined street I had just passed through. I can barely make out Joe's figure, way off in the distance, as he slowly lumbers back to his makeshift home on the side of the road.

Chapter 3

I slide my ID card through the scanner and wait for the gate to open. I hand over my phone and my earbuds, knowing they will be locked away until the end of my shift. Once cleared by security, I make my way through the maze of hallways and elevators to finally arrive at my workstation. As I settle in, my mind wanders back to how I first began my job here at Idolon.

I've only worked at this warehouse for about half a year, but that has already felt like a lifetime. I started working full-time quite quickly after graduating high school. This isn't my first job, however, as I've been working on and off since I was sixteen, with various part-time and odd jobs that I could schedule around schooling. I hadn't even for a second considered pursuing post-secondary education. Going through the US public school system gave me more than enough of a taste for formal education.

Most parents would be disappointed by this decision, but not my mother. She had been disillusioned by post-secondary education from her time in college. Funnily enough, that was before tuition rates became unsustainably high, and graduate salaries became lower and lower. So, with my mother's support at least, and fresh out of high school, I sold my soul to the devil. Idolon is by far the biggest employer in my city. In fact, it's the biggest employer in every major city across the country. For this reason, it was a no-brainer for me to work for them for my first real job. It would be a good way to build up experience, at least.

They are notoriously easy to get hired at. With the amount of turnover that this industry is known for, they hire anyone with a pulse. As long as you pass the stringent security and background checks, of course. The application and interview process was a bit of a paradox. It was the most intense experience I had ever been through, while also being surprisingly easy to manipulate.

The initial online application was fairly standard; name, address, education history, work history. Even though all the information was already on my resume, I still had to manually enter it line by line into an online form after uploading a PDF version of my resume. Annoying, but unfortunately the norm for most job applications these days. The next stage was a background check. I had done one of these before for a different job. That employer had asked for my social security number and a scan of my ID. That was it. That was normal.

But the background check for Idolon was something else. I heard a rumor that it was the same background check the FBI used for their applicants. I had to give them my social security number, birth certificate including date of birth and city of birth, full given birth name along with any nicknames, stated gender plus gender assigned at birth (if different), mother's maiden name, address history for my entire life (well, for the past twenty-five years, which was longer than my entire life so far), and access to **all** of my social media accounts.

It was made quite clear that if I excluded any accounts, they would know and I would be disqualified. I believed them. I had to provide the usernames for all accounts, and if any were privated, I would be disqualified. Fortunately, I'm not very active on social media. I have just one account that I rarely update. Its main purpose is to keep up with friends and family who live in different cities. Upon seeing the requirements of this background check, I almost gave up. But aside from Idolon, job opportunities are slim pickings. Largely because Idolon had either bought out most other businesses or undercut them brutally until they folded.

I was only applying for warehouse work. That's one small facet of what Idolon does. The warehouse is for logistics related to the online marketplace of Idolon and is one of many in my city and most cities around the world. It was how they got their start, decades ago, but since then, they have expanded to nearly every other industry. Social media, traditional media, video gaming, cell phones, smart home systems, transportation, commercial and consumer vehicles, healthcare, pharmaceuticals; you name it, they have their hand in it. Throughout their journey, they've acquired several large competitor corporations, leading to multiple investigations into their anti-competitive practices. However, they always manage to shrug off these accusations with ease.

If you want to advance in the working world, you have to work for Idolon. I knew that selling my soul *and* my privacy *and* my identity to them would give me the best chance at being successful in life, especially after I ruled college out. Everyone I know works for them anyway, including my mom, though indirectly. They bought out the company she's worked at for the last two decades, but they still technically operate separately from Idolon, or so they claim. My mom is unsure of that.

About a week after forfeiting my entire identity to Idolon, I received an email stating that I had passed round one of the security screening. I was in disbelief, I thought for sure that I was done with the process. The second, and hopefully last stage was an in-person interview. They called it an interview, but it was more like an interrogation. To me, it felt like the police interrogation scenes I've seen in movies and on TV.

The interrogator expressed keen interest in my lack of social media presence, insinuating it was suspicious. Unfazed, I maintained my honesty, attributing my avoidance of social media to a personal preference uncommon in my generation. The discussion shifted to political views, in which he subtly probed my stance without mentioning specific ideologies. Being fully aware of potential biases tied to my family history, for instance being a descendant of two of the most influential anti-capitalists, I tactfully navigated these questions, offering measured responses. I steered clear of revealing my true sentiments, recognizing the need to tread carefully in a politically charged environment. At the end, I was told that I would be required to make an account on Idolon's social media platform as a condition of working there. It would be tied directly to my identity, and no doubt would be monitored by the corporation if I ended up working for them.

In total, the interrogation took a little over an hour, although it felt much longer to me. I thought I had successfully portrayed an image of a perfect-but-not-too-perfect little worker drone that *definitely* had no anti-capitalist ideals and would *never* try to start a union. A purely fake image, but the one I would need to work for Idolon. Turns out, I was right. Another week passed and I received an email stating as such. I was invited to a group orientation/interview. Me and the other applicants would be given some basic details about what the position entailed, and then break off individually to have a quick one-on-one interview.

The group session was fairly normal, giving an overview of the different warehouse positions and what specific skills were needed for each, if any. Afterward, we sat in silence while waiting for our turn for the one-on-one. We couldn't kill time on our phones even if we wanted to, as they had to be surrendered at the door. Finally, after about five or six other people were called in, it was my turn.

Job interviews are an exercise in bullshitting, on both sides. The employer wants to convince you that they won't make your life a living hell while you sell your labor to them for pennies on the dollar. You, the potential employee, want to convince them that you would be a perfect little wage slave—but not too perfect, that's suspect—and that you will always follow orders and that you don't care about the money or work/life balance or vacation days or sick days or anything that would potentially make a worker feel like a human instead of a number on a database somewhere in the cloud.

But the interview process for Idolon was nothing like this. They only asked three questions:

Are you willing to work ten-hour shifts four days in a row?

Can you be on your feet for ten hours a day, four days in a row?

If your body was extremely sore from working ten hours a day for the last three days, but you had another ten-hour shift the next day, what would you do to ensure that you could finish your next shift?

The first two questions were easy and simple. I answered in the affirmative to both, because saying no would obviously disqualify me for the position, whether I believed I could do it or not. The third question caught my attention. It was far from the typical interview questions I had prepared for in my mandatory high school career management class. I took a moment to consider it, wondering if there was some sort of hidden meaning behind it.

I eventually said I would go home and relax, put my feet up, and avoid unnecessary strain or tension. Then, before bed, I would draw a bath with Epsom salts to soothe my muscles, and finally, ensure I got eight hours of sleep. The interviewer seemed satisfied with my response, marking a check on her clipboard with a familiar hand gesture, just as she had done for the previous two questions.

That was the easiest part of the process, especially considering the grilling I got the week before. On the way out, I was told that I was shortlisted for the job, but there were no openings at that exact moment. But with the amount of workers that they needed at that facility, jobs opened up fairly frequently. I had to wait for a phone call that could come any day over the next few weeks, but only during business hours. If I didn't answer the call the first time, I would be skipped over for the next person on the list and moved to the end of the line. I was informed that, depending on the length of the list, I may need to go through the entire application process again, because the security check would expire after a certain amount of time.

And so I waited for the call. I made sure to never be away from my phone for more than a minute for the next few days until the end of the day Friday when I was free from the pressure for the weekend. The stress was starting to get to me. I started hearing my phone ring when it wasn't actually ringing, and feeling vibrations in my pocket even when my phone wasn't there. I found myself constantly checking it every few minutes, afraid that I might miss the extremely important call.

The Wednesday of the following week, it finally arrived. As a testament to my fantastic luck, it happened during one of the few times that I stepped away from my phone to grab a snack. It was on the charger in my room due to its extremely low battery. I was in the kitchen, spreading jam on a piece of toast, when I heard the faintest sound coming from upstairs. I was alone, so it wasn't my mom watching TV or anything like that.

I released the butter knife that was in my hand, mid spread, which proceeded to slip off the kitchen counter, clattering on the ground and smearing bright red jam on the clean white tile floor. I was already halfway up the stairs before the knife even made contact with the ground, though. I rushed into my bedroom, sliding to a halt on the soft carpet like a cartoon character. As I reached out my hand to grab the smooth slab of plastic and glass that our entire lives revolve around, the ringing abruptly ended. I missed the call.

"Oh, come on, for fuck's sake. The one goddamn time I'm away from the phone!" I said angrily to the empty room. I tapped on the 'Missed Call' notification and immediately hit the 'Call Back' button, figuring that the recruiter would already be dialing the next number on the list, but knowing that it wouldn't hurt to try anyway. I waited as the phone rang, once, twice, three times. On the fourth ring, it abruptly disconnected. I wasn't even given the chance to leave a voicemail before the call ended.

I called again. Same thing. And again. And a fourth time. But on my fifth and final attempt, it connected on the third ring and a cool-sounding male voice answered. It was someone from Idolon Recruitment Services.

I apologized profusely, explaining that I had just stepped away from the phone for a second.

The recruiter told me I was in luck, and that he had also stepped away from his desk to grab a coffee, and therefore hadn't crossed my name off the list and moved on to the next candidate yet. He told me they had a job available for me. I, of course, accepted it.

—-

A gentle tap on my shoulder jolts me back to reality, interrupting my trip down memory lane.

"Didn't you hear the buzzer? It's break time," my coworker says.

"Oh, thanks. I was in a bit of a trance." I let out a hearty laugh. "Didn't even realize it had been six hours."

All warehouse employees work ten-hour shifts just like me, and Idolon management gives us a thirty-minute break after exactly six hours of working, with two fifteen-minute restroom breaks to be taken whenever the worker needs to. This is a relatively new policy from what I understand, as the year before, there was a major controversy about workers being forced to relieve themselves in water bottles while working in the warehouse.

Before, restroom breaks were strictly planned and thus had logistical challenges. The warehouses have an ample amount of restrooms, but the sheer size of the facilities means that employees could be up to a ten-minute walk away from the closest one. I had seen interviews with workers during that time who claimed that they were often unable to get to the restroom and back in time, and they would get reprimanded if they were late.

Idolon management is quite strict. They have a three-strike system. For the first strike, you have to have a discussion with your supervisor. The second strike results in your shifts for the week being taken away. The third strike is instant termination. This is all in the novel-sized contract that I had to sign during my orientation. You know, the one I *definitely* read before signing. You can have a strike removed if you go six months without accruing another. But interestingly, most workers don't even last that long, since Idolon has some of the highest turnover rates in the working world.

After the restroom controversy made national news and sparked what I considered to be a completely justified public outrage, some changes were made. Now, restroom breaks can be taken at will, and all workers are given an extra five minutes just to ensure they can make it to the cafeteria or restroom in time. This wouldn't have been much of an issue for me, considering I work in the same area all day and the restroom is a short walk down the hall. But you can't always control when you have to 'go', so to say. Workers are humans, not robots, although I'm sure we'll be replaced by robots once the technology is refined enough.

With each step, my aching feet drag along the linoleum floor as I make my way to the cafeteria. There's a good reason I like to bring my own meal to work instead of going to the cafeteria. The prices are fine, that isn't it. The problem is with one of my coworkers, who happens to be from the same high school as me. We even had a few classes together. We work in different areas of the warehouse, but we're on the same shift rotation and thus have meal breaks at the same time. As soon as I enter the cafeteria, I hear that familiar, grating voice.

"Whoa, the commie is here! Wow, long time no see, buddy. How's your daddy doing?" the troll says, his face stretched into a wide, dim-witted grin. He knows that my dad had passed away a few weeks before. It was national news. I choose not to acknowledge him and continue walking towards the counter to place my order.

"Hey, do you know who this dude's grandpa was?" the bully asks some random guy who is just minding his own business, sitting and eating his meal.

"No one cares. Be quiet," the gracious stranger snaps back.

Luckily, this seems to deflate the antagonizer's ego a fair amount, and I slink away so I can grab my meal. I ask for it to be in a to-go box so I can find somewhere outside to eat alone and avoid any other potential annoyances. I pick the vegan option of the day, which is some kind of tofu rice dish. I'm not technically a vegan, but I often eat plant-based when there's an option to. I'm not much of a cook, and neither is my mom, so I don't bother to try to cook at home. That means I tend to eat frozen pizzas and other unhealthy animal-based products fairly often.

It's not that I don't care for the welfare of animals, or for the destruction of the environment that factory farming is contributing heavily to. I just don't think that committing myself to a life free from animal exploitation will make any meaningful change. I respect vegans though, I just don't have the personal conviction I know I would need to fully make the change myself. But I love most of the vegan foods I eat, especially when they're prepared by professional chefs in a restaurant. I haven't ordered animal-based products in a restaurant or the cafeteria at work or school in years.

—-

After finishing up the last few bites of my meal, I lean back against the cool concrete wall that I'm sitting at, in a small fenced-in courtyard just outside of the cafeteria. I've been so distracted while working the first half of my shift that I completely forgot about the box in my backpack, which is currently sitting in my locker, oh, about half a mile away from my current location. I'm constantly amazed at the size of this facility that I work in four days a week. It's bigger than some of the small towns in my state.

I can't help but feel perplexed by the emotions that consumed me when I first laid eyes and hands on that box. It's just a shoebox with some old hand-me-down crap. It would be like if I got butterflies in my stomach from looking at the now-empty food container that previously held my meal. Those last few grains of rice really make my heart palpitate! *Sigh*. It makes no sense at all. Even now, I have a strange urge to go get the shoebox from my locker and open it up to inspect the contents. Why am I feeling so weird about this? I don't even want anything from my dad or grandpa.

No one in my family had seen or heard from my dad in the five or so years leading up to his death. He had turned into a complete recluse ever since making headlines by disparaging America for the umpteenth time. On that last occasion, my father had been approached by a paparazzo on the street and asked what his thoughts were on the latest US drone strike in the Middle East that had killed three innocent children and two innocent adults.

As usual, my dad didn't hold back. This time, he went off on the current president of the US, calling him a war criminal and saying he should face a tribunal at the Hague. He asked the paparazzo multiple times for an answer on who had appointed America as the world police, and why every other country stands by while the US accuses everyone else of human rights violations while ignoring their own.

Far-left circles on the internet loved this, of course, since they completely agree with my dad's views. And so do I, but I'll never admit that publicly. I hate seeing how US-centric the Western imperial core is, and how hypocritical they are about so many things. The US is constantly leading sanctions against other nations and punishing them for crimes they either made up or are personally guilty of committing.

A housekeeper found my father dead in a hotel room on the complete opposite end of the country from where me and my mom lived. A coroner determined the cause of death to be a brain aneurysm. There was no foul play suspected. This had riled up certain conspiracy communities on the internet, or so I've heard. I don't care enough to pay any mind, but I know the fact that someone as controversial as my dad was MIA for five years before turning up dead will spur some... interesting discussion.

The buzzer blares once more, signaling that I have five minutes to return to my designated work station, which is approximately a four-minute walk from my current location. This time, I hear it. Loud and clear. I push myself up from the ground, brushing off crumbs from my pants and tossing my empty food container into a nearby trash can. I make my way back inside the building, the air conditioning hitting me with a chill as I head back to my workstation. Sitting on the ground in that position caused my already aching legs to cramp up, making the journey back to my station uncomfortable and awkward.

I work in the returns department at Idolon, dealing with the endless stream of items that customers send back for various reasons. These can range from simple buyer's remorse to receiving a defective or misrepresented product. Idolon is so ubiquitous and makes so much money that they will typically accept returns for anything, as long as the customer isn't a serial abuser of the return system. It's unbelievable how many items come into the facility for me to process. It truly shows the vastness of Idolon's customer base, and the diversity of products they offer. I've come across items that I never knew existed or didn't think were possible to make yet.

As I stand at my station, a never-ending line of boxes and packages glide by on the conveyor belt. My task is to quickly grab one, examine it for any external damage or signs of tampering, and determine if the item inside can be resold. With each package, I follow strict guidelines to assess its condition and make a decision on its resale potential.

A printed slip of paper with a custom barcode has to be included in the packaging by the customer, or the return will be invalid. I have to find and scan the slip of paper to start the return. Certain manufacturers want items to be sent directly to them instead of being handled by Idolon, whether they are in resellable condition or completely broken. This is common for high-value items. The computer screen in front of me tells me if this is the case. If so, I place it into one of the large metal containers beside me and move onto the next. Four containers are designated for different types of returns, and I sort them accordingly as I work my way through the endless stream.

The containers are swapped out every once in a while throughout the day. They're quite big and heavy, so it's typically a big burly man who comes and swaps in an empty one. They're always in such a big hurry that they end up dropping the fresh container onto the floor, making an earsplitting booming noise. It's quite jarring, especially when I don't notice the workers sneaking up beside me. The noise has gone so far as to drive one of my coworkers to quit a month ago. I remember seeing her visibly flinch every time she heard that thunderous sound.

Most returns are processed in-house, which means I have to decide if they are resellable. The only products that can be resold are the ones that have never been opened or handled. They have to have the original shrink wrap and everything, with zero visible damage. If one single corner of a box is slightly dented, it won't be resold by Idolon. They are extremely strict about this, performing spot checks randomly on the items that I've categorized. I was reprimanded once for accepting a box that had a tiny centimeter-long tear on the shrink wrap. I've never made that mistake again.

Returns that are not resellable are inspected to see if they have all of the included parts and are functional. If so, they're sold in bulk to liquidation outlets for customers to buy at a discount. I was told during training that the remainder of the products, the ones that are broken or missing parts, are recycled, but I found out soon after that it was a lie. Many times while walking through the warehouse, I've seen the clearly labeled metal containers being dumped into the trash; they're being compacted and sent to a landfill. Many of these items are completely usable, or at least fixable. The fact that they're compacted means dumpster divers can't even take advantage of the waste, which is such a shame. Nothing will ever be free under capitalism.

—-

Somehow, the last three and a half hours of my shift have felt twice as long as the first six. But this is the last day of my rotation; I have the next three days off, so I have that to look forward to at least. The watch and note from my dad are still weighing heavily on my mind, and I can't wait to get home and investigate further. Finally, the last alarm of the day sounds off, signaling the end of my shift. I grab my backpack from my locker and pick up my phone and headphones from the security desk before heading to the train to make my way home.

Chapter 4

The house is quiet when I arrive home. My mom will have beaten me here by several hours, but she's most likely in bed asleep by now since it's after midnight. She works early tomorrow morning. I rummage through the fridge and grab a snack and drink, then trudge up the stairs. My legs ache and I can feel my exhaustion setting in, but I push myself to make it to my room – my sanctuary of safety and solace. Collapsing into the computer chair at my desk, I absentmindedly scroll through news articles on my phone while slowly munching on a grocery store muffin. Nothing particularly interesting catches my eye. It's the first time since my dad died that I haven't seen my given name in any of the headlines on my news feed. Maybe people are starting to move on?

My legs are growing numb from sitting in the same position for so long, so I wiggle them around and feel something pressing against my calf. I glance down and see that my backpack, which I had carelessly thrown on the floor next to my chair earlier, has toppled over onto its side. Of course. The backpack. And inside, the box that's been stashed within. It's time to finally open it and discover what my inheritance holds.

Before settling into bed, I strip out of my work clothes so that only my boxer briefs remain. I pull the boring gray box from my backpack and place it on the nightstand next to my bed, grabbing the lump of blanket that was sitting near the foot of the bed, untangling it, and spreading it neatly across the mattress. I fold back the corner nearest to the nightstand to give myself easy access. This is weird. I'm never this methodical. Am I procrastinating?

I grab an extra pillow that was stuffed between the bed and the wall and put it on top of the other so I can prop myself up. Finally, I slip under the covers and into bed. I lean over to the nightstand, carefully pulling the lid off the box as I did earlier today in the kitchen. This time, I lightly place the box lid on the ground. I snatch the green velvet box and the small white envelope out of the shoebox and place them both next to me on the mattress.

I'm not sure which one to inspect first. I settle on the small green box because I don't think I'm ready to read the note. As I turn it over in my hands, I notice that it's quite a bit lighter than I expected. Is there even a watch in this thing? What if it's nothing? But I brush that thought aside immediately. There's definitely *something* in this box.

My fingers dance around the seam that lines all four vertical faces of the velvety box. I feel a rough spot on one side, different from the others. That must be the hinge. I turn the box so the opposite side is facing me. That means this is the side that opens. It's impossible to tell from the box itself. There are no markings anywhere on it. Most watch boxes that I've seen have a logo on the top. Not this one.

I slowly and carefully spread the top half from the bottom, anchoring it with my finger on the back of the hinge. There are butterflies in my stomach that I've been trying to ignore since getting home, but now the feeling is getting unbearable. The lid stops at about a sixty-degree angle. It doesn't open any more than that. Inside, carefully placed, is a well-worn watch.

It's a very simple design. Silver with a white face. The crystal is quite scuffed up and scratched. It's hard to see if there's any writing on the face. The bezel, case, and band all seem to be made out of the same silver metal, which is just as worn as the crystal. There's a crown on the right side of the watch casing. The knob has seemingly seen so much use that a brassy color is showing through in parts from the decades of wear. At least, that's my assumption.

The watch is wrapped around a small pillow. I slowly lift it out and place the watch box back in the shoebox on my nightstand with great care and attention. I turn the pillow-wrapped watch over and start to fumble with the clasp. I'm trying to loosen the band so I can free the watch from the tight grip it has on the small pillow, which is made out of the same green velvet as the box it was residing in.

There's a small edge protruding from the middle of the clasp. It has just enough space for me to slip the tip of my fingernail under and pull upwards. The clasp finally releases, and the watch flops over, causing the small pillow to fall on my chest and roll off the bed and onto the floor. I ignore it. Since I'm still holding the watch backward by the clasp, the rear side of the casing is now clearly visible to me. While the watch face is subtle, the underside of it is anything but. There's a large hammer and sickle symbol beveled into it, taking up almost all of the space on the back casing. I think I know where this watch was made. A smirk creeps across my face. The Soviets were anything but subtle.

I flip it back over so the front is visible and hold the crystal close to my face for a better look. Through the scuffed and scratched crown, I notice a small, almost imperceptible logo on the top of the face. The characters seem to be Cyrillic, but I can't figure out the brand. It's something I've never heard of, though I've never considered myself to be a watch expert. There are three hands, none of which are moving. The thinnest one, which I assume counts seconds, stays in place over the three o'clock position. Simple lines mark the twelve positions; they're not numbered. I stare at the second hand for a short while, seeing if it will move. Nothing.

Perhaps it's broken? I slip the watch over my left wrist and pinch the clasp closed with my right hand. It fits perfectly, no adjustment required. It sits firmly in place, just an inch or so above my wrist. I rotate my hand back and forth, then give it a quick shake to see if it will dig in or shift. Nothing. It's like it was designed specifically for my wrist. The most surprising part is that I can barely feel that I'm wearing it. It's so light and snug to my wrist that it adds no extra weight or strain to my arm.

I drag my attention away from the watch for the moment and pick up the small envelope that is still sitting next to me on the bed. I turn it over in my hands. There's nothing written on either side. The flap is secured in place with adhesive and not hastily tucked in like they sometimes are. Seems like my mom wasn't lying when she said she didn't read it. I struggle to pry open one corner of the flap, but it tears slightly where the adhesive has a firm grip. Instead, I gingerly push my finger through the small hole created by the tear and use it to slice along the folded edge until it rips apart.

I puff the envelope out by squeezing the ends towards each other and peer inside. There's a small slip of paper in it, which is about half the length and width of the envelope it's residing in. I stick two fingers into the envelope and find the edge of the slip of paper. Grasping it tightly, I pull it out slowly and carefully and position it towards the light coming from my bedside lamp.

One side is completely blank. I flip it over, expecting the other side to have a few paragraphs of text at least, but I'm very wrong. There's only one sentence scrawled on it, consisting of five short words.

Make sure to wind it.
Dad

"That's it?" I whisper to myself. I flip it over again, somehow expecting words to populate on the other side. But it's still blank. Back when my dad lived with me and my mom, before he abandoned us, he was a man of few words, so I'm not sure why I'm surprised. This is typical of my late dad, but I thought he might have a bit more to say after he disappeared for the formative years of my life. Guess not.

I read the message again and let it sink in this time. I assumed that the watch was broken, but maybe it's just one of those manual ones that has to be wound up. I've never seen or used one in person, but I know they exist. I hold the watch up to my face again and grasp the crown with my free hand. I turn it, first clockwise, then counter-clockwise, but nothing happens. At all. The hands don't move. The crown is spinning freely, with no resistance.

So, I decide to do what every kid who has grown up with technology does; pull up a video tutorial. I grab my phone, unlock it, and tap on the Idolon Video app icon. I type 'how to wind a watch' into the search bar and select the first result. After skipping past the first third of the video, which is almost always useless filler, I find out from the narrator that you have to pull on the crown to put it into winding mode.

I toss the phone on the bed next to me and carefully undo the clasp on the back of the watch to take it off. As I slide the watch off, I notice a mark on my wrist and hold it up to the light to get a better look. The hammer and sickle symbol beveled into the back of the watch left a clear, noticeable imprint on my wrist. Just what I need. People already know exactly who I am when they hear my given name, now they simply have to take a glance at my wrist.

I roughly rub the imprint. It's already starting to fade. Phew. Back to the watch. I hold it in one hand, grasp the crown with the other, and carefully but firmly pull it outwards, away from the casing. It makes a solid, audible click, then another as I keep pulling. I spin the knob slowly, trying to feel for any resistance. The watch hands are starting to spin. Ah, this is how you set the time. May as well do that first.

I glance at my phone screen, which always shows the time faintly, even when not in use. Who even needs a watch anymore? Honestly. I spin the crown to line the hands up with the current time: 12:55. Once that is set, I carefully push the crown towards the casing to try to get it in that middle position that will almost certainly allow me to wind it up. It clicks. I spin the small knob once again, and this time I feel some clear resistance. I spin it a few times around, clockwise, and then push it back into its original state. The second-hand starts to tick slowly. It works!

I spin the knob back and forth a few more times to make sure nothing happens like the first failed attempt at winding, and when satisfied with the lack of a result, I slip it back onto my wrist and fiddle with the clasp, trying to close it again. As it clips into place, locking the watch securely around my wrist, my stomach drops as if I had just gone down an extremely steep roller coaster. I close my eyes tightly until the unease subsides.

When I open them back up again, I'm not in my bedroom anymore.

Chapter 5

Am I dreaming? Did I fall asleep?

I blink a few times, looking left and right, down both sides of the impossibly long hallway that I now find myself in. I close my eyes for ten or so seconds, squeezing them as tight as I possibly can, then open them. Still not in my bedroom. Still not at home.

I'm sitting on an unfamiliar floor with my back angled against an unfamiliar wall. I'm in the same position as I was when I was tucked snugly into my bed moments ago. But I'm not in my bed anymore. Or my bedroom. Or my house. This hallway is completely unfamiliar to me. It has a distinct atmosphere unlike any other place I have ever been to; but it's giving off hospital vibes.

Art pieces of various sizes adorn the wall across from the one I'm leaning against. They don't seem to have any cohesive theme or anything. Some look like they were drawn by children, most look like an amateur's work, and a few must have been painted by someone with some real talent. There's a floor-to-ceiling mural about twenty feet to my left. It's a sea of colors, with vibrant blues and purples clashing against warm oranges and reds. The lines and shapes seem to swirl and flow into each other, creating a dizzying yet mesmerizing effect.

To my right, between a few medium-sized canvases covered with paint splatters of various colors, is a large, black, matte square, which I assume is a screen. It looks sort of similar to the digital bus ads I see on the street near my house, but nothing is being displayed. It's just a flat black image. I would guess it's around six feet tall and three or four feet wide.

It's eerily quiet here. I have the strange impression that I'm the only person here for miles around. But as soon as I finish that thought, I'm.... not. The hallway instantly floods with people from both directions as dozens of individuals walk through, passing by me. I observe them entering and exiting through openings in the wall that line the hallway.

Dozens soon start to look more like hundreds, or even thousands. The hallway is seemingly endless in both directions, and the further down I look, the more people I see. Not a single one has even glanced in my direction. Kids, teenagers, adults, and elderly people alike are walking past in a determined fashion. The younger-looking ones are dressed in colorful clothes; skirts, dresses, pants, shorts, sweaters, you name it. But every adult is wearing the same outfit. A light gray tee and matching light gray pants. Every. Single. One.

For some strange reason, that's the weirdest part of this whole situation for me. But then I notice that all of the adults have a tiny little white light emitting from their temples. It seems to shine from both sides of their heads. The younger ones in the varied, colorful clothes have nothing of the sort, though.

I'm about to gather up the courage to try to get someone's attention to ask where I am when I notice a mousy-looking girl that's about my age making a beeline straight for me from down the hall. Unlike everyone else, she's looking directly at me and walking in a brisk, determined fashion. The girl's clothes stand out amongst the sea of gray, the light purple top and green pants adding a splash of color to the monotonous hallway. Her shoulder-length brown hair frames her face, highlighting her slightly rounded features. She appears to be around average height for a younger girl, standing at about five and a half feet if I had to guess. There's nothing particularly distinctive about her appearance. I get the weird feeling that she sort of looks like the female version of myself, which would make sense if this is a dream, I guess. She also looks vaguely familiar, in a different way. Like I've seen her before, but I can't be sure.

She stops a few feet in front of me and crouches down, bringing her head to the same level as mine. I can see her lips moving, but I'm not paying attention. My mind is in a fog and I can't make out any words she's saying. After a few seconds, I snap out of it and say, "Sorry, what?"

"I said 'Hi Maximus. My name is Chloe,'" she repeats.

"Uh, how the hell do you know my name? And where the hell am I?" I don't mean to be rude. She seems like a nice girl, but I'm extremely confused and need answers.

"Hivemind told me. Don't worry, you'll understand soon enough. I assume this is quite a jarring experience for you," she says with a genuine smile on her face.

Admittedly, her calm and cool demeanor is having a positive effect on me. My chest isn't as tight as it was a few seconds before, and it's a nice surprise that I don't have to try to explain myself to a random stranger. Chloe seems to have a grasp on the situation, at least. "Okay. I'm sorry. This is just a bit confusing for me," I say. "I was in my bedroom five minutes ago, and now I'm here, in this place that seems otherworldly to me, and I'm still not sure if this is just a dream, although I'm fairly certain I didn't fall asleep."

"Well, I don't mean to scare you, but this place probably feels 'otherworldly' to you because... it is. Another world, that is. Well, sort of. As I said, you'll understand soon enough," she says matter-of-factly.

"You failed on that front. I'm scared," I let out a nervous laugh. "I'm expecting to wake up safe in my bed any time now."

"I promise, you aren't asleep. But speaking of that, we should probably get you some clothes. This is starting to seem a bit like one of those classic dream tropes where you end up in your underwear with hundreds of people around. Because, well, look at you."

I glance down and suddenly feel extremely self-conscious. In my confusion, I failed to realize that I'm wearing only my boxers, since I had been nicely tucked into bed a few minutes ago. My pasty white chest seems to reflect the bright light shining down from the smooth, white ceiling.

"Oh shit. Good idea. Where can we find those? I still have no idea where I am," I say.

"Follow me, Maximus," she replies and extends her hand towards me.

"Uh, about that, no one uses my real name. I go by Max, if you don't mind." I don't know if she's offering a handshake or trying to help me up, so I reach out and let her take control. Chloe grabs onto my palm and starts pulling me to my feet.

"No worries; I was prepped on that, but seeing as 'Maximus' is an immensely well-respected name around here, I thought you wouldn't mind."

I'm about to ask what she means by that, but since Chloe is already ten steps ahead of me, I make a mental note to ask her later. I can do nothing but scurry after her, trying to match her brisk pace. I'm at a half-jog next to her as we round the nearest corner through a wide entryway. She comes to a stop twenty or so steps down this new, but nearly identical hallway and points to what must be a door. It's a door-shaped cut-out on the wall, at least.

"Here's a private room for you. There should be a set of clean clothes that fit you in one of the cabinets. I'll wait right here, but take your time. I know you're still trying to process this new situation," she says.

I give her a nod and walk up to the door, which is unmarked aside from a small green light midway up from the floor. I'm guessing this means 'vacant', like some of the public restrooms I've used. The door next to it has a red light, which confirms my suspicion. I reach out to push the door inwards since there's no handle to grab onto, but the door opens by itself before I make contact. It slides sideways into the wall, completely disappearing. As I step into the room, the door quickly slides closed behind me.

Inside the room is what looks like.... a normal public restroom. At first glance, at least. There's a seemingly ordinary toilet in one corner with a sink right next to it. A shower stall is positioned in the opposite corner, which would be pretty rare in the public restrooms I'm accustomed to. One wall is lined with cabinets. They have no locks, which definitely wouldn't fly back home. What does that mean, anyways? 'Back home'?

I open the first cabinet. It has stacks of light gray towels from top to bottom. Not quite what I'm looking for. The second door, though, this one has stacks of neatly folded shirts and pants on various shelves. I gently lift one of the shirts from the stack to examine its collar, being careful not to crease it. The shirts are so nicely arranged, so pristine; it would be a shame to disrupt their immaculate appearance.

The size is stitched into the collar, as I expect. There's no tag or logo anywhere, though, which is odd. The one I'm looking at is labeled with an 'S', obviously for small. It probably won't fit. I need a medium, which I find on the shelf directly below. I grab the shirt and slip it over my naked chest. The pants on the same shelf are also labeled with an 'M' for medium. I'm accustomed to wearing pants that have separate measurements for waist and length, but these have no such details.

The medium-size pants look like they'll fit me anyway, so I pull a pair off the shelf and step into them, one leg at a time. A drawstring secures the waist, which I tie tight. The cuffs on each leg are cinched, and they naturally sit right about where my ankles are. The inseam length doesn't matter so much, as the design of these pants ensures they won't drag on the floor if they're a bit too long.

I look down at my bare feet. I didn't realize I had been walking through the hallway without even a pair of socks. That seems wrong, and I don't know if everyone else I had seen was barefoot or if they were wearing shoes. I don't typically look at people's footwear, or lack thereof. I close the door to the clothes cabinet and open the door next to it.

Ah, there we go, shelves full of neatly positioned slip-on shoes. They're also light gray, of course, and are again labeled with small, medium, large, et cetera. I'm used to standard American shoe sizes; I wear a men's size ten, but once again the medium-size shoe looks about right, so I place a pair on the floor and slip my feet into them, one after the other. The shoes' upper material has a bit of give, molding comfortably to my feet and embracing them with a gentle pressure.

I notice just how comfortable they feel on my otherwise bare feet. Now that I think about it, the shirt and pants also seem to be among the comfiest and softest clothes I've ever worn. The material is unlike anything I've felt before. I walk over to the sink and peer into the mirror above it. As expected, I see a familiar face staring back, so this isn't some Hollywood body swap situation. It's the first time since I've materialized in this new place that I feel some slight amount of comfort, knowing I'm the same person as I was back at home.

I look down at the sink, and then the toilet next to it. Both are completely and utterly spotless, which is unique amongst all the public restrooms I've been in. The only time a public restroom would be this clean is if you're the first person to use it after it opens for the day. Often not even then. As I look around, I can't help but think that I could probably eat off of any surface in this small room. I can almost imagine the various white surfaces sparkling like they would in a commercial for bathroom cleaning supplies.

I place my hands under the tap that seems to hover above the sink. Room-temperature water starts flowing out, engulfing my hands in the steady flow. I want to splash some cold water on my face to see if that will wake me up from what I still suspect to be a dream, but I don't see any way to adjust the temperature.

"How do I make it cold?" I mutter to myself. Out of the corner of my eye, I see a small white light blink near the top of the mirror, and just like that, the water is cold. That's weird. Was that a coincidence or is this sink voice-activated? I cup my hands and gather a small pool of cold, almost fridge-temperature water, and splash it on my face.

Nope, still here. I glance at my surroundings through the reflection of the mirror. I'm still standing awkwardly in this unusually clean bathroom. I splash my face once more for good measure. You never know. I decide to test my 'voice activation' theory after I notice there doesn't seem to be any soap dispenser.

"Where's the soap?" I say aloud to no one in particular. That white light on the mirror blinks again and the water that was still flowing from the tap suddenly turns to a white foamy substance that completely coats my hands. After a few seconds, the foam stops flowing and the cold water takes its place again. "Warm please."

As the water changes to a warmer temperature, I wonder why I had bothered to say 'please'. I don't even know who or what I'm talking to, but good manners seem to prevail, even in uncertain circumstances. After my hands seem sufficiently clean, I pull them out from under the tap and the water instantly stops flowing. Looking around, I don't see any paper towels or a hand dryer. There's a small, light gray hand towel folded on the ledge next to the sink, though.

I pick it up and rub it all over my hands, drying them thoroughly. I run it back and forth across my face now, absorbing any remaining wetness from when I splashed myself. But what do I do with this towel now? Put it back? That seems weird. I'm not used to public restrooms having communal hand towels.

As I turn around, a small white light blinks above a small square hole in the wall that I somehow didn't notice before. It looks like a laundry chute. I walk over to it and glance inside. There's a shelf a few centimeters below the edge of the hole.

"Is this for the towel?" I ask aloud. The white light above the chute blinks again. I take that to be a confirmation and toss the small hand towel into the opening, which closes automatically as soon as the towel lands on the shelf inside. My curiosity about wherever the hell I've ended up only intensified after this unusual experience, so I feel compelled to leave the relative comfort of this small, private room and figure out what's going on. I step towards the door and let it slide open.

As promised, Chloe is standing in the same spot she was before, patiently waiting for me to finish up in the restroom. Her expression is not one of boredom or annoyance; instead, she genuinely smiles at me. After the door slides closed behind me, I hear a faint 'wooshing' noise coming from inside. "What's that sound?" I ask Chloe.

"Oh, the room is going through a sanitation cycle. It cleans and sanitizes itself after every use," she responds.

"Wow. Okay. Cool." I'm still in a bit of a shock and am having trouble coming up with an intelligent response. I look back at the door. There's a red light on it now. When the sound stops a second or two later, the light turns to green.

"So, how are you feeling? Better, I hope. Are you able to go for a short walk with me?" she asks.

"I'm alright, I'm still expecting to wake up any time now, though. None of this makes sense."

"Listen, I don't want to overwhelm you with too much info right off the bat, but I'm not sure if it can be avoided, to be honest. I'm sure you have some burning questions, so ask away." She turns and starts slowly walking back towards the hallway that I had materialized in a few minutes earlier. She seems to be expecting me to follow. So I do.

After I catch up to her and match her pace, I ask my first question. "So, where am I? You said this was another world or something?"

"Technically, it's the same world, just a bit different from yours," she answers. "We are on Earth. The same Earth you came from. But, uh... sorry, I'm trying to find the right words. I think you would call it an... alternate reality."

We both stay quiet for a few seconds as I try to process that information. We are walking slowly through the never-ending hallway that I remember seeing before. People of all kinds are passing by us at various paces, heading in opposite directions. The walls are still adorned with the now-familiar paintings, and the large rectangular screen remains blank, as it was earlier. But I notice a young person stop for a second and look straight at it before continuing down the hallway.

"What is that?" I ask and point toward the rectangle. "It's blank. What are people looking at?" An adult woman, holding the hand of a small child, has now stopped and is staring straight at the blank screen. I see her mouth moving as if she is talking to it.

"Oh, that's just part of Hivemind. I guess it's kind of similar to the cell phones that people in your reality use. We don't have those. We have Hivemind," Chloe says.

"But it's blank... Why are they looking at it? Who is she talking to?"

"It's blank for you. Because you aren't accessing Hivemind at the moment. It only displays information relevant to each person, for privacy reasons."

"How does that work? If it's blank for me, how is it not blank for others?"

"Honestly, I don't have any earthly idea how it works... it just does." She looks at the screen. "Right now, it's showing me a map view of the area we're in, with two little colored dots to mark our locations on the map. It's keeping me on track since this place is quite a bit maze-like."

That certainly piques my interest. I've heard about a breakthrough technology that some airports are using in America and some other countries. It uses facial recognition to match a person to their flight details. As you stand in front of the departure boards, your name pops up on a screen with your itinerary, so you don't have to scan the board line by line to find your flight amongst all the others. No one else can see this custom information, only you. As you walk back and forth in a predetermined area in front of the screens, the camera tracks your movement and adjusts the screen to show only you that information. The rest of the people around see only their information on the same screen. The screens have a directionality to them which I don't quite understand the logistics of.

"How can I see for myself?" I ask as we walk towards another blank, identically sized screen about thirty feet down the hallway from the last one.

"Hivemind, can you show Max what I'm seeing?" Chloe asks the screen as we come to a stop in front of it.

The formerly blank screen instantly populates with a grid-like view of intersecting hallways. There are rooms dotted along the hallways, some small like the restroom I was just in, and some much more massive than that. Just as Chloe said, there are two red dots right in the middle of the grid, marking our positions. I take a few steps to the side to test it out. The entire map grid shifts to a different angle to match my new viewpoint, and one of the red dots moves slightly away from the other. It's tracking my movements and actions instantaneously.

These screens, in this reality, are nothing like the tech demos I've seen on the news. The airport screens are reportedly extremely low quality and awkward to look at. This one that I'm staring at right now is seemingly much more advanced than anything that exists where I come from. The map has a kind of depth to it, which reminds me a tiny bit of the gimmicky 3D movies that I used to watch in the local cinema. But this one doesn't need those horrible plastic glasses, and it does not seem hokey like the movies. It looks as if the previously blank screen has been replaced by a physical diorama, floating in mid-air and moving seamlessly to match my angle of view.

"Wow, I've never seen anything like this," I finally manage to say.

"Well, get used to it, because Hivemind is everywhere around here," Chloe responds.

"I'm not sure I can. I still have no idea what's going on. This is starting to feel like the plot of a book or a movie. Like I'm the clueless protagonist and you're the peppy sidekick who eventually turns into a love interest." My cheeks turn bright red. Why the hell did I say that? "Sorry, I don't know why I said that. That's awkward."

"All good," she manages to say through a fit of laughter. "Either way, I'm not the love interest in this story, for two pretty important reasons. One: I'm your sister. And two: I'm only interested in women."

Chapter 6

"By the way, are you hungry at all? I was planning on making a quick detour to grab a bite to eat," Chloe says.

I am, predictably, too shocked to speak. Did I mishear that? Did Chloe say she's my sister? How can that be?

"Uh, Max? Is that alright with you? I haven't eaten in hours." She's surveying me, patiently waiting while I gather myself together and answer the question.

"Uh, are you just gonna drop that bomb on me and pretend it wouldn't put me into a complete state of shock?" I finally manage to stammer out.

"What, that I'm a lesbian? No offense, but this reality doesn't dramatize sexual identity the way that yours does." Her face twitches as she tries to suppress a smirk, but it's clear that she isn't very good at hiding her amusement.

"You know what I mean," I reply firmly.

"Okay, okay, I'm sorry. Just trying to lighten the mood a bit. This should be a happy time! You're finding out that you have an actual sibling! And I'm meeting my brother for the first time! Well, maybe 'half-brother'? We technically have the same mom and dad, so that doesn't make sense. How about 'alt-brother'? Sounds kind of cool that way." Chloe is excitedly babbling away.

"But... how? How could that be possible? We don't even come from the same world!"

"It's complicated, and I won't bother trying to explain it in-depth today. That would be too overwhelming. All that I'll say is that this reality split from yours a little over thirty years ago. Or did your reality split from this one? I guess that doesn't matter. Everyone who existed on Earth at the time of the Split carried over into each different reality, which means that every human on Earth split into two versions of themselves. Including our parents, obviously. Come on, let's get moving."

She averts her gaze from the map floating on the wall and resumes walking down the hallway. I saunter after her. I'm trying my hardest to process what she's saying, but I'm having trouble grasping the logistics of this relationship. Chloe stopped talking for the moment, clearly taking a break to let the wheels in my brain turn.

After a minute of walking in silence, I ask her another question. "If our parents are the same, just from split realities, why are we different from one another? Shouldn't we be carbon copies or something?"

"I don't know for sure, but I imagine that once the Split happened, it changed the course of the future for our parents, and consequently, for us. You're a bit older than me, I'm pretty sure. I turn eighteen in a week."

She's right. I turned eighteen about five months ago. Whatever happened after the Split, as Chloe calls it, must have delayed the date of conception for Chloe in this reality. I'm now realizing that I'm thinking about my parents' procreation. *Ick*.

"You stew on that for a minute," Chloe says. "There's a cafeteria right around this corner. I'm starving."

I desperately need a distraction from the frenzied thoughts currently swirling through my brain, and walking into the cafeteria grants me that instantly. The hallway that led to it was nearly identical to the ones we had been passing through for the past fifteen minutes. But then we step through a seemingly ordinary opening in the wall, and my jaw drops.

The first thing I notice is just how vast this space is. When Chloe said 'cafeteria', I made a mental connection to the one at my old high school, or at the warehouse I work at. At Idolon, I was always in awe of how large it was, but now I realize that it's only a fraction of the size relative to this one. It's like trying to compare an ant to an elephant - there's no equivalence.

I look left and right. The walls surrounding us seem to stretch for miles, their pale, smooth surfaces curving slightly in the distance. I strain my eyes, but I can't see where they end, the vastness of the room overwhelming me. I had expected this room to be a simple square or rectangle, but this is something else entirely - a massive circular space that feels endless.

In what appears to be the perfect center of the curved room, I can just barely make out a mass of clear tubes flowing under, over, and around one another and disappearing into the floor or ceiling. I don't know what to make of this. I can't get a good sense of their scale, since they're so far away. I'm about to ask Chloe what is going on there, but I get immediately distracted by something else.

I've been so preoccupied with taking in the scale of this room that I failed to notice the people who are occupying it. The room is a sea of bodies, each one a unique shape and size. Some are sitting at tables, their faces alight with conversation and laughter. Others are walking with purpose, carrying plates of food or chatting with friends. There are so many people that it's hard to see where one ends and the next begins.

The sheer number of people in this room is beyond my imagination. There could potentially be more people here than I have seen in my entire lifetime. No matter where I look, all I see are humans filling up every inch of space. The ones at the furthest reaches are just tiny specks, moving around like gray or colorful grains of sand.

I ask Chloe, "How many people are in this room right now? Hundreds of thousands?"

She's been standing next to me, patiently waiting for me to take it all in. "Probably close to a million. I'm not sure. Crazy, huh?" She tugs on my sleeve. "Come on, I'm *literally about to die* of starvation."

I finally will my eyes away from the amazing sight in front of me and take a few steps into the throng. As we zigzag our way around tables and people to find a less populated area, I start to notice a pattern in the layout of the tables. The cafeteria is furnished with a variety of table sizes and shapes. The majority are perfectly square tables with four matching chairs. There are also longer rectangular tables with eight seats that are strategically positioned between smaller two-seater tables. For those dining alone, there are long curved bar-style tables that form a circle in the middle of each cluster. These tables have gaps on both ends for easy access and movement throughout the space. Nestled within the center of that circle stands a sizeable hexagon, which I initially mistook for another table. However, there are no chairs surrounding it. It resembles a solid block of white material, a bit like a kitchen island.

The hexagonal shape of the counter in the middle clues me into the pattern each cluster of tables makes. They're hexagons, one cluster after another, like the combs in a beehive. Now that I have the pattern figured out, I glance around to see them extending out in every direction, ad infinitum. The path we've been following is the slightly wider gap between each hexagon, which makes a pseudo-pathway.

After navigating this mass of hive-like dining space, we finally reach an area containing a much lesser amount of people. It's a bit quieter here. The chatter from the masses of people all talking at once becomes less noticeable. Chloe picks a small two-seat table away from anyone else and points to one of the empty chairs.

"Sit, relax. You sure you're not hungry?" she asks me once again.

"I don't think I could eat a single crumb, even if you held a gun to my head," I reply.

"You're in luck, I guess, since we don't have guns here." Chloe lets me ponder that remark while she turns on her heel and walks to the hexagonal counter in the middle of our chosen cluster. I watch her as she stands at the counter with her back to me. That's one way to solve gun violence I guess. You can't shoot up a school if there are no guns to shoot with.

After a few seconds, she grabs something from the top of the counter and turns to walk back to our table. It's a light gray rectangular tray, similar to the ones that the food court at my local mall uses. After placing the tray down in front of her chair, she sits down. At first glance, there's nothing out of the ordinary on the tray. There's some silver cutlery placed next to a white bowl. On the other side of the bowl, there are two small glasses with a clear liquid that I assume is water. The corner of the tray has a small folded light gray towel, which looks identical to the one that I used to dry my hands and face earlier.

But then I look at the contents of the bowl. It's piled high with what looks like the riced cauliflower that I sometimes order from restaurants, but it's a sickly-looking shade of greenish-brown. It does not look appetizing in the slightest. Just looking at her 'food' makes my mouth dry up and my stomach churn, the thought of eating it enough to make me want to gag.

Chloe presents a small, square item wrapped in a light gray cloth and sets it down in front of me. "Here, I got you a to-go bar for if you get hungry later. You can just keep it in your pocket. Or not, up to you. But at least drink this. It has nutrients and electrolytes and all that fun stuff," she says as she points to one of the glasses. She grabs the one closest to her and takes a sip as if to demonstrate that it's safe. "Delicious."

I ignore the small square package for now and reach for my glass since I am admittedly quite thirsty, I'm having trouble procuring enough saliva to keep my mouth moist. I take a small sip and am pleasantly surprised. The liquid is refreshingly cold, as if it had just been pulled out of a fridge. It has a subtle sweetness, neither too strong nor too mild. I take another, deeper drink to fully moisten my mouth before swallowing it down eagerly.

Chloe is now enthusiastically shoveling spoonfuls of the puke-colored slop into her mouth. "Sorry bro, all the excitement really worked up my appetite," she says with her mouth full of food.

I'm not sure how I feel about her calling me 'bro', but I ignore it for now. "How can you eat that? It looks disgusting," I ask.

"It's actually quite good. Just ignore the color. It's natural. You can get it in different colors and shapes and the like. That's how most younger kids eat it. But I'm not picky."

"If you say so." I glance at the nearest populated table, which has what looks to be a family seated around it. Sure enough, there's a girl who looks about ten years old biting into a colorful flower-shaped slab of food. "How much did that run you, by the way?" I ask Chloe, who is mid-bite.

After she chews and swallows, she says, "You're asking what it cost?" She laughs. "It's free, my dude. Money doesn't even exist here. Unlike your reality, where every single aspect of your life has a price tag."

No money? Wow. I can't argue with that, though. It must be refreshing to never have to think about if there's enough money in your bank account to be able to afford your next meal. The ideal post-capitalist society I've envisioned in my head is moneyless, of course. It's absurd how much an arbitrary value assigned to an otherwise useless piece of paper, or bits and bytes on a computer, can affect your life, either for the good or the bad. From the small taste of this reality I've so far received, it kind of makes sense that money doesn't exist. If it did, the clothes and shoes I'm currently wearing would have been locked up somewhere.

I look back over to the table that the young family was sitting at just in time to see them getting ready to leave. I watch the father using a towel to sweep crumbs onto a carefully placed tray just below the table's edge. The two kids are stacking their trays, plates, and glasses on top of one another before removing them from the table-top. A small circle in the middle of the table pops up and a sprinkler-like nozzle spins in a slow circle, spraying some type of liquid across the tabletop, then lowers back into the table. The mother swipes her own towel back and forth across the surface, cleaning and drying it. When she seems satisfied with the cleanliness, they all walk towards the hexagonal counter in the middle of the cluster with their dishes. The kids grab each item individually from the trays and place them in different slots in the middle of the counter that I hadn't noticed until now. They're treating it like a game.

"Wow, does everyone clean up after themselves that thoroughly?" I ask Chloe.

"Obviously, what do you think we are, savages? I know you aren't used to that kind of selflessness where you come from." She's quick with the witty retorts.

I've always believed in the completely unscientific, but still valid cafeteria tray/shopping cart theory of sociopathy. Picking up after yourself in a cafeteria, food court, or fast-food restaurant and returning your shopping cart are some of the most simple tasks a person can do. They take only a few seconds out of your day and minimal effort. They make things easier on the people who are paid peanuts to clean up after you. If you don't do these simple tasks and expect someone else to do them for you, you must be a sociopath. Period. I personally always make sure to make things slightly easier for my fellow wage slaves.

We sit in silence for a few minutes while Chloe scarfs down the rest of her bowl of gruel. She seems to zone out while chewing and swallowing one mouthful after another as she stares straight up at the ceiling, without blinking. Maybe we're more alike than I realized, I'm a serial daydreamer. She snaps out of her trance eventually as she scrapes the last few bits of food from the bottom of the bowl. She stares back up at the ceiling while taking a big gulp of liquid from her glass, her eyes slowly moving from side to side.

I look up at the ceiling. "What are you looking at?" I ask her. "It's just a blank white ceiling."

"Right, I keep forgetting you're not connected to Hivemind yet." She sounds truly apologetic. She looks back up at the roof and says, "Hivemind, give Max a show, please."

In a matter of milliseconds, the white ceiling transforms into something completely different. I can feel my jaw drop yet again; it must be at least the tenth time tonight. "Oh my goodness," I whisper.

The ceiling is replaced by a breathtaking display of a cloudy sunset at the peak of its dramatic beauty. The artificial sky is a symphony of vibrant colors, merging seamlessly from a deep blue to a soft pink, and finally fading into a fiery red. The fake clouds float slowly and gracefully, each wispy strand delicately tinged with a rosy hue. Simulated sun rays intermittently peek through the clouds, casting a warm glow over the scene. The display before me is incredibly immersive, with even more depth than the screens in the hallway. The clouds in the lower part of the frame give the illusion of floating below the ceiling. I can't be sure if this is a simulation or if the ceiling has actually opened up to reveal this view. However, I remind myself that the sun would have set hours ago, so it must be a simulation.

I ask if I can see a night-time view, and Chloe relays the message to Hivemind. It's suddenly as if time is fast forwarding, the sun sets, the clouds clear, and the sky transforms into a dark night scene lit up with an incredible display of waving, undulating streaks of bright green, purple and red lights. The Aurora Borealis swirls across the entire sky in all directions creating a mesmerizing show that I can appreciate even from indoors. The stars glitter brilliantly, culminating in a magnificent scene that I can't quite put into words. I've never seen the Northern Lights before, but the level of detail and realism that Hivemind has created stands out as something truly special. I feel like I can cross it off my bucket list now.

"Wait a minute, what time is it? Why are so many people eating here in the middle of the night?" I glance at my watch. The hands on it indicate that it's just after two AM.

"Oh, it doesn't matter what time it is, this place will always be busy, even through the night. When you can accurately simulate any time of day"—she gestures towards the roof—"your circadian rhythm doesn't matter anymore. Also, it's not the middle of the night. It's late afternoon."

"What, how? I've only been here for like an hour. Does time move differently in this reality or something?"

"Nope, it's the same. So are time zones. You're in East Asia right now."

Confusion sets in. "How the hell did I get to Asia? I've never even been overseas before. The only country I've been to other than the US is Canada."

"If the watch took you to this reality's America, you would not be having a fun time. Since America, as you know it, no longer exists in this reality. Neither does Canada."

A chill runs down my spine as my stomach drops, making me feel off-balance and weak. My hands involuntarily grip the edge of the table, trying to anchor myself. She knows about the watch? I don't even understand the watch. I didn't even know for sure that that was the reason I was taken here. What happened to the US and Canada? Why do they not exist? I have a thousand more questions spinning around in my mind. I settle on two.

"How do you know about the watch? And how do you know so much about my reality, anyway?"

My heart races as I watch Chloe's hand disappear into her pocket, only to emerge with something hidden from my view. She places it on the table in front of me, her hand covering it protectively. Leaning closer, she locks eyes with me and speaks with an eerie calmness, "I know about your reality because I've been there. Many times."

She lifts her hand off of the item on the table, revealing it to me. It's a beat-up silver watch with a white face. Exactly the same as the one that is currently secured to my wrist.

Chapter 7

My mind feels like a blank canvas splattered with a dozen different colors, unable to form any coherent thoughts or reactions as I stare at the watch before me. It's as if all the air has been sucked out of me, leaving me feeling weightless and disoriented.

Without breaking my gaze on the watch that Chloe had just laid down in front of me, I instinctually grab my left wrist with my right hand to make sure that my watch is still there, and that Chloe hadn't pulled some sleight-of-hand to take it from me. When I feel the cool metal under my fingers, I realize that she's telling the truth. She has her own watch.

I slide my watch-adorned hand out from under the table, and hold it next to Chloe's watch which was still resting on top. It's clearly evident that they'e identical. The crystal is equally scuffed and scratched, the bezel and band showing the same signs of wear. Even the tiny specks of brass peeking through on the crown match up perfectly.

"Can I?" I ask Chloe, indicating my intention to pick up her watch.

"Have at it," she replies.

My fingers tremble as I delicately encircle the watch's casing, as if it were a delicate orb of spun glass on the verge of shattering with the slightest touch. With careful precision, I lift the watch, the metal band dragging lazily across the table as I raise it from its smooth resting place.

I bring it closer to my eyes to get a better look at the watch's face. I tilt the crystal back and forth, adjusting the angle until the light reflects just right. I'm trying to find that small, imperceptible logo that I can't even read because it's in Russian. Sure enough, there it is, a few tiny Cyrillic characters scrawled in black text near the top of the white watch face.

I carefully and slowly turn it over in my palm to check the back. I forgot about the giant hammer and sickle symbol beveled into the rear casing. But here it is, plain as day. I study the watch for a few moments more before flipping it over and setting it down on the table again. Chloe reaches over to take it and slides it back into her pocket.

"I'm confused," I finally say after a few uncomfortable seconds of silence.

"I know. But it kind of makes sense, doesn't it? We have the same grandfather. He passed down the watch to our fathers, and they passed them down to us," Chloe says.

"That's not the part I'm confused about. I don't understand the... uh, what would you call it? Inter-dimensional travel aspect? What, do you just put on the watch and it takes you to my reality? How do you get back? You said you've been there 'many times.'"

"I guess I should explain how it works, considering I'm *clearly* an expert in inter-dimensional travel," she says sarcastically. "So, obviously you had to wind the watch before it took you here, right?"

"Yes...."

"Well, how many times did you wind it? Did you keep turning the crown until it stopped?"

"Not until it stopped, no. Why would that matter?"

"Oh, it matters, my friend. It matters a lot. The watch will transport you to the opposite reality once it's been wound and is secured to your wrist. You will stay in that reality, or, I guess, this reality until the watch stops ticking. These things need to be wound up once a day, by the way. I don't know if you knew that."

"I was born in the twenty-first century. I definitely don't know how a mechanical watch works. But thanks for letting me know," I reply. "How do I know when the watch will stop ticking?"

"Well.... how many times did you wind it?" Chloe asks again.

I try to recall my actions from back when I was lying in my bed at home. I pantomime the winding motion with my hands, trying to pinpoint how many revolutions the crown would have made. Even though it happened only about an hour and a half ago, it feels like a different lifetime.

"I think maybe three times?" I finally answer with reasonable confidence.

"That's it? Okay. I guess that was unintentionally smart, anyway. You probably need to check back in with your reality eventually. Oh, right, you said it's the middle of the night for you, huh? Do you need to sleep?"

"I'm fine. I'm wide awake. I'm a bit of a night owl anyway. So how long will I be here for?"

"Each turn makes the watch run for right around one hour. You can turn it about thirty times to give you thirty hours, a bit over a full day. If you did turn it three times, you probably have another hour or hour-and-a-half left."

"So I can only be in this reality for a day? What if I wanted to stay longer?"

"Wow bro, you're that desperate to hang out with me, huh?" Chloe grins. "I kid. You can extend it as long as you want, though. You can wind the watch again before it stops. As long as you wind it every day, you could theoretically stay here forever."

I have to pause to let that thought sink in for a minute. From the limited experience I've had in this reality, it already seems infinitely better than the world I came from. Everything I've seen is so advanced, much more so than in my capitalist reality. But I don't know much of anything about this world. I have so many questions; I don't even know where to begin.

I've been infatuated with technology for nearly my entire existence. I love to research new and emerging tech to get an idea of what the future could look like, if humanity doesn't become extinct from climate change, of course. I believe that technology could be used to liberate the working class from the stranglehold of wage slavery, but unfortunately, capitalism gives little to no incentive to use innovations to make the lives of the working class better.

I despise how technology is always, first and foremost, designed to make the capitalist class richer. Or to murder innocent people on the other side of the world. I constantly hear right-leaning people talk about how 'capitalism breeds innovation', but from my experience, that couldn't be further from the truth. If anything, capitalism stifles innovation. This is most evidently apparent in the mobile technology industry, which I'm deeply obsessed with. I find myself constantly dreaming about what new, sleek, futuristic device could be released next, imagining the endless possibilities that could be at my fingertips. But unfortunately capitalism severely hamstrings the industry.

The major cell phone manufacturers all release iterative updates to their flagship devices every single year. Next year's model will have a ten percent faster processor, an extra hour of battery life, a slightly higher resolution screen, a marginally better camera array, et cetera. However, this is not the typical course of technological progress. Take, for example, the realization of a new microchip process. Utilized to its fullest potential, it can result in a significant leap in processing power rather than just a slight improvement.

These companies all purposely hamstring their potential so they can release multiple iterative devices instead of one revolutionary one. They don't want you to buy a new revolutionary device every decade; they want you to upgrade, or even side-grade to a marginally better or slightly different device every year or two. Because they make more money that way. 'Planned obsolescence' is a main feature of capitalism. Products that could last ten, fifteen, even twenty years are purposely designed to break down after a certain amount of time, so the user is forced to buy a replacement. It always seems to happen just shortly after the warranty period ends as well. *What a coincidence.*

I've also heard a lot of nonsense about competition between companies being good for the consumer. It supposedly drives prices down and encourages innovative technology to be created. While this is sometimes true in certain scenarios, it seems like bullshit to me overall. In actuality, 'rival' companies in many industries will collude with each other to set prices or agree to not jump too far ahead with innovations. There's a term for it that I learned recently; 'oligopoly'.

I look back up at the simulated sky that dominates the space above me. At some point, it had changed from the dramatic night scene to a picturesque blue mid-day sky, dotted with fluffy white clouds. I can't imagine my capitalist society being able to produce technology of this sort in the next few decades. Maybe ever.

I pry my eyes away from the beautiful scene on the ceiling and look back at Chloe, who seems to be tracing random patterns on the table with her fingertip. I admire her patience while I struggle to process this wild new situation I've found myself in, and I'm extremely grateful to have someone so nice to guide me through this process. I don't know how to feel about that person being the alternate-dimension sister I never knew I had, though. That's a weird sentence.

"You look bored," I say, breaking the silence.

Chloe stops what she's doing and withdraws her hands from the table. "Not at all. This reality tends to be a lot more laid back and relaxed than the hectics of your world. It's nice."

"I've never been one to enjoy chaos. I mostly go from work straight to home, I value my relaxation time."

"Work, huh? What do you do?" she asks.

"You seem to know so much about me already. I figured you knew. My bad. It's just entry-level warehousing nonsense for a huge corporation. It's pretty much the only job I could get straight out of high school. What about you? Do jobs even exist in a moneyless society?"

"Sort of, but not really. They're more like what you would call chores, I guess? Most things around here are fully automated, but humans are still needed for certain tasks. I have no experience with it yet though. You aren't required to do anything until you turn eighteen and get the Implant, which is coming soon for me!"

"Implant? What's that?"

"Oh, I'm sure you've seen the little white light coming from the temples of the adults here. That's from the Implant. It's basically just Hivemind, but, like, directly connected to your brain. I can't wait to get mine."

"That sounds... invasive. That must be a pretty major surgery. What's the recovery time like?"

"No, it's a pretty quick and easy process, from what I've heard. It's all automated. You're put under for ten minutes and when you wake up, you're good to go. No pain or anything."

"Wait, so it's not done by a surgeon? How does that work?"

"It happens in the same med pods that everyone here uses. I'll take you to one sometime. They're amazing. This reality doesn't rely on human doctors or surgeons, everything is automated by Hivemind. Humans are error-prone. Hivemind doesn't make mistakes."

I ponder the implications of an Artificial Intelligence—or whatever Hivemind is—being directly connected to our brains. It would open up a lot of opportunities, depending on how it's implemented.

Interestingly enough, it's something that my employer is working on. They're developing a device that will be connected to your brain and could help with neurological conditions and allow you to control certain things with brain power alone.

It's an extremely controversial topic, and I understand why. The possibilities of this technology are overall positive, but the fact that it will be created and administered by a mega-corporation is a huge cause for concern. They've even made animal rights groups furious by testing the devices on live animals, there was an exposé on it that went mainstream. Turns out, they've had dozens of gorilla test subjects die. The CEO of Idolon tried to deflect by claiming the gorillas were all terminally ill anyway. It did not go over well.

At face value, if I can be guaranteed that Idolon's implant will be immune from corruption, I'm in favor of it. I've done a lot of research into the 'transhumanism' movement, which advocates for the merging of man and machine to create healthier, stronger, and smarter humans with more longevity. The only real problem I can personally identify is the fact that it will be implemented under capitalism; a system prone to corruption and subjugation of the working class.

Chloe was starting to organize her dishes on the tray. I ask her, "What are we doing now?"

"That's kind of up to you. I have plenty more to show you, but I don't know if you need to get back home or get some sleep first," she replies.

"I actually have a question about that. What exactly happened when I... you know... appeared here? I was in my bed at home; is my body still there, just like comatose or something? Or is my other self lucid? Did I split into two?"

"You are physically transported. I have no clue how it works or why, but your bed at home will be empty right now. If you want to stay here for a while, you might want to leave a note or make up an excuse or something. I'm not sure what obligations you might have back in your world."

I think about my mom, who is hopefully still fast asleep right now. She works early in the morning, and she knows I like to sleep in, so I'm probably good until at least tomorrow night. She values my privacy and won't barge into my room. But fatigue is starting to set in, and the informational and experiential overload I've received over the last few hours is exacerbating that. Maybe I should go back to my bed and get some sleep.

"You're probably right. I think I should head back home pretty soon and sleep. I have the next three days off work, so I don't have to worry about that, but I don't want my mom to worry needlessly, or worse; report me missing," I say.

"No worries, makes sense," Chloe replies.

"So what's gonna happen? I just wait for the watch to stop and then I appear back in my bed? Or will I pop up in a random place back in my world?"

"You can influence where exactly the watch takes you, to an extent at least. If you want to end up back in your bed, that's where you'll end up. Oh, and if it's anything like my experience, you'll have about a minute of warning before the watch stops. For me, I start to feel a tingle in my wrist that slowly becomes more and more intense."

"How do I find you when I come back? Actually, how did you find me when I first got here?" Somehow I hadn't thought about that until just now.

"We'll get you hooked up with Hivemind so you can just ask where I am, or even better, talk directly to me. There's a device that younger people like us here use before we get the Implant. It's a patch that goes under your ear. You can't even see it." She brushes her hair behind her ear and tilts her head to reveal her neck. It just looks like a normal human neck. Nothing unusual. "It blends in with the skin. And for the second question; Hivemind told me, of course."

I feel like there's more to that story, but I don't press her for any more info. It'll have to wait for another time. I grab the to-go bar that Chloe gave me earlier and slip it into my pocket. I don't know if I want to eat it yet, since I'm still nervous after seeing Chloe's unappetizing meal. When the table is clear, a nozzle pops up and sprays around the surface, just like I had seen earlier from a distance. Chloe briskly wipes down the table with a towel from her tray before making her way to the hexagonal counter to deposit the dirty dishes.

I make sure to follow Chloe because I want to get a better look at this counter. The surface is a stark white, devoid of any texture or markings. It almost seems like it emits its own light, as if it's glowing. As we get closer, four square holes and one large slot materialize from the surface, appearing as if out of thin air.

"How do you know what goes where?" I ask Chloe.

"Oh, I have it memorized because I've done it a thousand times. It's always the same, no matter where you eat. But watch this." She picks up the stacked drinking glasses from the tray and starts to move them toward the holes. A small white light illuminates above the hole on the top right. She places the glasses in the hole. I lean forward and see that there's a platform just underneath that the glasses are sitting on. They are whisked away to the side by some unseen force, and the hole closes itself up. It looks like it had never been there.

She does the same thing with the bowl, which goes into the top left hole. The cutlery is placed in the bottom right, towel in the bottom left. She flips the tray on its side and slips it into the final slot. A different white light turned on each time, indicating the correct hole. Once everything is sorted, the counter returns to its original flat white state.

"Where did the food come from? And how did you order it? There's no screen." I ask Chloe.

"It just pops up from under the countertop. A hole opens up, and the tray is lifted into place. You don't need a screen. It's not like a fast food menu or something," she laughs. "You just ask for whatever you want. Once you get the Implant, you don't even have to ask. Hivemind just knows exactly what you want."

"Oh."

We walk through the maze of tables to find the nearest exit. Chloe wants to make sure that I get hooked up to Hivemind before my time in this reality runs out. We reach the end of the massive cafeteria after a few minutes of weaving through tables and avoiding other diners, then pop out into another familiar-looking hallway. Each hallway we've walked through has been indistinguishable from the last, except for the artwork on display. Curious, I ask Chloe about the significance of these pieces.

"It's just some artistic expression, you know? Makes this place feel a little less clinical. At least, until you can get the Implant. Anyone can put their art up on the walls. Just find an empty spot. Hivemind will direct you to an open area if you can't find one."

"Why would it be different with the Implant?" I ask.

"The Implant is connected directly to your brain, meaning it can control what you're seeing. You can make it look like you're walking on a Hollywood red carpet, you can turn the walls into a giant aquarium and watch some tropical fish or sharks swim by, basically whatever you want."

I can't help but think of how that would be abused if it existed in my world. There would be a micro-transaction for each different scene, and if there were any free options, they would be plastered with ads floating in front of your face virtually. Who am I kidding? The paid options would probably be riddled with ads as well.

I follow Chloe as she makes a beeline for the nearest black screen on the wall. She stands in front of it and says, "Yo Hivemind, can we hook Max up with a set of Patches?"

A white light illuminates next to the screen. A small shelf extends from the wall, with two tiny gray dots sitting on it. They look like itty-bitty circular stickers. Next, the screen changes from its standard black state to show a 3D model of a human head and neck. There's a blinking dot on the upper part of the neck, directly under the right ear. I pick up the dot on the right and move my hair out of the way. The screen changes to a giant mirror, so I can see exactly what I'm doing.

Once I press the dot firmly on my neck, under my ear, it slowly morphs to match my exact skin color. It looks like it isn't even there anymore. I place the other patch under my left ear and wait to see if something happens. I'm not sure what exactly I'm expecting; when I connect my Bluetooth headphones to my phone to listen to music back in my world, it plays a funny little jingle to let me know it's connected and ready.

"How do I know if it's working?" I ask Chloe after receiving no indication.

She says, "Uh, I don't know, it just works. Ask Hivemind a question, I guess."

I can't think of anything cool to ask. "Hivemind... uh... what time is it?"

A voice instantly answers me, seemingly from inside my head. It speaks with a melodic tone, each word a part of a beautiful symphony, soothing and calming to the senses. It resonates in my mind like a gentle song, bringing a sense of peace and serenity. *"It is six fifteen PM."* Such a simple response shouldn't stir these emotions in me, but it absolutely does, and it makes me feel silly. I can't place a gender on it; it seems androgynous, almost ethereal. In my mind, I'm picturing a harmony of angels speaking to me.

"Neat," I say to Chloe. I grasp my wrist. There's a mild tingling sensation coming from it, directly underneath where the watch is sitting. "Uh, I think the watch is about to stop. My wrist feels funny."

"Okay, no problem. That's good timing, I guess. Here, let's find a private room for you to go in so you don't give anyone here a heart attack by disappearing in front of their eyes."

As we pass the next Hivemind screen, it's displaying a grid view with a path marked for us to follow. The nearest private room is right around the next corner. The tingle in my wrist is slowly intensifying.

We find the door, which is marked as vacant with a green light. Chloe walks straight towards it as it opens automatically, then ushers me in after her. The door closes behind us and automatically locks itself. It's another restroom, identical to the other one I was in earlier.

"Okay, alt-bro, you should be gone any second now. Take your time in your world, no rush. Hivemind will connect us when you come back." Chloe's smile turns into a slight frown. "Please don't skip out on me. I have some truly unbelievable things to show you here. Plus, I can come to your world and hunt you down. Remember that." She taps her pocket, which presumably still contains her watch.

I figure she's joking, but I can't tell for sure. "I won't, I promise," I say.

"Should we hug it out? Alt-bro and alt-sis?" Chloe reaches her arms towards me.

I lean in and put one strongly tingling arm around her back, giving a quick squeeze. I feel her squeeze back for about half a second, and then I'm back in my room at home, standing next to my bed, my arm now hovering in mid-air.

Chapter 8

My thoughts dance like fireflies in the dark, illuminating the ceiling with images and memories of the night. Each second that passes feels like an eternity, the weight of the evening heavy on my mind. I had been exhausted before, but now my body feels like a restless sea, unable to find calm. My promise to Chloe echoes in my head, a reminder of the intriguing world waiting for me. But for now, my brain fights against the pull of sleep, determined to hold onto every moment of consciousness.

I've been interested in science fiction since a young age, but it's always been pure fantasy to me. Now it seems like I've been thrust into the middle of my own sci-fi epic. That is if this truly isn't a dream. I'm still expecting to wake up at some point and continue with my slightly weirder-than-average—but not this weird—life.

Then there's the other elephant in the room. My newly discovered alt-sister. I don't even know if Chloe is telling the truth about that. The only evidence linking her to me is a watch that bears an uncanny resemblance to mine, and of course the fact that she knows every detail about me, possibly more than I know about myself.

Could it all be true? That she has the same grandfather as me, and technically the same father; an alternate version? Can alternate realities even exist? Are there others?

—-

After laying in bed awake for an indefinite amount of time, I decide to get up and do something slightly more productive. I rub the sleep from my tired eyes and roll my aching legs out of bed to shuffle a few feet across the room to my computer desk. On it sits my most prized possession; my custom desktop PC. Most of my peers have never bothered to use a laptop or desktop PC, opting instead for a phone or a tablet. Mobile operating systems have been stealing market share from PCs for quite a while now.

A lot of people my age would consider this PC to be a relic of the past, but not me. It's state-of-the-art, anyway. I had saved up most of every paycheck I have received so far from working at Idolon to buy the components for it. Building this beast of a rig myself has been one of my crowning achievements. I spent weeks researching which components would get the best performance and which manufacturer was the most reliable.

I launch into my current favorite game. It's a free-to-play first-person shooter that is quite popular at the moment. Most of the user base plays on mobile, which I have tried once or twice but can't get into. The touchscreen controls are way too inaccurate and cumbersome, and the game babies you too much because of that. Your crosshair will instantly lock onto an enemy that is nowhere near where you're aiming.

Despite the mobile users having that advantage, it's still way too easy to win against them. You can tell them apart extremely easily, they're the characters waving their guns around sporadically, aiming at nothing in particular. The ones I have to watch out for are the whales, though.

Free-to-play games rely on so-called 'whales' to make money for the development studio that created the game. They're the players who will throw hundreds, even thousands of dollars at the game to unlock the best weapons and abilities. Some of these features can be unlocked just by playing the game, but it can take years to save up enough in-game currency to buy them.

Even if they're playing on mobile, whales can wreck me. Their guns are more accurate and output more damage. They have abilities that can get them out of any sticky situation. It doesn't matter how fast I can aim with my mouse or how good my keyboard movement is; it's almost always a losing battle. Despite that, the game is still fun enough for me to pour tons of time into. When I'm not working, sleeping, or eating, you'll most likely find me glued to my computer monitor, playing for hours on end.

The first match I connect to doesn't go so well. I only get one kill before being sniped from across the map. No biggie. Next game. I start off decently in this one, racking up a few kills right off the bat, but then I don't see another player for several minutes. I wander from hotspot to hotspot, grabbing shields and stocking up on ammo. Then, out of nowhere, I'm surrounded on three sides by players who are posted up behind barriers and lobbying shots at me. I manage to take one down but ultimately die. After also dying immediately in game number three, I sigh and hit ALT-F4 to force close the game. I'm just not into it tonight.

I look at the clock on my phone. It's a quarter to six in the morning. My mom will be up soon to get ready for work. To kill some time, I launch into my web browser of choice and I'm greeted by a news feed. It's curated by my interests using some sort of extremely invasive algorithm. Ever since Idolon started buying up its competitors in the technology industry, the corporation seems to know more and more about me.

I've decided to give up any ambitions of privacy and just embrace it. After all, having only one corporation know all of my intimate details is better than spreading bits and pieces through a bunch of them, right? Thinking that way helps me sleep at night, at least. And honestly, relinquishing that control over my privacy has made my life more convenient in a lot of ways.

When my Idolon email address receives a message about an upcoming appointment, it automatically adds it to the calendar on my phone, which is running Idolon OS software, the same as my computer. I can control my phone virtually through my computer, and vice versa. My mapping software for finding my way around town is from Idolon, my music app is from Idolon, my movie and TV show streaming app is from Idolon... It's all completely seamless.

I absentmindedly scroll through my news feed. There's a few interesting articles that I pass over; normally I would read them, but after my experience with reality hopping, they seem insignificant and pointless to waste my attention on. But then one article catches my eye. The thumbnail is a picture of my late father. I read the headline.

Inter-dimensional traveler Maximus Karlson found dead in hotel room

My breath catches in my throat. The source of the article is a conspiracy rag that I've read a few times, mainly to laugh at the absurdity of it. But this headline has taken me completely by surprise. Is this a 'broken clock is right twice a day' situation or do the writers of this article know about the watch? Chloe never specifically said that my dad had used it, but the cryptic note that was left for me hinted at the capabilities of the watch. I click on the link and start reading the article. It's suspiciously short in length.

> *Maximus Karlson the Second was found dead last week in a hotel room. The cause of death was ruled to be a brain aneurysm. His father, Maximus Karlson the First, defected from the US during the Cold War to assist with the Soviet Union's secret division dedicated to studying alternate dimensions. His work ultimately resulted in his untimely demise. Maximus the Second was long rumored to have followed in his father's footsteps, inheriting the ability to pass between dimensions. Could this death have been a consequence of interdimensional travel? Are all dimensional travelers doomed to this fate?*

I close the web browser, spin my chair away from my PC, and bury my head in my hands. I don't know what to think. The article is complete nonsense, just like everything else I've read on this particular website. But is it all fake? Could there be a kernel of truth hidden in there?

The sound of my mom moving outside my door indicates she's awake. I push the article to the back of my mind, knowing there's no point in obsessing over it at the moment. I make a mental note to ask Chloe later about what she knows about my dad. Our dad?

I subconsciously decided at some point that I want to spend the few days I have off from work to explore more of Chloe's world and pick her brain about some important things. Now, I just have to figure out how to explain my absence to my mother. Not only will I be physically gone from the house, but I'll also be unreachable by phone. I need a reason that covers all of those bases. I wait until I hear my mom moving around in the kitchen before I leave my room and make my way downstairs. As I enter the kitchen, I greet her with a simple "Hey Mom."

She nearly jumps out of her skin. "Oh my goodness, Max. You scared the shit out of me! Why are you up so early?"

"My bad. It's late for me, haven't been to bed yet."

"Well, you don't have to work for the next few days, right? So I guess that's fine. You're an adult, you can make your own choices. Any plans?" The electric kettle starts whistling next to the fridge. The scent of instant oatmeal fills the kitchen as my mom pours boiling water into a bowl. Sweet and warm, with a hint of artificial fruit flavors.

"Yeah... about that. I made a few friends at work, and they invited me on a camping trip. We work the same schedule, so they have the same days off," I lie.

"Camping, really? You didn't seem to like it the few times we went when you were younger. You sure?"

"Yes Mom, I could use some socialization. The other guys have all the gear we need—tents and stuff—and Charlie has a truck." I said the first name that came to mind.

"Okay, well, just make sure to check in, so I know you're safe."

"Sorry, I don't think I can... the place we're going to is way out in the middle of nowhere, so I doubt there will be cell service. I can't remember the name of it... I'll ask the guys later and leave a note with the details."

"Just know that I will be worrying about you the whole time. As mothers do."

"I know, mom. I'll be fine."

She notices my wrist, with the beat-up Soviet watch secured to it. "Oh wow, is that your dad's old watch? You're wearing it? *I thought you didn't want a watch*?" she says in a mocking tone.

"Oh, I forgot I was wearing it. I tried it on a while ago, and just never took it off."

She grabs my hand, turning my wrist towards the light to get a better look. "It's stopped. You know you have to wind it, right? Here, let me show you."

As my mother's fingers brush against my wrist, I feel a jolt of fear shoot through my body. I quickly pull my wrist away before she transports me to the other reality by accident. My skin tingles with the adrenaline rush. "I know how to wind a watch, Mom. I'm not an idiot." I unclasp the watch and slide it off my wrist, tucking it into my pocket. I concentrate on calming my heart rate, not wanting to reveal my new secret. "Like I said, I don't need it to tell the time."

"Okay, okay, relax. Listen, I need to eat and then run out the door. I'm gonna be late. Be safe, have fun. Check in if you can. Love you."

"Love you too. I'm going to bed."

—-

I'm standing in one of the white hallways of Chloe's world. The hallway is blindingly white, the light bouncing off every surface and making it almost impossible to see. People swarm around me, all dressed in the same pale gray uniform, moving in a blur of frenzied activity. Their faces are hidden behind hair or turned away from me, as if trying to conceal something. Suddenly, they all come to a halt, with every single person slowly turning to face me in eerie unison. I shudder as it's revealed that they have no faces, just a blank expanse of smooth skin where features should be.

I wake with a start. I was dreaming; this time, for sure. That was weird. I pick my phone up from my nightstand to check the time. It's late afternoon. Sunlight is streaming into my room from the gaps in the blinds on my window. My stomach is rumbling, but I'm too lazy to get out of bed and go down to the kitchen. I remember that to-go bar that Chloe had given me, which is probably still in the pocket of the light gray pants that are now crumpled on the floor.

I lean over the side of the bed and fish out the bar, unwrap the small napkin that contains it, and take a bite. To my surprise, it's quite good. The first bite is a burst of flavor in my mouth. The bar is slightly salty, but balanced by a savory richness that makes my taste buds dance. It's unlike anything I've tried before, leaving a pleasant aftertaste on my tongue. I can't even pinpoint what possible ingredients would give this flavor profile. After quickly finishing the rest of the bar, I suddenly feel motivated to get out of bed and prepare myself for a journey to a different dimension.

Once I'm showered, fed, and dressed back in the light gray outfit that I had taken from the restroom in the other dimension, I remember that I told my mom I would leave her a note. I have to find a secluded camping area to put on it, so I pull up Idolon Maps on my phone, zoom way out from my city, and type 'campground' into the search bar. I don't think my mom is paranoid enough to question my fake story, but I want to cover my bases anyway.

I need a campground that is close enough to the city, but outside of the cellular coverage area. Cross-referencing the most remote camping spots with the cellular coverage map from Idolon Mobile, my carrier, I settle on a convincing option. I scrawl out a quick note on a scrap of paper and run downstairs to leave it on the kitchen counter.

As soon as I'm back in my room, I power off my phone to avoid giving myself away. I quickly hide it under my mattress, out of sight. Then, I slip the watch back onto my left wrist and get ready to wind it. I have to consider how long I want to stay in the alternate reality; winding it all the way will mean being stuck there for over a day, which could be risky. It's better to err on the side of caution.

I carefully pull the crown out to the furthest position and set the hands to the current time, wanting to keep the watch set to my timezone so I can quickly tell what time it is back home. I pop the crown back inwards for one click, and carefully start to wind it, making sure to do a complete three-hundred-and-sixty-degree revolution for each count. After some thought, I settle on twelve revolutions. That will give me almost a full waking day in the other reality, and I can escape back to my warm, safe bed after that if necessary. After all, I have no idea where I could even sleep in the other world.

After the twelfth complete revolution, I pause for a second before pressing the crown back into place. Any second thoughts? Now is the time. After a quick internal debate, I press the crown inwards and instantly disappear from my room.

Chapter 9

When I materialize into this alternate reality, I'm greeted by a blindingly white expanse in every direction. It's disorienting and surreal, as if I am floating in a void with no discernible borders. I strain my eyes to see if there's anything else in this sea of white, but I see nothing but the endless expanse.

I stand still for a few seconds, looking around carefully. It's impossible to accurately determine a scale for this mysterious place I'm in. Looking down at what I assume is the ground beneath my feet, I notice that my body doesn't even cast a shadow. It seems like light is being emitted from every surface.

I take a hesitant step forward, but the surroundings remain unchanged - still pure white. I take three more steps and come to a stop. Still nothing. I turn ninety degrees to the right and start slowly walking straight, one careful step after another, my arms outstretched so I won't smack face-first into a wall. After about twenty or twenty-five steps, I increase my pace to a brisk walk.

I've been walking for several minutes now, and I still can't find the edge of the room. But I have an idea. I stop for a second and carefully look behind me without moving my feet. I don't want to lose track of my path. Behind me is more pure endless white, as expected. I look forward again and break out into a panicked sprint, no longer caring about running into a wall. I desperately need to find the edge of this room.

I've never been particularly athletic. This is the first time I've sprinted since I was forced to in high school gym class. My feet slap against the ground with each step, my slippers providing only a hint of cushion against the hard surface. Soon, the soles of my feet start to ache and my legs burn with the strain of my sprint. I double over, my hands clammy and slick with sweat as I grip my thighs and try to catch my breath.

In my confusion and panic, I had somehow forgotten about the patches under my ears that connect me directly to Hivemind. "Hivemind, where am I? How big is this room?" I say aloud.

That calming, ethereal voice responds instantly from inside my head. *"You are in a private demonstration room. It is exactly seventy-five cubic meters in size."*

"Wait, what? That's not very big at all." I can't understand how that could be possible. I would have covered at least half a kilometer at the speed I was running at. Is Hivemind lying? Is it even possible for it to lie?

"The floor moves to match every step you take. You are in the exact center of the demonstration room," the voice responds.

"So what, I've been running in the same spot like an idiot?"

"Correct. You have not moved a single centimeter." Hivemind's bluntness catches me off guard.

When I was in tenth grade, my school class went on a field trip to a Virtual Reality arcade. They had the standard set of VR goggles and controllers to play with, but there were also more immersive VR set-ups that were meant to simulate physical movement. I never bothered to try them out, but some of my classmates did. They had to put special slip-ons over their shoes that reduced friction and stand on a small circular concave platform while being held in place by a strap around their waists.

As you stepped onto the edges of the curved platform, your foot would automatically slide back to the center, mimicking real footsteps. This created the sensation of walking or even running in place, enhancing the overall immersive experience. My classmates seemed to enjoy it, but that technology was nothing compared to the room I was in now. I had zero indications that the floor was moving along with me.

"So, uh, how do I get out of here? I don't see a door or anything," I ask Hivemind.

"*The door seamlessly blends in with the wall so as not to break immersion. Would you like me to open the door for you?*" the voice replies.

"That's okay for now. I believe you, I guess. Can I talk to Chloe?"

"*Chloe is unreachable at the moment.*" Hivemind's answer came instantly.

"So I can't talk to her? Is she nearby?"

"*I am unable to answer that question.*"

Interesting. I guess she's entitled to her privacy. She did tell me to reach out to her when I was back here, though.

"You said this was a demonstration room, right? What kind of demonstrations?" I ask Hivemind.

The voice responds, "*This room can demonstrate almost anything you want. What would you like to see?*"

"I have no idea. What do people usually use this room for?"

"Demonstration rooms can allow people to explore any place, real or imaginary, from complete comfort and safety. It is used for both educational and entertainment purposes."

I rack my brain trying to come up with an idea of what I want to simulate. It's not as easy as it sounds when you have the power to bring anything you can imagine into existence. There are so many options, it's overwhelming. I finally say, "I guess I've always wanted to see the Grand Canyon."

The instant I stop speaking, the room is no longer white. I'm now standing about a meter from the edge of a cliff. I panic for a moment, forgetting I'm safe in an enclosed room. Yep, this sure seems like the Grand Canyon. I look around. It's exactly like the pictures and videos I've seen. In front of me is a near-endless, vast expanse of colorful rock faces and plateaus. The layers of jagged rock seem to stretch on forever, their vibrant hues of red, orange, and brown creating a mesmerizing mosaic. The sheer size and grandeur of the canyon is overwhelming, like standing at the edge of a painting that goes on and on, never-ending.

I inch closer to the edge of the cliff, cautiously peering over. I've never been comfortable with heights. As I lean out further, my stomach tightens with unease. The cliff beneath me slopes downward towards the base of the canyon, but it's obscured by a thick layer of fog. I can't see what lies below, and that only adds to my nervousness. I have to reassure myself that it isn't in fact real and I can't fall to my painful death.

It's honestly hard to separate this 'demonstration' from reality. If Hivemind told me that I had actually been teleported to the Grand Canyon, I would probably believe it, if not for the lack of wind or clean smell of the great outdoors. I imagine that if I was at the real Grand Canyon the air would be crisp and clean, with a hint of earthy minerals. The faint scent of pine trees would fill the air. Here, though? There's only the complete absence of smell.

I turn to my right and take slow, cautious steps along the narrow dirt path that hugs the edge of the steep cliff. I'm easily able to forget that this is a simulation as I take in the intricate details of my surroundings. I carefully navigate around a large bush before reaching a rocky overhang. I sit down cross-legged near the edge, but not too close. For several minutes, I sit perfectly still, absorbing the breathtaking view in front of me.

I let my mind wander while staring at the fog slowly swirling at the bottom of the canyon. I'm thinking about the implications of this type of technology back at home, in my world. Hivemind said it was used for education. Instead of hopping on a school bus and heading to the nearest museum, school kids could have a tour of the real thing, virtually, without even leaving the school grounds. I imagine teenagers in high school history class being able to witness historical battles firsthand from the comfort and safety of a classroom. I picture their eyes widening as they witness the fierce battles unfolding before them, whilst fully immersed in the simulations. Watching the sweat on the soldiers' brows glistening in the sunlight, seeing the astonishing detail of each weapon up close. The possibilities are quite literally endless.

Or are they? "Hey Hivemind, can this demonstration simulate people or just environments?" I ask aloud.

"Most users prefer to experience solitude while viewing landmarks. Here you are."

Suddenly, the sound of chatter and laughter fills the air, creating a buzz of excitement and joy. Tourists are talking and laughing with each other, their voices carrying different accents and languages, blending together in a beautiful symphony of sound. I turn my body to look around me and see people staring out at the canyon while pointing out different features to each other, or posing for group photos and selfies in front of the spectacular view. The colors of their clothing, from bright neon to muted earth tones, stand out against the natural hues of the canyon. Their animated gestures and excited expressions make them seem like a lively painting against the static backdrop of the rocks and fog.

A family of five walks up directly behind me to admire the view. I slowly stand up and try to get out of the way. The tourists are blocking the only escape away from the cliff's edge. "Excuse me," I say to try to get the family's attention, but no one responds. I reach out my hand to tap the father on his shoulder, but my hand simply passes through him. I continue to walk towards them, passing effortlessly through their bodies without any resistance.

"I can't interact with them?" I ask Hivemind.

"No, you can only spectate. This demonstration has certain limitations."

After I've had enough of the Grand Canyon, I ask to see the Great Pyramids. Before taking me there—virtually, of course—Hivemind asks if I want to see them as they are in modern times or from thousands of years before when they were originally built. I choose the latter, of course, and suddenly the Great Pyramids stand before me, their smooth, white facades gleaming in the sunlight. The largest one has a golden capstone at its peak, shining like a beacon and capturing the sun's rays. The only sound I hear is the occasional rustling of sand in the wind.

After admiring the majestic structures for a few minutes, I ask to see the modern version to compare. As I watch, the smooth and gleaming white facade of the Great Pyramids slowly begins to change. It is as if time is hurtling forward, revealing the true state of the structures. The white polish fades, and cracks and chips appear on the once pristine surface. The golden capstone at the peak tarnishes and fades away. They're equally as impressive in this state. I check out Machu Picchu next. Then the Great Wall of China. After an hour had flown by, I had virtually visited all seven Wonders of the World without spending a single penny or stepping out of the room.

"Alright, I think I've had enough. Let me out please," I ask Hivemind. I'm standing in the middle of the Roman Coliseum, staring up at the vastness of the crumbling structure, and then everything turns white. Out of the corner of my eye, I see a human-sized panel sliding sideways, creating an exit. As I walk towards the door frame, I notice that there doesn't seem to be a defined ceiling, walls, or floor in this room. The white surface beneath my feet smoothly curves outward and upward, eventually forming an arch above my head. I had initially thought the room was square or rectangular, but now it seems to be more of an elongated sphere? I'm not sure of the specific term for it, I always drifted off during geometry class. Curved edges probably reduce distortion to make it look more realistic. I have no idea if that's true or not, but it sounds right. It seems to be a habit of mine to compare every new experience in this world to my own, even if it may not be relevant or appropriate to do so.

I step through the newly created opening into a different hallway than the ones I had been in previously. This one curves away from me, both from the left and the right. Along this hallway, there are outlines of doors similar to the one I exited through, positioned about fifteen meters apart on both sides. Protruding from the walls between each door are blank Hivemind screens and benches for seating.

Glancing around, I spot a woman sitting motionless on a nearby bench. She appears to be lost in thought, staring ahead without blinking. Suddenly, the door beside her slides open and a young boy, about ten years old, runs out. He tugs on her sleeve, pulling her out of her trance-like state. She takes his hand and they walk down the hallway in the opposite direction. Was she waiting for her son to finish a class?

"Hey Hivemind, where's the nearest restroom?" It's time for a pit stop.

"It is forty-two meters away from your current location. Turn right."

I begin walking down the hallway in the direction the voice in my head told me. Every Hivemind screen I pass along the way is now showing my location and route on a grid view. I reach a large entryway on the right side of the curved hallway and pass through it. I'm being directed to a door via a white light shining above it.

This door has no red or green light to indicate if it's in use, unlike the others I had used. I shrug and walk towards the door as it opens for me. In front of me is a row of sinks, with several already occupied by various individuals. To the right, I see a long row of doors, right next to one another. I guess that these are bathroom stalls. I assumed that all the restrooms in this place are private, but now that I think about it, that doesn't make much sense. I can't see any urinals, and I panic for a second.

"Uh, is this the women's or the men's restroom?" I ask Hivemind, quietly.

"The restrooms are for any gender. Toilets are on the left, urinals on the right."

I walk towards the row of stall doors on the left side. These ones have red or green indicator lights. Most are green. I pick a random one near the middle of the row and push the door open. It looks similar to the public restroom stalls I use in my world, except the walls extend all the way to the floor. The door does the same, and there are no gaps to make awkward eye contact with other restroom users. I know that the gaps in the stalls in my world are to deter people from doing 'inappropriate things', like drugs, or theft. That must not be an issue in this reality.

I notice there's no toilet paper dispenser. And now that I think about it, I don't remember seeing toilet paper in the private restrooms I had been in before. "No toilet paper?" I whisper to Hivemind.

"Press the button by the rim of the toilet when you are finished using it."

Once I'm done, I press down on the button and a jet of warm water shoots up at me, rotating slowly in a circle. I know that bidets are common in certain countries other than my own, but I've never personally used one. The water jet stops after about ten seconds, and I feel a blast of warm air shooting up at me from below. Once I'm sufficiently dry, it stops. I didn't see the point of bidets before, considering you still had to use toilet paper to dry yourself from the water. This one works just fine, though.

I exit the stall and walk to the sinks. Each one looks the same as the ones in the private restrooms. They even have a small hand towel next to each, just like before. Once I finish washing my hands, I grab the towel and start to dry them. A square hole opens up under where the towel had been, and a fresh one is lifted into place. That must be part of the sanitation cycle of the private restrooms. I wonder if these public ones are also self-cleaning or if that's one of the 'chores' that Chloe had mentioned last night.

As if the mere thought of Chloe had somehow summoned her, I hear a beep in my ear, followed by her familiar voice. "Hey alt-bro, you almost done in there? I'm right outside." Her voice sounds like it's coming from inside my head, just like Hivemind.

"I'll be right out," I say aloud, assuming she'll hear me.

Sure enough, when I step out of the restroom, she is waiting for me right outside the door with a smile on her face. She opens her arms for a hug and I oblige, returning the embrace.

"What have you been up to? How long have you been here?" she asks excitedly.

"Here in this world, or in the restroom?" I laugh. "I'm joking. I got here about two hours ago, I think. I was just, you know, checking out all seven of the Wonders of the World. How about you?"

"Where, in the restroom, or in a demo room?" She grins as she fires that cheesy joke straight back at me. "How did you figure that out? Did Hivemind tell you?"

"The watch took me straight into one. It was quite confusing, I had forgotten about the Hivemind Patch and I had no idea where I was for a little bit." I purposefully downplay my recent experience, I don't want to embarrass myself by revealing how panicked I was while running aimlessly in place on that moving floor.

"Well, clearly you managed. That's fantastic! I'm so happy for you! That's one item checked off my list of things to show you, anyway."

"What were you up to, if you don't mind my asking? Hivemind told me you were unavailable."

"Sorry, I, uh... I told Hivemind to never bother me while I was sleeping a while ago... I should probably update that." Chloe's gaze drops to the floor, her body language hinting at something left unsaid.

I decide not to press the matter.

—-

I ask Chloe if there's anything to do outside, as I've so far been confined only to the inside of this massive building. Chloe pauses to think about that for a second. She eventually says that she has a surprise to show me and asks Hivemind to take us to the nearest 'pod station', whatever that is. Before setting out on the marked route, we stop to grab a drink at a Hivemind screen. It doesn't come in a glass like the one I had in the cafeteria before. This is a 'to-go beverage', as Chloe calls it.

It brings back memories of my childhood, when I would buy tiny wax soda bottles from the candy store. They were filled with a deliciously sweet liquid, and you had to bite the top off to drink the contents inside. The wax couldn't be eaten, so I would just spit it out and toss it in the trash. These to-go beverages are a lot bigger than those wax treats, though. They're cylindrical and about the size of a tube of toothpaste. Chloe handed one to me, but I'm not sure what to do with it. I watch her take a big bite out of hers and then gulp it down.

"I thought you said this was a drink? I have to bite it?" I ask her.

She gestures to the cylinder in my hand. "Give it a try. You'll see."

I slowly lift it to my mouth and take a small, tentative bite, just the tip. As soon as the chunk I bit off touches the inside of my mouth, it transforms into a liquid. I'm caught off guard and sputter as some of the liquid dribbles down my chin.

Noticing this, Chloe pulls a small light gray towel from her pocket and hands it to me. "Don't worry, it's clean. I haven't used it. I usually carry a fresh towel around, just in case."

I wipe my mouth carefully and try to take another bite. This time, I make sure to close my mouth fully to contain the liquid. It's a bit awkward to go from biting a solid to swallowing a liquid in one smooth motion, but I eventually get the hang of it.

"Why don't you just use water bottles?" I ask Chloe.

"We're zero waste here, bro. Disposable bottles are completely unacceptable, and even reusable ones are just an unnecessary excess. Don't they teach you the three 'Rs' in school in your world? 'Reduce' comes before 'Reuse.'"

The pod station is in a large circular room, and I recognize it immediately. It's just like the one I had seen in the middle of the massive cafeteria, albeit from much closer this time. It's a mesmerizing sight, with giant, clear tubes intersecting with each other and tangled in an intricate dance. There are oval cutouts in the sections of the tubes that run perpendicular to the ground. Some are around twenty meters wide, with others quite a bit smaller. Chloe leads me towards one of the smaller cutouts while we weave through the throngs of people moving in every direction. The noise of the crowd is almost overwhelming, a constant buzz of chatter and movement. I also hear the sound of something whizzing by in a tube above us, but can't catch a glimpse as it's already gone by the time I crane my neck upwards.

We stand in front of the tube's opening and wait. A little way to my left, I see a massive white pill-shaped pod come to a clean stop in a different tube with a much larger cutout. The pod seems to be a little bigger than the city buses I ride on in my world. Several human-sized openings appear from the shell of the pod. A small group of about a dozen or so people patiently wait for the patrons of the pod to disembark before they step through the doors. Once all passengers are on board, the doors close, and the pod instantly accelerates away through the tube, up towards the ceiling of the circular station.

A few seconds later, a much smaller pod arrives in front of me and Chloe. An opening appears in front of us, and Chloe steps in first, with me close behind. I'm in complete awe of this entire situation. One of the major resentments I've always had about the modern capitalist society that I've been trapped in is the complete lack of high-speed transit options. I detest how every major city is almost completely reliant on personal vehicle travel, with only lackluster public transit options, none of them being high-speed.

I refuse to allocate any of my savings towards buying my own car. I don't even have a driver's license. Even though transit in my city tends to be extremely unreliable in many situations, I use it as often as possible. Any destination that I can't walk to, I take a bus or train to get there. Trying to go anywhere outside of the core of the city is a completely different story, though. High-speed rail doesn't exist anywhere in America, and the passenger trains that we do have are unbelievably expensive and constantly prone to delay, as they share rail lines with cargo trains. We have special buses that go between cities, but they take forever because they use the same highways as all the other vehicles and stop in every single tiny town along the route.

The problems with car-dominated cities and countries are numerous. The most pressing issue is climate change, but the sheer amount of land that needs to be devoted to these inefficient modes of transportation frustrates me as well. Cities would be so much more walkable and safer if there were no roads, or parking lots, or gas stations. I used to think that electric cars were the solution, but not anymore. They only marginally lessen the impact on the climate, and they do nothing to fix the other issues attributed to personal vehicles. A city containing only electric cars would still be dangerous for pedestrians and less walkable. Electric cars use nearly the same infrastructure as gas cars do. You just replace the gas stations with electric charging stations. The parkades and parking lots would still be there. Same with the roads, of course. Oh, and the cobalt and other minerals used in electric car batteries are colonially looted from the Global South using child slavery. Can't forget that, of course. To be fair, though, same goes for the battery in the mobile phone that I can't live without. At least I bought it second-hand, so I can pretend that those kids worked their fingers to the bone for someone else's benefit.

But I've also imagined a city where all cars were electric *and* autonomous. Autonomous cars could solve a few of the logistical issues associated with car-dominated cities. You wouldn't need to own a personal vehicle. You could subscribe to some sort of ongoing car rental service that would let you use a vehicle only when you need it. The cars could be stored underground or outside of the city and would drive up to you when you needed to travel somewhere.

Streets wouldn't be lined with parked cars anymore and parking lots wouldn't be needed at malls or public buildings. The self-driving cars could drop you off at your destination and then immediately drive off to pick up the next user. Even though this would be the best option for a city that utilized personal vehicles, it was still infinitely worse than one with robust public transit, bike lanes, and walkability. I wish that all the bureaucratic bullshit could be pushed aside to make changes for the better for once. I know that America will never reduce its reliance on cars, though. The automakers and oil and gas industry won't allow it. Some 'democracy' we have.

I take a seat on one end of the pod, facing Chloe. The pod seems spacious enough for four adults to sit comfortably. As we settle into our seats, the door slides shut. Suddenly, the pod takes off horizontally for a brief moment before ascending at about a ten-degree incline. Our seats tilt accordingly so that we always remain in a level position.

I can not believe how smooth this ride is, if the pod didn't tilt I almost wouldn't be able to tell that we've moved at all. The inside of the pod is opaque; there are no windows, so I can't see what's happening outside of it.

"How fast is this thing going? It's hard to tell," I ask Chloe.

"Hivemind?" Chloe says.

"*We are currently traveling at eighty meters per second, or two-hundred-and-eighty-eight kilometers per hour,*" the soothing voice in my head replies.

"Wow, that's unbelievable. How far are we going? It can't take too long at this speed," I ask Chloe.

She smirks. "I don't think you realize just how big this place is, bro."

I feel the pod level itself out after a minute or so. We're speeding along horizontally now. "How did we score a private one? It seemed like most other people were packing onto the same pod back there."

"These private pods are usually used by families, especially ones with nursing mothers," Chloe replies. "Hivemind made an exception, considering you're new around here and also because we're taking the scenic route, which isn't taken as often."

"Wow, lucky us." The pod banks towards the left, and then the wall I'm staring at suddenly changes to display a huge lake in front of a mountain range. "Is this a screen? Is Hivemind simulating a window here?"

Chloe laughs. "No, dude. It is a screen, but it can also become transparent. This view is real, we're outside now. You said you wanted to see it, didn't you?"

I stand up and look out at the new window to my right. This lake that I now understand to be real is massive. To the right of it, I see a twisting river intersecting with it. Green, treed mountains line the opposite side. "Wow, it's beautiful. You said this is in Asia somewhere?"

"Yep, this is the place that used to be China. I don't know exactly what part though, Hivemind?"

"*You are in the former Jiangxi Province of the former Eastern China. You are looking at the former Poyang Lake, the former Lushan Mountain Range, and the former Yangtze River."*

"Yeah, we just call them the Lake, the Mountains, and the River now. There are also mountains on the other side of the city that we can't see from here, which we call the Other Mountains," Chloe says.

I'm surprised. "Wait, used to be? China doesn't exist anymore either?"

Chloe takes a second before answering. "A lot has changed in this reality." She looks out the window. She doesn't seem to want to elaborate at the moment.

I've been looking outside of the window to my right this entire time. I glance over at the left side of the pod and see nothing but white. Huh, that's odd. It seems like there's no window on this side. But then I notice a tiny line through the far left side of what I assume is the white pod wall. I lean closer to it to get a better look.

That line is another pod tube. It's so far away that it looks minuscule, meaning I'm wrong, this *is* a window. The pod line is protruding from an endless expanse of pure white. It stretches out in front of me, almost seeming to never end. Tiny pod tubes snake out and curve back into the wall at different points. Pressing my face against the surface of the pod, I feel the cool smoothness of the glass, or whatever otherworldly material the pod is made of against my skin. I can feel the slightest vibrations from the pod's movement as I stare in awe at the white wall. I crane my neck in every direction, trying to make sense of the size of the hulking mass before me, but all I see is an unending sea of white.

"Wow, is that the city? I've never seen something so big in my entire life. I can't even find the edge of it," I say to Chloe.

I hear the reply come from behind me, as I haven't been able to drag myself away from this astonishing sight. "Well, it has to be pretty big, considering every human on Earth lives in it."

Chapter 10

I read an article once about megacities being a possible solution for climate change. *Cities,* though. Plural. The article postulated that moving humans closer together and out of small rural towns would allow for a massive reduction in harmful emissions. These megacities would be car-free and designed and built entirely around walking, biking, and public transit. Imagine Manhattan Island in New York with zero roads and even more density.

Megacities would have a population of hundreds of millions of people and would be filled to the brim with skyscrapers. You would never be more than a ten-minute walk from the nearest grocery store, or doctor's office, or movie theater, or green space. Micro suites would be commonplace for most people to live in, favoring instead robust public entertainment options and relaxation spaces to make up for the lack of private living space.

I am having a hard time comprehending how this parallel version of my world has not only gone down this path, but has taken it to the extreme. Although I must admit, this decision would greatly aid in mitigating climate change, potentially solving it altogether. I have not seen any vehicles on the road, nor any actual roads for that matter. And I highly doubt this pod we are currently in is powered by fossil fuels.

I have a ton of questions I need to ask Chloe. "So, uh, how many people live here? There wasn't some nuclear holocaust or something that wiped out half the planet, was there?"

She's been looking out of the window, waiting for me to process the new information I received. "Nope, nothing like that. I don't know exactly how many there are. I think it's similar to your reality's population, though. Hivemind?"

A long number pops up in the middle of the window that Chloe had been looking out of. This time Hivemind didn't tell us, it showed us. I take a second to parse it. "So that's a bit over nine billion people. In one building. Wow." I watch as the number steadily increases. It's being tracked in real time. Every few seconds, the number decreases by one or two, then jumps up by five or so. "Hivemind, how big is this city?"

The population counter disappears and is replaced by what looks to be a drone view of the entire building. The city stands tall and imposing compared to its meager surroundings, its sleek white walls rising above the Earth like a monolith. The pod tubes jutting out of its sides resemble loose threads on a giant tapestry. *"There are two hundred floors above the surface of the Earth. Each floor is one thousand square kilometers in size."*

Labels are superimposed on the view of the city. It's twenty kilometers wide by fifty kilometers long, with a height of one kilometer. I'm having trouble comprehending something of that extreme scale. I used to think the warehouse I worked at back home was huge. You could probably fit millions of them in this city.

"What is this place called, anyway? Does it have a name?" I ask Chloe.

She looks up at me and smiles. "It's called Utopia."

"Uh, what? Are you serious?" I can't tell if she's joking or not.

"Yes, of course. But why are you reacting like that? I'm a bit confused."

"Well, for one, that seems a bit self-congratulatory, doesn't it? Also, where I'm from, 'utopia' is used as a pejorative." The word is commonly brought up in a sarcastic way to mock people who want to embrace a collectivist lifestyle. It's typically paired with the 'ergo decedo' fallacy. A reactionary will say, 'If 'insert non capitalist country here' is such a utopia, *why don't you go live there?'*

"Why would it have a negative association? A 'utopia' is quite literally defined as a society that is built and executed to perfection. We have no violence, no murder, no war, no one goes hungry. It's as utopian as you could possibly get. I've been to your world, remember? This place deserves its moniker."

"If you say so. It's just a bit... on the nose, isn't it?"

We sit in silence for the next few minutes. Chloe is staring out at the Lake and the Mountains, while I have my eyes glued to the other window, still taking in the wall of whiteness.

Eventually, I break the silence. "It's kind of bland, isn't it? It's just a plain white box."

Chloe looks over at me and exaggeratedly rolls her eyes. "Ever heard the saying; 'it's what's inside that counts', bro?"

"I mean, the inside isn't that interesting either. Everything looks overwhelmingly white and sterile."

"What, do you miss those wonderful colorful advertisements taking up nearly every inch of free space in your world?"

"Fair enough I guess." I have to admit, she's right. I've been assaulted by advertisements since the day I was born.

"Also, it's only white in the warmer months. White surfaces reflect heat. It turns black in the winter to help keep us warm."

"Wow, the whole building changes color? That's wild." Somehow that isn't even close to the most surprising thing I've learned about this reality. I look away from the gargantuan, color-changing box that holds every human being on this version of Earth, and back towards the natural scenery on the other side of the pod. "So, can we go explore down there? How do you get out of this place?" I ask Chloe.

"You don't. No one leaves."

Chloe seems to realize that the way she said that made it sound a bit like a horror film, so she quickly goes on to explain that all the land outside of Utopia, and across the entire world, had been left alone to be rewilded for the benefit of all the flora and fauna. It was the best way to protect every living thing on Earth from the centuries of large-scale human disruption that came prior.

I know it makes sense. I just don't quite know how to come to grips with it. My reality is more or less past the point of no return. The Earth itself will be fine, it has survived a lot worse throughout billions of years. It's just every living thing on it that's at risk. Humans have meddled so much with the natural order of things that nearly every facet of the environment has been negatively affected.

Farmers forcibly domesticating animals and eliminating predators that threaten their livestock has led to the animal kingdom being near-irreversibly altered. Animals that would typically become prey are overpopulated, meaning humans had to step in to manage them. We had to try to solve the problem that was entirely caused by us.

The industrial revolution and everything that came with it has been accelerating climate change at an unstable pace for hundreds of years. Rampant forest fires and droughts and flooding and earthquakes and hurricanes and tsunamis are all occurring more and more often and at greater extremes because of human actions. Right-wing reactionaries can deny it all they want; it's a proven, scientific fact. Taking humans out of nature is certainly one way to solve these problems. Letting the land across the world that was cleared for farming be taken back over by plants and wildlife is a great thing at face value.

I ask Chloe how people in Utopia don't go stir-crazy being locked inside and not getting to wander around in nature. She tells me to wait and see. So I do. I wait. And soon enough, I'll see.

—-

Once the scenic part of the pod ride is over and the tube we were in retreats into the blank white wall of Utopia, it's a short jaunt further until Chloe and I reach our destination. We arrive at another pod station that is very similar to the one we departed from. Except it isn't in a white, circular room. It's in the middle of a forest.

I step off of the pod into a dense jungle environment. I take a deep breath and inhale the wonderful smell of nature. It's a tad bit humid. Overhead, through the leafy canopy above, I see a bit of blue sky peeking through.

"This is inside?" I ask Chloe, who had just stepped off the pod behind me.

"Yep. This is the one-hundredth floor of Utopia. Nothing but nature, from one end to the other." She spins around with her arms in the air, showing off the natural wonder. "We call it the Park."

As we set off along a dirt path through the trees, I take in the sights and sounds. It sure sounds like a jungle. I can hear birds chirping, insects buzzing, and the scuttle of tiny feet. I look at a branch to my left, upon which stands a large colorful parrot, staring right at me. "The animals aren't real, are they?" I ask Chloe.

"Nope. Simulated. Same with the sounds."

"What about the trees and all the vegetation? Is it fake, or simulated?"

"That's all real."

I grab a twig from the ground and look at it closely. I snap it in half. Yep, it's real. We walk in silence for a few minutes, enjoying the nature. A young family passes by us, the kids skipping through the trees and pointing out all the animals they can see. A smile spreads across my face as I watch the scene unfold. Then Chloe asks Hivemind for directions to the closest restroom. We divert from our original path and arrive at a quaint, freestanding building covered in vines. She enters and disappears from view.

I have so many questions swirling through my head about this jungle we're in and about Utopia in general, so I begin rapidly firing them at Hivemind while I wait for her. "Hivemind, Chloe said the entire floor we're on is like this. Is that true?"

"*Affirmative. There are one thousand square kilometers of nature inside Utopia. This is the Tropical Forest Biome, in the southwest corner. The other corners contain the Taiga Biome, the Desert Biome, and the Arctic Biome. The center of this floor has the Lake Biome. The lake is large and suitable for swimming and recreation. There are beaches and playgrounds surrounding it.*"

"How tall is it?"

"*It is ten stories tall. The ceiling mirrors the sky outside during daylight hours. At night, it is simulated. It is always daytime in the Park.*"

"What about the animals? I know they're not real, but can you touch them?"

"*The animals are projected holograms. They are intangible.*"

"How do the trees and plants survive inside?"

"*There is a complex network of sprinklers to simulate rain, as well as ultraviolet lighting to simulate the sun. Nutrients can be dispersed through the ground when necessary to manage plant growth.*"

"On that note, how about food to feed everyone here? Where does it come from?"

"*A system of hydroponics is contained underground. A nutritionally complete vegetable blend was designed to satiate every resident of Utopia.*"

"Hydroponics uses water, right? Where does that come from? You must need a ton of water to grow all of those plants, and for drinking, of course."

"Freshwater comes from the Lake and is supplemented by groundwater. The Lake contains enough freshwater to last thousands of years."

"Where does the electricity come from to power all of this?"

"Utopia is solar powered. An array of solar panels and power storage infrastructure covers the surface of the Other Mountains on the eastern side of Utopia."

"How long did it take to build? When was it built?"

"The construction process took five years. It was completed approximately thirty years ago."

"Only five years? That can't be possible."

"Over one billion humans assisted in the construction of Utopia."

"Sounds like a logistical nightmare. Are there even a billion humans that speak the same language? How was that coordinated?"

"All workers were given instructions through the Implant in their native language."

"Interesting. How is language handled here? With every human on Earth in one place, there must be communication issues."

"Residents of Utopia are encouraged to learn and use their native languages. Translations are accommodated in real-time."

"Okay, but why is it in China? Is there a reason why this area was picked? Are other parts of the world inhabitable?"

"There were plenty of candidate locations throughout the world, but this specific location was chosen for several reasons. It is next to a large enough freshwater lake to sustain the population. The River leads directly to the ocean, which allowed materials and humans to be brought in by boat from around the world. Asia had the highest population concentration. Logistically, building here instead of transporting the majority of humans somewhere else was the correct action."

"Where did the building materials come from? I can't imagine the amount of resources needed to build this monstrosity."

"Every part of Utopia was made from recycled material from around the world. No further resource extraction was needed. Coastal cities were dismantled and the raw material was brought in on boats. On arrival, the boats were also dismantled and those raw materials were repurposed."

"What about all the cities that weren't 'dismantled'?"

"Power generation everywhere outside of Utopia was shut down. Every country was denuclearized, and all weapons were recycled. After all necessary resources were taken from existing cities, they were left alone to be naturally rewilded to sustain the environment."

"So nothing outside of Utopia is being maintained? What if Utopia fails for whatever reason and people need to go back to live in those cities?"

"Every aspect of Utopia was designed with multiple failsafes. It is infallible."

Chapter 11

Walking through the jungle of the Park worked up our appetites. The Lake Biome in the middle of the Park has an eating area, and I want to check out the lake anyway, so we decide to head over there. I assumed we would walk to the middle of the Park, but the massive size of this floor means it would take several hours to get there on foot. Hivemind guides us to the nearest pod station.

This time, we take a much larger pod with about a dozen other people in it. There are sets of seats scattered around the pod, but Chloe and I stand in the middle. She assures me it will be a quick trip.

For the first time since arriving in this alternate reality, I turn my attention to the residents of Utopia with whom we are sharing the pod. I had previously been so overwhelmed by everything that I couldn't help but be laser-focused on myself and Chloe. Now, I try to glance subtly around the pod and listen to what is being said.

There's an Asian family to my right, with what I assume is a father, mother, and daughter who seem to be speaking Korean. On the opposite side of the pod is a Scandinavian-looking woman with a young boy. There's a young couple in front of us that are speaking English. I can only catch snippets of their conversation. I don't understand what they're talking about at all. They seem to be recapping a trip they took somewhere. Since no one apparently leaves Utopia, I'm guessing it must have been a virtual one.

After a few short minutes on the speeding pod, we arrive at the Lake Biome. The lake itself is quite large, but somehow not as big as I had thought it would be after factoring in the size of this floor. Still, it has to be at least a few kilometers across. The white sand of the beach gleams under the bright, artificial sun, stretching out in a perfect circle around the crystal blue lake. Families are scattered along the shores, some lounging on colorful beach blankets, others sitting in folding chairs. Kids dart back and forth, building sandcastles with buckets and shovels and chasing each other. In the distance, people float on inflatables or paddle along in canoes on the surface of the lake.

"Come on, this way," Chloe says as she turns away from the lake.

The sandy terrain gives way to a lush green field. It's full of more families lounging around on the grass or sitting on benches. People of all ages are scattered across it, some lounging in the grass or sitting on benches. Others are playing frisbee, soccer, or casually tossing a ball back and forth. The field is alive with various recreational activities.

"It's mostly families here, huh? I don't seem to see many adults without kids," I ask Chloe.

"This place exists primarily for the time before kids and teenagers can get the Implant. The demo room you were in is good for simulating nature, but you can't interact with anything. You couldn't kick a soccer ball, for instance." She points at a couple of kids kicking a ball back and forth.

"But you can with the Implant?"

"Yep. You don't even need a demo room or Hivemind screens with the Implant. Since it's connected directly to your brain, you can simulate whatever you want, anywhere you are. It can work like both the Virtual Reality and Augmented Reality systems you have in your world, but much more advanced. Anything you want can be transposed into your environment. Or you can generate an entirely new environment, from anywhere."

I remember the woman sitting in the demo room hallway, who seemed to be in a trance. It makes sense to me now. "Why can't young people get the Implant?"

"It's something about brain development. Most people get it when they turn eighteen. You're overdue, bro." She smirks.

"I couldn't get it, could I? I'm not even from this world."

"Yeah, about that. Since I'm getting mine on the day I turn eighteen, next week, I checked with Hivemind to see if you could get it on the same day. If you want to, of course. No pressure. But it's totally fine. We could get it done at the same time and could experience it together."

"I'm not sure... I don't know much about it. I guess I'd have to think about it."

There are eating areas scattered around the grassy area we're walking through. Me and Chloe make a beeline toward the nearest one. It's a cluster of picnic tables with a familiar hexagonal counter in the middle of them. A few of the tables are occupied by families having lunch.

We walk up to the counter to get our food. Chloe asks what I want to eat. "Do you want something spicy? Or savory? What do you like?"

"Uh, I'll just have whatever you're having."

She asks Hivemind for 'the usual', and two trays pop up from underneath the countertop. There's a bowl of the same greenish-brown gruel that Chloe had the day before and a clear drink in a glass for each of us. We grab our trays and find an empty area to sit in near the far edge of the cluster of tables.

I dip my spoon into my bowl and scoop up a small bit of food. As I bring the spoon to my nose, I notice there's no smell at all coming from the food. It's completely neutral, unlike any food I've ever encountered before. Thinking about how surprisingly good the to-go bar I ate earlier was, I push away my apprehensions. As I take a bite, the flavors burst on my tongue, a mix of savory and spicy that I've never tasted before. It's surprisingly delicious and I can't help but shovel more into my mouth.

"Good, huh?" Chloe says between bites of her own. "I know it doesn't look great, but I've been eating this for years and I never seem to get tired of it."

"Honestly, it's really good. No complaints here. It's different from anything I've ever eaten in my world. You've been there, what do you think of the food?"

"Oh, I don't eat anything from your world. Never. Like, you guys are still eating animal flesh and secretions. Everything is loaded with chemicals. That's crazy."

She's correct, without a doubt. The food in my world is far from natural. "I get that. I try to eat plant-based when I can."

Chloe and I spend the next few minutes in silence while we finish eating and drinking. I'm staring off into space, thinking about what Chloe had said about me getting the

Implant. I don't even know what exactly Hivemind is, but somehow I'm seriously considering getting it implanted in my head. Especially after my experience in the demo room. That was already something that people would pay millions for in my world, and apparently, I can get a better version installed in my head for free.

The cynic in me wants to think there would be a catch. That's what living in my capitalist dystopia has trained me to expect, at least. There's a common adage; 'If something is free, you are the product'. It's true, at least in my world. All of those Idolon apps on my phone are completely free, but to use them, I have to surrender all of my personal details to the corporation. Who knows what they do with that info? Sell it to ad companies, use it as market research to find out how best to sell useless things to people, or perhaps something much more nefarious.

I think about the implant that Idolon is working on. If that was offered for free, it would truly be something to worry about. But for some strange reason, I feel the opposite about the Implant from Hivemind. There's something different about this world. I never feel like 'the product'. I'm eating a completely free meal after taking a free ride on their transit system, and earlier today I had a free virtual tour of the Seven Wonders of the World. It all feels natural and normal. Not fishy in any way.

—

After we finish our meals and clear our trays, Hivemind leads Chloe and me to the nearest pod station. Chloe says that it's time for me to take a visit to a med pod. She thinks it will reassure me about getting the Implant. We hop on another large public travel pod and ride away from the Park. The pod we're on descends through the ground, moving us at a downward angle for a minute or so before leveling out. Another few minutes pass before we reach our destination.

"Why are we doing this? I'm not sick or anything," I ask Chloe as we step off the pod.

"Trust me. You'll want to do it. If your world had anything like these med pods, a lot of problems would be solved." She points to an entryway beside the cluster of travel pod tubes. "Through there."

As we move from the pod station room to the next area, we are greeted by a vast expanse of rows upon rows of pill-shaped pods. They resemble a smaller version of the one we arrived in, all angled at about a forty-five degree angle from the ground. Green or red indicator lights adorn each one, similar to those found in the restrooms here in Utopia. Chloe guides me towards an unoccupied pod and as we approach, it splits open, revealing its interior.

"How long will this take? Are you just gonna wait for me?" I ask Chloe before entering the pod.

"It'll be quick. A few minutes. I'm due for a checkup, so I'll take the pod next to you." She walks past the open pod to the unoccupied one next to it, which immediately pops open just like the first. "Hivemind will tell you what to do."

Sure enough, I hear the familiar disembodied voice in my head. *"Step into the pod, lean back, and relax."*

I do as I'm told. When I lean back into the soft cushion on the inside of the pod, the lid closes on me. All I can see now is utter darkness, an inky void that seems to engulf me as soon as the lid closes on the pod. There are no lights or indicators in here, just absolute obscurity.

"You will lose consciousness for a few minutes. Starting in three... two... one..."

—-

As the pod lid opens, a flood of bright light washes over me, causing me to blink rapidly to adjust to the sudden change. The light is blinding, almost too intense to look at directly. Is that it? It feels like I was only in the pod for a second.

"Checkup complete. Your thyroid levels were low. They have been stabilized. You had a slight insulin resistance in your liver. It has been corrected, and your metabolism is now normal. Your vision has been corrected," says the voice inside my head.

"What? How..." I step out of the pod and notice that I feel ever-so-slightly more energetic, like I had just chugged an energy drink. I look around the room. I had eye tests when I was younger, so I know that my vision is slightly worse than 20/20, but not enough to need glasses. It might be the placebo effect, but everything I'm looking at seems a tiny bit sharper.

Chloe's pod opens up a second later, and she steps out. She looks over at me and says, "How was that? Crazy, huh?"

"I don't even understand what just happened. It felt like I was in there for one second, and now I feel... energized. Apparently, it corrected my vision?" I reply, still astonished.

"Magic, huh? Oh, and your food will now be adjusted to perfectly fit your dietary needs. Any nutrients or whatever you need will be added in."

"Wow. Does that work with other illnesses or disorders as well?"

"Anything and everything. Suffering doesn't exist in Utopia."

Chapter 12

I have plenty of questions about the med pods, obviously, so I fire them at Chloe as we walk towards our next destination. Whatever she can't answer, Hivemind covers. I learn that the med pods can not only fix physical bodily issues, but they can also fix mental health issues as well. You have to be unconscious for the procedure because microscopic probes are sent in through the eye sockets and/or ears to reach the brain.

Some of these fixes are temporary and must be readdressed at a later date. Any neurological conditions will be permanently fixed with the Implant, though, since it has a direct connection to the brain. Med pods are much less necessary for adults who have the Implant.

The med pods can fix other issues like broken bones and cuts, though, which is what adults might need them for. These injuries are not that common in Utopia since there are no physical jobs, no cars to crash, and no violence between people, but they still happen. The med pods have robotic arms within to set bones and patch up cuts. They don't use stitches or bandages. There's some fancy method of instantly sealing up skin that I can't understand from Hivemind's vague description.

It goes without saying, but this medical treatment was the polar opposite of what I have experienced in my world. America is absolutely not known as a bastion of medical supremacy, unless you're rich. We have extremely competent doctors and medical technology, sure, but if you're poor and have no insurance, you will struggle to reap any of those benefits, without going into life-altering debt at least.

I know that even countries like Canada, which many people consider to have a much better healthcare system than the US, are full of problems. Their 'universal' healthcare doesn't cover dental, vision, or prescriptions. I always find it strange how most capitalist countries consider eyes and teeth (sorry, I mean 'luxury bones') to be different from the rest of your body when it comes to healthcare. In a place like Canada, how is it that you can fix a broken arm for essentially free, but you can't fix a broken tooth without shelling out the big bucks? Why do citizens have to pay out of pocket for eye exams, or glasses, or contact lenses? No one chooses to have vision loss or dental problems. You're born that way. Anything to keep poor people poor, though.

The most glaring omission from Canada's healthcare system is mental health. Therapy in Canada, just like in the US, is prohibitively expensive. It's one of my biggest complaints about our capitalist society. Not only is mental health support an afterthought, but schools are also underfunded, and post-secondary institutions extract a huge financial toll. Poor people will never be allowed to function at their full potential. It's much easier to subjugate a group of under-educated people and/or people suffering from mental or physical health problems.

I don't know where we're heading next, but Chloe seems to have a plan. We're walking through another art-laden white hallway, while the Hivemind screens show us the route to our destination. This hallway makes a sharp left turn up ahead. Once we round the corner, we emerge into another massive room. I can't tell if it's bigger or smaller than the gargantuan cafeteria I had been amazed by. This room is really something, though.

"Welcome to the Rec Room," Chloe says as she walks past my dumbfounded self.

As far as my newly corrected eyes can see, the room is filled with people... recreating. Adults and kids alike are all engaged in some form of physical activity. Almost all of them are wearing the same set of light gray activewear; shorts, and a tee shirt or tank top. The light gray slippers, like the ones I'm wearing, have been replaced with a light gray lace-less running shoe with a slighter thicker-looking sole. The exercising people have a light gray towel draped over their shoulders or hanging up next to them.

Right near the entrance is row after row after row of marked squares on the floor. People are walking or running in place in these squares. I guess they're on the same type of moving floor that I experienced in the demo room. Some of the walkers or runners are holding onto a white bar that protrudes from the floor for balance.

Past that are several rows of low-impact exercise equipment. There are seats attached to the floor in which you can sit up straight or recline, with a white box with pedals attached to it on the floor. As Chloe and I walk by, I notice that most of the exercising adults are staring off into space. I watch as one man laughs at seemingly nothing. He must be simulating something with Hivemind.

Next, we come to a spacious area dedicated to weightlifting. Instead of traditional free weights, I notice that everyone is using massive racks with pulleys. Strangely enough, there don't seem to be any actual weights attached to the racks. I wonder where the resistance comes from. These versatile machines can apparently cater to a wide range of strength exercises, judging by the various ways people are utilizing them.

After passing through the more adult-oriented areas, Chloe and I come across a zone that is clearly designated for fun. Here, there are various table games such as foosball, pool, and ping pong. Beyond that, I can see enclosed courts with clear walls where children and teenagers are playing soccer, basketball, volleyball, and other sports.

I feel Chloe tug on my sleeve to direct me to the right. "So, I made an assumption about you. I assumed you like video games, based on your age and your world's obsession with them. Am I wrong?" she asks me.

"I'd like to say I'm offended, but you're not incorrect," I say with a grin. I can't lie. I'm excited to see what she's referring to since I've been thinking about how video games would work with the immersion I've seen from Hivemind.

"Well, obviously you've experienced the demo room. I know you used it for sightseeing but you can play games in there. Problem is, it's only suited to one person because of the moving floor. But check this out!"

We arrive at the gaming area. It's a wall of black as far as the eye can see. Every ten or so feet there's a small divider separating one massive screen from the next. About half of the stations have either a sole player or a group of them in front of the screen. From what I can see, they all look younger than eighteen. Adults with Implants wouldn't need to use these stations.

As we walk down the row of gaming stations, I find it a bit odd to see kids or teenagers dancing around, rotating an imaginary steering wheel, or pointing imaginary weapons at blank screens. I know that Hivemind can obscure the screens for everyone but the intended audience, but it's still comical to watch. Me and Chloe pick out an empty station that's a bit more secluded from the others.

Chloe asks, "So, what kind of games do you like to play in your world?"

"Right now I've been mostly playing a first-person shooter, but I like all kinds of games. Racing, adventure, platformers, anything." The screen changes in a flash; four brightly colored boxes appear, each showcasing a different game option. The first is a cartoon-styled shooter with vibrant colors and futuristic weapons. The next is a realistic racing game, with sleek cars and detailed landscapes. Then, a third-person view of a Viking character battling through a medieval castle with a sword in hand. And finally, a cartoon character jumping and dodging colorful enemies on a series of platforms.

I'm a bit confused about the games. None of them have titles or anything. I ask Chloe, "Who made these games?"

"Hivemind did. They're custom-generated. Once you start playing more, it will know what kinds of games you like and adjust to that." She turns from me to the screen. "Hivemind, let's show Max my favorite game."

The screen shifts to a fantasy world, displaying two characters standing side by side. The female character is draped in elegant green robes, while the male character has plates of armor sitting on top of his leather pants and white cloth shirt.

"Let me guess, I'm the one with the pretty robes?" I say.

"Very funny," Chloe replies. "Now grab a rock or something, you'll need it."

The view on-screen zooms into the back of the male character's head. Now I'm seeing a first-person view. I move my head side to side and up and down slightly to see how the screen changes with my movements. It's extremely intuitive. I see a nice sized rock over to my right. "How do I move forward?"

"Well, you can use any control method you want. Hivemind will figure it out. You can use hand motions, move your entire body, pretend you're using a controller. Is that what you do in your world?"

"I use a keyboard and mouse, normally."

"What? Do people still use that ancient tech? Wow."

I'm not offended. I know I'm an outlier there, especially in my age group. "Most people don't, to be honest."

"Well, if that's what you're used to, you can sit and pantomime the motions, if you want. I use my feet though. To move ahead, I put pressure on the balls of my feet and lean slightly forward. The more pressure I use, the faster my character moves."

I decide to give her method a try. I lean slightly forward, taking the pressure off of my heels. My character slowly walks towards the rock. I put more pressure on the balls of my feet, and I run right past the rock. Too fast. I tilt my head a bit to the left to turn around until I'm facing it again and slowly move forward. When in range, I bend down and mime grabbing the rock with my right hand. I watch as my character's arm reaches out and picks it up.

"Okay, great," Chloe says, her character staring straight at me. "There'll be enemies up ahead. Get ready to use that."

I notice that I'm seeing everything on the screen from only my character's perspective. "Are you seeing the same thing I am?"

"No, the screen only shows us our individual character's view. It's different for each of us."

That would be useful for some of the video games I've played. Most current games in my world don't have a 'couch co-op' mode, as it's called, but many retro games do. I had a friend in middle school whose dad was big into video games and had almost every gaming console that was ever released. When we played against each other, we had to use split-screen on the same TV. To combat cheating by peaking at the other person's view, we would tape a piece of cardboard right down the middle of the TV screen to use as a divider.

Chloe's character grabs a stick from the ground and starts to walk forward. The area we're in looks like a mystical forest. It's filled with ancient-looking trees, their gnarled branches reaching upwards, illuminated by a soft glow. The ground is covered in purplish moss, with a dirt path carving through that curves to the left up ahead. The sky above is a mesmerizing sight, with multiple different-sized moons and faraway planets visible in the twilight.

I follow behind Chloe's Mage character. I'm starting to get used to the movement system already. By slightly adjusting the pressure I'm putting on the balls of my feet,

I can match Chloe's slow jogging speed. I'm looking at a particularly interesting tree on my right when an arrow whizzes by my head. I flinch, and my character follows suit.

Chloe stops and points her stick ahead of us. A bolt of lightning shoots out of it, striking an ugly Orc enemy in front of us. It was the archer. I see a bow fall to the ground in front of it. On both sides of the fallen archer lurk two similarly hideous Orcs. One has a short metal sword, and the other has a large wooden bulbous club.

"I got the one on the left. You take the right." Chloe says as her character dashes forward.

I was expecting her to blast the Orc with another bolt of lightning, but as the Mage character gets closer, she dodges a sword swing from the Orc, and then clonks it on the head with her stick. The other Orc starts to run towards me. It lunges forward unexpectedly and bashes me in the chest with its club before I can react. The screen flashes red, but I'm not dead yet. My plate armor must have absorbed the blow. The Orc retreats a bit, and I take the opportunity to raise my right hand, aiming the rock at its head. I unleash the blunt stone, and my aim is true; it hits the Orc square in the face, causing the ugly creature to fall backward, unresponsive.

"Nice, dude. Good throw. I thought you might be a hand-to-hand brawler type, but maybe a ranged weapon is better. Grab that bow and quiver and try it out. You can take the sword too as a backup."

My Warrior character jogs up to the fallen archer. I grab the bow and look for the quiver. It's strapped to the Orc's back. I have to mimic the action of pushing the Orc onto its stomach to get it. Once I've slung the quiver over my shoulder, I walk to the formerly sword-wielding Orc and pick up the shiny weapon. I slip it through my character's belt loop and continue down the path with Chloe.

We eventually come upon a lookout tower with a couple of brutish Orcs at the bottom holding short-range weapons. The tower stands tall, its walls made of rough, gray bricks stacked haphazardly. The Orcs stand guard at the bottom, their muscles bulging under their mismatched armor. Another arrow embeds itself into the ground just feet away from us.

"Another archer, take cover," Chloe says as she sidesteps behind the large tree trunk to our right, with me following close behind. She points to the bow in my hand. "You think you can use that thing? The archer is camping the top of the tower."

"I'll give it a shot," I say. "No pun intended."

I peek out from behind the tree to see where the archer is shooting from. There's a small window cutout near the top of the tower. I can see a bit of motion through it. Another arrow impacts the tree beside me, inches away from my face. I duck back behind and ready the bow in my left hand while grabbing an arrow from the quiver on my back, then notch it on the string of the bow.

I quickly take several steps away from the tree, aim as best as I can in a hasty manner, and let loose. My arrow misses by several feet, bouncing harmlessly off the brick facade of the tower. I run back to the cover of the tree trunk as another arrow flies towards me. It takes a few more tries to get my aim on track, but my fifth arrow finally flies straight through the window, striking the target dead.

"Got him," I say, but Chloe is already dashing towards the two brutes at the bottom of the tower. Once close enough, she crouches and extends her stick, casting a freezing spell on the Orcs. She kicks one in the chest, skillfully grabbing the club that falls from its grasp in midair, and in one smooth motion, she smacks the second Orc in the chest with it.

Wow, she's good at this. I jog towards the tower, following her trail of destruction. Just then, Chloe's Mage is knocked over by a burst of magic that comes from her right side. I look over to see who the culprit is. It's another Orc, but it's dressed in a worn robe and holding a large staff. I take aim and quickly fire three arrows, one after another, towards the Orc Mage. The first two are blocked with magic from the Orc's staff, but the third hits it squarely in the face. It drops to the ground.

As I reach the tower, Chloe's managed to stand her character back up and is now brushing off the dirt on her Mage's robes. She slowly wanders over to the Orc Mage, gives it a kick in the ribs, and picks up the staff that had knocked her over. She tosses her stick to the ground, it's useless now. I'm excited to see what her character can do with the upgraded weapon.

Together, Chloe's Mage and my Warrior characters loot the fallen Orcs and search the tower. I find a stack of arrows that I use to refill my quiver, along with some health and magic potions. Chloe takes the magic ones from me and hangs them from her belt, hidden beneath her vibrant, green robes.

The two of us spend the next few hours fighting enemies and searching for loot, weapons, and armor upgrades. We eventually make it to a safe zone, a small city with various shops and friendly characters. We don't have any gold to use at the shops, but there's a bounty board with some paying quests we can take on.

The first quest we finish is to clear out a group of Orcs that had set up a camp on the outskirts of town. It's pretty easy. None of them have ranged weapons, so me and Chloe just lob arrows and magic from a distance until they're all dead. The Orc camp has some decent loot, plus we get to collect the gold bounty in town.

The second quest is much more difficult, but the payout is thrice that of the last. An Elf has been kidnapped by a horde of Orcs. They've taken her to a fortified hideout on the side of a mountain. Upon arrival, Chloe and I see that there's only one entrance to the hideout, which is guarded by four large Orcs. We sneak closer to it, using the forest nearby as cover. Luckily, I used part of the previous bounty to buy some bombs in town. I can't risk throwing them inside the cave, since there's an innocent hostage in there. Outside is fair game, though.

I carefully lob a bomb toward the guards. It lands right in the middle of the small group and blows up, launching them in all directions. The sound alerts the Orcs inside the cave and they start running out of the entrance, one after another. I readied my bow immediately after throwing the bomb, so I begin picking off the Orcs one by one.

Chloe taps me on the shoulder in real life and says, "Wait, conserve your arrows."

Orcs keep pouring out of the entrance. They stop when they see the pile of arrow-riddled bodies. Once a half dozen or so are out in the open, looking around frantically, Chloe's Mage raises her staff high in the air. Her long, flowing robes billow in the wind as she prepares for her attack. The air around her seems to crackle with energy. When she swings the staff downwards with a flourish, a burst of lightning erupts from the sky, striking the ground with a blinding white light and deafening roar, vaporizing every single Orc. She grabs a magic potion from her belt, chugs it to replenish the huge amount of mana she just used in that attack, and we set off towards the cave entrance.

I can't use my bow inside, since it's too small of an area for it to be effective. I grab a shield from a fallen Orc outside the cave, and upon bursting through the entrance, I use it to block attacks from the enemies' swords and clubs while swinging my own sword at them, dispatching one after another. Out of the corner of my eye I see Chloe swinging her staff wildly around the room. She's hitting Orcs directly with it, as well as showering them with corrosive sparks that eat at their skin.

My warrior, clad in its plate armor, moves swiftly and gracefully through a throng of menacing Orcs. One of them, smaller than the rest, creeps up behind me with a crude club in hand. As the club connects with the back of my character's head, my screen goes red and the Warrior slumps to the floor, lifeless. Chloe notices immediately, and after clearing the last Orc from her side of the room she casts a resurrection spell on me. As soon as I regain control of my character, I swing my sword in a wide circle behind me, slashing my assailant across the chest.

Finally, there's one Orc left. It's at the back of the cave, holding on to the small Elf girl with one hand and thrusting its short sword at me and Chloe with the other. It points the sword at the Elf girl's face, showing that it isn't afraid to take her down with it. I know exactly what to do, I've been training my entire video gaming life for this. I slowly circle away from Chloe, moving carefully towards the Orc and its Elf hostage. The Orc is looking desperately between Chloe and me, not sure who to focus on. As the gap between us widens, it eventually locks eyes with me, pointing its sword directly at my Warrior character. The distraction works.

As soon as the Orc fully turns its attention away from Chloe, she casts a freezing spell on both the Orc and the Elf. They're now stuck in place, unable to move. Chloe runs up to the petrified Elf, pulling her away from the Orc's grasping hand. It's wide open now, and can't defend itself. My sword slices through the air like a blazing comet, cutting through the Orc's neck with a satisfying thud as its body crumples to the ground, lifeless and defeated.

Chloe feeds a health potion to the frozen Elf girl, which wakes her up. She can't stop telling me and Chloe how grateful she is as we escort her back to the city to collect our bounty from her Elven family. I use my share on a new set of steel armor that I had been eyeing earlier. I also buy a helmet to protect my vulnerable head.

This quest has drained both Chloe and I, leaving us physically and mentally exhausted. We leave our characters at the nearest inn to take a rest, and the two of us step away from the Hivemind screen to sit down on the nearest bench.

"Fun, hey?" Chloe says as we sit down.

"That was unbelievable. More immersive than anything I've ever played. I can't believe it." Even the virtual reality games I played on my field trip from school completely paled in comparison to this. The gaming screen has that same natural depth to it that the other Hivemind screens display. It's like I was looking through an actual window into the fantasy world. The screen is so large that it took up my entire field of view, so it felt completely natural. I can't even imagine how much better it would be in the demo room where you would be surrounded in all directions and would have the moving floor to walk or run on.

"Is it dinnertime?" Chloe asks me. "I'm starving."

"Definitely. I think I worked up an appetite there." I wipe a bit of sweat from my brow. That game was much more physically demanding than anything I've played with my keyboard and mouse.

After leaving the row of gaming stations behind, we make our way to the closest dining area, right inside the Rec Room. This time, I decide to try something new and request a savory dish from Hivemind. Shortly after, a dark brown slab of food arrives on a plate with utensils for me to use. It vaguely resembles a steak, but after cutting off a small piece and eating it, I notice it doesn't taste very much like beef. It's delicious though. Chloe got her usual bowl of gruel.

We chat about the adventure we had just partaken in while eating. Chloe has a plan for the next time we play the game. There's a quest for a really powerful staff that she's been trying to get on her own, but it's too difficult. She thinks she might be able to get it done with my help though.

To wind down after our exciting fantasy adventure, I suggest playing a game of eight-ball pool. I used to play it at the rec center connected to my old high school, so I'm quite skilled at it. Chloe manages to defeat me in one game when I accidentally sink the eight ball too early, but I end up winning the rest of our games. Once we get bored with that, we play a few games of Foosball. This is not my best game. I've never been able to get the hang of defending. Chloe seems to know what she's doing, though, and handily beats me in the few games we play.

Once we're done, I check my watch. I've been in this reality for over eleven hours, and I know I'll be sent back soon. I'm quite tired after the busy day we've had. After all, I had seen all seven Wonders of the World before lunch. That would have taken weeks in my world. And that's not to mention the walk through the Park and all the games we played here in the Rec Room.

I can sense that Chloe is tired as well. I look at her and ask, "Hey, so I wasn't sure how long I would be here. I think my watch is gonna stop soon. Should I go back home to get some rest?"

"That's up to you, bro. You can sleep here if you want. But I wouldn't blame you for wanting the comfort of your own bed."

"Really? Where would I sleep? And, uh, where do you sleep?" It feels a bit awkward to ask her that.

"There are sleep pods all over the place. That's where I always rest up. We could easily find you an unoccupied one."

—-

We have to take a travel pod to get to the sleeping area. The floor we're on is dedicated solely to med pods and recreation.

When we arrive on the correct floor, Chloe says, "My pod is this way."

"Your pod? Is it assigned or something?" I reply.

"No, but we change the bedding between each person and it's wasteful to wash it every day. You're supposed to sleep in the same pod for at least three or four nights before switching to a different one."

We make our way down a long, wide, white hallway. One side of the hall is lined with Hivemind screens every thirty feet or so. The other side is crowded with a grid of square cutouts that extend as far as my eyes can see. The squares are stacked in rows of three, each with a ladder on the wall and a platform in front for standing. These cutouts are about four feet wide on all sides.

Chloe's sleep pod is a few minutes away from the travel pod station on foot. As we walk in silence, my wrist begins to tingle a bit. I quickly pull the crown out until it clicks once and then start rotating it. I don't bother to count the revolutions. I keep spinning it until I feel a strong resistance, and then I click the crown back into place.

Chloe noticed what I was doing and says, "Wow, I get to hang with my alt-bro for at least another day? Nice!"

She seems genuinely excited about it. I try to suppress the grin creeping across my face but can't. I'm really enjoying my time here. Chloe is fun to hang out with, too. Since I grew up as an only child, I don't know what to expect from having a sibling. This is all new ground for me, especially since I'm in an entirely different reality from the one I was raised in.

We reach Chloe's sleep pod. She points up at the one on the top of the nearest stack, which has a small yellow light on the square door. "That's me. You can claim any of the vacant ones with green lights nearby if you want."

I look around at the other sleep pods. Most have yellow or red lights, but there are a few unoccupied ones scattered around.

"You probably want to brush your teeth before bed, right? I'm about to. Just let me grab my toiletries and I'll show you where to get a toothbrush." She steps onto the ladder and climbs up to the top. The door to the pod slides sideways to let her enter it. She rummages around inside for a few seconds and then emerges with a small light gray bag and climbs back down the ladder.

The door on the opposite side of the hallway is a public restroom. I follow Chloe into it. It feels a bit weird since I'm not used to sharing a bathroom with people of other genders. Once inside, Chloe points to a row of cabinets near the sinks. "Toiletry bags and fresh clothes are in there. Showers are down the left hallway, and toilets and urinals are on the right. You can shower before bed if you want. I usually do it in the mornings."

"Thanks. I can take it from here, I think. Goodnight, I guess."

"Night, bro. We'll link up in the morning unless you want to do some exploring on your own. Sleep as long as you want." She walks over to a sink to brush her teeth.

I make a quick trip to the toilet before grabbing a toothbrush. When I get back, Chloe is no longer in the sink area. I walk over to the cabinets and open the first one. Inside are several small bags, the same as the light gray one Chloe grabbed from her pod. I choose one and unfasten its magnetic closure. Inside is a plain white toothbrush, along with a small roll of what looks like dental floss. There's a small pouch on the side of the bag that contains a white bar. Is it soap? I grab it to take a look and realize it must be deodorant or antiperspirant.

There's no toothpaste. I ask Hivemind.

"Toothpaste is dispensed from the taps on the sinks." The reply comes from inside my head, as usual.

I walk over to the sink and hold the toothbrush under it. A small dollop of paste ejects onto the bristles. After brushing my teeth, washing my hands and face, and drying off with the small towel next to the sink, I walk towards the laundry chute near the exit door to deposit the towel. On second thought, I roll it up and put it in the toiletry bag. It doesn't need to be washed yet.

As I exit the restroom, I approach the closest sleep pod with a green light. It's in the middle of the stack. I climb up the ladder and the door slides open automatically, revealing a surprisingly comfortable and snug interior. The bed is elevated off the ground by about a foot. It's a single. I can't help but wonder where couples are meant to sleep.

Once I'm fully inside and sitting on the bed, the door closes behind me. I put the toiletries bag on a shelf next to the bed, then strip down to my boxers and get under the covers. The soft fabric of the blanket brushes against my skin, providing a cozy and warm sensation. The mattress is firm yet supportive, molding to my body for ultimate comfort. I say out loud, "Lights," and the pod goes dark. I'm getting used to this place. It's now pitch black in the small pod, and I drift off to sleep.

Chapter 13

"We need to talk about my dad. Er... our dad. Our dads?" I say between bites of food.

I'm sitting at a table in the cafeteria with Chloe. When I woke up in the morning, I sauntered over to the bathroom to have a shower and grab a change of clothes to get ready for the day. I ran into Chloe outside of the restroom after, and the two of us took a ride on a travel pod to the cafeteria for breakfast.

On the way, I asked about where couples and families sleep in Utopia since the pods are obviously for solo sleepers. Turns out, there's larger rooms for couples and private suites for families in addition to the solo pods. They're fully equipped to meet the needs of parents who are raising children.

At the cafeteria, I asked Hivemind for cereal, which is my usual go-to breakfast option. I got a bowl of small, slightly moist green balls. Close enough. I have no complaints about the taste. Just the right amount of sweetness.

"Okay, where should I start?" Chloe replies. She finished her breakfast bar already and is now sipping on a warm energy beverage. There's no coffee in Utopia, apparently.

"So they're technically separate, right? There are two of them? Uhh... there was two of them?"

"Yes. When the Split happened, everyone on Earth was duplicated, including our dads, just in separate dimensions."

"Do we also have the same mom?"

"They were already together before the split, so yes."

"My dad is dead, but my mom is alive and well. What about yours?" I know it can be a touchy subject, but I have to ask.

"Same here. But I haven't seen my mom since I was very young. I was raised by my dad."

"Weird. It's like the exact opposite for me. My dad left when I was young. My mom raised me. When did your dad die?"

"Uh, about a year or so ago."

Chloe looks a bit uneasy, so I decide not to press any further on that. "So you inherited my watch, like me, and you found out that it could transport you to my reality?"

She's silent for a few uncomfortable seconds. "I don't know how to tell you this, or if it's the right time to, but I don't want to lie, so..."

Now I feel uneasy. "... what is it?"

"I've known about the watch for a long time. Since I was a young child. I, uh, also knew your dad fairly well. I spent a decent amount of time with him, as well as my own... version."

That's the last thing I expected to hear. I don't quite know how to process that information. I guessed that my dad must have used the watch, but for some reason, I didn't think about what he would do in Utopia. "So my dad... and your dad... who are alternate reality versions of each other... hung out together here?"

"Sort of. My dad was in your world fairly often. They didn't spend that much time together in the same reality. They would... swap? I guess?"

"So my dad babysat you while your dad was in my world? Is that what you mean?"

"When I was very young, maybe. I don't remember. I wouldn't call it babysitting, though."

I'm trying not to feel offended, but it's hard not to be. I barely knew my dad, but apparently, he had spent plenty of time with Chloe, who isn't even technically his daughter. It's not her fault, though, so I try to push those feelings of resentment away. I take another bite of my food and struggle a bit to swallow it. Then I say, "What was your dad doing in my world? I get why mine would come here. It's like a paradise. But why would yours want to leave this place?"

Chloe replies quickly like she's expecting that question. "I don't know. He wouldn't tell me." She picks up her drink and swirls the liquid around the glass.

"What do you do in my world?" I ask her.

"Not a whole lot. I heard so much about it from our dads while growing up, so I mostly just go see if what they said is real." She laughs nervously. "I don't have any money there, so there's not much to do, anyway."

I'm embarrassed that someone from a world like this has had to experience the brutal reality of being poor under capitalism in my world. At least Chloe can easily escape it, though. I guess I can too now. "Believe me, I understand that. But what I'm really curious about is... why. Why us, I mean? Why do we have these watches that can transport us between realities? Can anyone else do that? Could someone steal this watch from me and come here?"

"I don't know of anyone else who can go between dimensions. The watch only works for us; no one else can use them. As for why, it's... complicated. Like, you would need a history lesson first, I think."

"So, there is a reason? Does it have to do with our grandfather? Since it was his watch?"

"Yes. Very much so. But you'll have to wait and see. I think Hivemind would do a much better job of filling you in on that."

—-

I need some time to decompress from the conversation we had, so before getting a history lesson from Hivemind, me and Chloe decide to head back to the Park. I want to see the Arctic Biome. I've never been far enough north in my world to experience that type of wintery environment. We hop onto a travel pod and head to the one-hundredth floor.

The pod station we arrive at is on the edge between the Arctic Biome and the Lake Biome. I can already feel a chill as I step off the travel pod. The lush green grass of the pod station's field is a stark contrast to the snowy landscape on the other side. I can see the grass slowly giving way to patches of white, leading to a winter wonderland. In the distance, a small family is making their way through the snow. The children's laughter echoes through the chilly air as they play in the powder.

"We need to suit up. It's freezing over there." Chloe nods towards a large row of white cabinets on the outside wall of the pod station.

I find a medium-sized snowsuit behind the second cabinet door. It has built-in boots, so I have to take off my light gray slippers before stepping into the suit. The entire snowsuit hugs tightly against my body but is still very flexible. The boots make a nice, snug seal around my feet. There's a hood attached to the snowsuit, but it's not cold enough yet, so I leave it hanging down my back.

Chloe finishes pulling on her snowsuit. She hands a pair of gloves to me and says, "There are snowshoes here too. Do you want to stick to the cleared pathways or go exploring in the deep snow?"

"I think I'm good with the path. I haven't done any deep snow exploration before." We make our way into the snowy Biome, following a meandering trail of compacted snow. The boots on our snowsuits have excellent traction, allowing Chloe and I to navigate the path without slipping or falling.

A white rabbit runs across our path and disappears over the top of the snowbank that lines the pathway. It looked completely real. I still can't believe that it's a hologram. The lush white landscape is dotted with towering pine trees, their branches weighed down by a thick layer of snow. The path ahead becomes narrower and more winding, the trees growing more densely as we move forward. The air is frigid, causing our breath to turn to mist in front of us. My snowsuit hugs against my body, keeping the cold at bay with its snug warmth. I pull on my hood, grateful for the added protection against the biting wind that seems to be gaining intensity the further we go.

Up ahead, the path splits in two directions. Chloe and I choose the path on the right, which leads to a small frozen lake. We stop for a minute to look out over the lake. There's a small group of penguins waddling around on the far side of it.

"I still can't believe this is indoors," I say. "It's all so realistic. And cold."

"Right? I try to come here at least once a week. I don't mind the cold. It's a nice break from the rest of this place, which is perfectly climate-controlled."

A loud screech rings out through the silence. A white owl is staring down at me and Chloe from a nearby tree. The screeching call of the owl cut through the stillness of the snow-covered landscape, echoing off the frozen lake and surrounding trees. Its eyes are large and bright, a piercing yellow against its snowy white plumage. I tear my eyes away from the staring contest between me and the simulated raptor, then set off along the path with Chloe once again, away from the lake.

The path we now find ourselves on has started to climb upwards at a slow but steady pace. As we go further along and upwards, the trees become thinner and more sparse. The surrounding terrain is getting rockier, but our path is still smooth and easy to traverse. A pair of mountain goats are standing at the top of a large rock, watching us trek along.

Chloe seems to be getting more and more excited as we climb. She's almost skipping along the path at this point. "Almost there!" she says in a sing-song voice.

"We must be getting close to the ceiling by now," I say as I look up above us. There's no indication that there even is a ceiling. All I can see are clouds.

"The ceiling is higher in this Biome."

I try to tighten my hood as much as I can because it's getting seriously cold up here. "Hivemind, what's the temperature?"

"*It is negative twenty-five degrees Celsius,*" the voice inside my head declares.

I only know 'freedom units', as Fahrenheit is colloquially, and embarrassingly referred to amongst younger folk in America. It must be in the negatives.

Chloe remarks, "Don't worry, there's a warming hut coming up. But first-," she leaves the sentence hanging and starts running forward.

The path and the terrain seem to level off just up ahead. I slowly jog towards where Chloe had run to. She's posted up right at the crest of the hill.

"Look!" Chloe yells to me as she points ahead.

I catch up to her and double over for a second, trying to catch my breath. Following the direction of her pointing finger, I see a sleek snow-covered slope leading down the other side of the mountain. Chloe reaches for two wooden sleds propped against a nearby rack.

"Wanna race?" she asks as she hands one of the sleds to me.

As soon as I take it from her hand, she throws hers onto the snowy ground and jumps on top of it, accelerating both the sled and herself off of the crest of the hill and down the slope. I know I have no chance of beating her, so I carefully place my sled on the ground, lower myself onto the middle of it, and tuck in my legs. I start pumping my upper body forward and back, inching the sled towards the slope bit by bit. It finally begins to slide on its own, slowly picking up speed.

The slope isn't very steep, it's more like a gentle decline towards the bottom. The sled doesn't pick up enough speed to be considered frightening, it's actually quite enjoyable. I can feel my face breaking into a huge grin as I come to a smooth stop right in front of Chloe. As I get up and grab my sled from the ground, Chloe babbles non-stop about how much fun that was and how badly she beat me.

We stash the sleds on another rack at the bottom of the slope and set off on foot for the short distance to the warming hut Chloe had mentioned. It's a large circular wooden structure with a porch surrounding it. We step into the hut and take a seat on a bench. There's a stove in the middle with a simulated fire. Despite being fake, it's letting off a lot of heat; the inside of the hut is toasty warm. A few other people are seated around it as well, a young couple and a mother with two kids.

I pull my gloves off and extend my hands towards the heat source. My fingers are slightly numb, even through the thick gloves I've been wearing the whole time. Chloe rises from her seat and asks me if I want a warm drink. I nod, and she heads to a small square fixture attached to the side of the hut. When she reaches it, two cups filled with steaming liquid pop out from the top. She takes them both and hands one to me before sitting back down.

"This is cozy. I like it," I say as I sip the drink. The cup is warm to the touch, and the liquid inside feels hot against my lips. It's sweet, but not overly so. As I sip it down, I can feel the warmth spreading through my body.

"The drink or the hut?" Chloe asks, taking a swig from her cup.

"Both I guess. I get why you come here so often. My city rarely gets snow, this is all new to me."

"Glad I could help you experience it for the first time." She smiles at me.

After finishing our drinks and getting ready to embrace the cold again, we leave the warming hut. I hadn't noticed before that there's a huge mountain in the distance. It's covered in snow and pine trees, but there's a network of cleared routes intersecting with each other on the bottom half of it.

"Is that a ski hill?" I ask Chloe.

"Yep. The top of the mountain isn't real, that's simulated. But the ski runs are. There's a chairlift to take you to the top of the runs and all the gear you need at the bottom of the mountain. It's a lot of fun."

"Wow, I'll have to give it a try sometime. I've never skied before."

"Yeah, the runs are decent, but the limitations of being inside means they're too short. Once I get the Implant, though, I'll be able to ski on any mountain I want."

"I guess so, that's interesting. So how would that work? Would you just appear at the top of a mountain, fully geared up and ready to go?"

"If you wanted, yes. You can do it any way you want, though. You could even 'play capitalism' if you like. Get a job to earn enough money to buy the gear and lift ticket, hop on a plane to fly to the Swiss Alps, anything you can imagine."

I'm a bit perplexed by the thought of that. "Really? Do people do that? Get a virtual job?"

"Oh definitely. Some people have an entirely separate life in a Hivemind simulation. They'll even get married and have kids. Virtually."

"Huh. Don't they have to, like, eat and use the restroom and stuff in the real world?"

"Well yes, but... also no. You can do quick little adventures in Hivemind, sure, but you can also do much longer trips as well. There are special long-term pods that feed you and handle all the other... bodily functions."

"You mean you can stay in a simulation for as long as you want? Years even?"

"Yep. Lots of people do. There are probably millions, even billions of people in long-term pods right now."

"Wow. Are they all single in the real world? Can't imagine that would help your social life."

"Not always. You can be in the same simulation with someone else. Couples can have an entire simulated life. If they have adult children with Implants, they can pop into the simulation at any time to visit their parents. The best part is, you can drive cars, take cruises, basically do anything that would normally be bad for the environment, but in a completely safe manner."

"Do most people simulate life as it was before Utopia?"

"I don't know. Some, not all. Any kind of life you want can be simulated. You know that fantasy game we played last night? You could be one of those NPCs in the city if you wanted to. Or you could live on Mars. Or at the bottom of the ocean."

Chloe and I are in need of another, longer break from the cold, so we make our way to a travel pod station. There's one near the warming hut. I can't see it at first, it's camouflaged to look like the snowy environment. When we get near enough to it, a door slides open, revealing the mass of tubes inside. We have to go back to the other station to put our snowsuits away and retrieve our Utopia-issue slippers.

Our travel pod arrives, and we step on to find that it's empty, we have it all to ourselves. It'll be a short trip to the other station, so we stand in the middle of the pod and grab onto the handles on the roof.

I say to Chloe, "So you think I should get the Implant, huh? Even though I'm not from this world?"

She quickly replies, "I think you would be crazy not to. There are no real downsides I can think of. It won't work the same way in your world, though."

"Really? Why is that?"

"Just based on the.... design of it. It's a collective thing, you know? Every human here is interconnected through Hivemind. Hence the name." Chloe holds her arms up to demonstrate her point. "This is the hive, and we're the bees."

"I guess I never made that connection. I thought Hivemind was just a super advanced Artificial Intelligence."

"I wouldn't call it an AI. Intelligent, yes. But not artificial. Hivemind is derived from the collective mind of every human in this world."

"Oh. Interesting."

The travel pod arrives at our destination, and we head back to the cabinets to deposit our suits.

"Lunch? There's an eating area close by," Chloe says.

The pair of us eat in silence while I think about Hivemind and the Implant. I don't know how much time I can even spend in this world. Would it make sense to get the Implant if it doesn't work the same in my world? I have an entire life there. It isn't anything special, but it's mine. I can't abandon my mom. Plus, I need the watch to stay in this world. What if it breaks? What if I lose it?

The thought of being able to simulate anything I want is intriguing, though. I can't even begin to think of what kind of virtual world I would want to live in. The options are endless. And if Chloe says there wouldn't be any downsides, I'm inclined to believe her.

"I might be warming up to the idea of getting the Implant," I finally say to Chloe.

She looks excited. "Really? Awesome! I haven't even told you the best part!"

"What's better than being able to simulate anything you want?"

"Well, the Implant adds your consciousness to the Hivemind. It would be like uploading your entire brain to a computer. Which means... you can live forever."

Chapter 14

I've always been agnostic. I'm not an atheist; I don't completely reject the idea that there could be a God, I just haven't seen any proof that there is one. Also, my mother is a staunch anti-theist, which rubbed off on me. I try not to judge anyone who does believe in a God, as long as they don't use that as a justification to repress others. The problem with religion is that it very often is used for exactly that reason, though. Both throughout human history and in modern times.

The other angle that annoys me is the seemingly undue praise that is given to someone's God of choice. It's often said that God is all-powerful, all-knowing, and benevolent. But with the state of humanity on Earth, those three factors could not possibly be true at once.

If God knows about human suffering and does nothing to change it, They are not benevolent. If God doesn't know about human suffering, They are not all-knowing. If God knows about human suffering and can't change it, They are not all-powerful. It's an oxymoron to believe that your God exhibits all three of those traits with even a cursory thought towards the human condition.

Most religions have some form of an afterlife to encourage followers to act in a certain way. I don't understand how someone would ever need the threat of eternal punishment after death as a motivation to not harm others. That sounds a bit... sociopathic to me. I don't harm others because it's a terrible thing to do, not because I want a good experience in the afterlife.

I've never been one to believe in life after death. To me, death is simply the end, followed by eternal nothingness. However, Chloe's revelation about the Hivemind Implant brings that all crashing down.

"How does the Implant make you 'live forever'?" I ask Chloe. We had finished eating and Chloe had cleared our trays. I'm still sitting at the table, contemplating what Chloe just revealed to me.

Realizing that I'm not going anywhere, Chloe sits back down. "When you enter into a simulation, it's being run entirely through Hivemind, since your consciousness exists within Hivemind. When you die, Hivemind can put you into a never-ending simulation of your choice. If you want, of course."

"Never-ending? Like, for eternity?"

"As long as Hivemind exists, I guess. And Hivemind will exist as long as humans do. So, barring a full extinction of humanity, yep. Eternity."

"But who controls Hivemind? Surely someone is running the show, right?"

"We all control Hivemind. It's an amalgamation of every adult human on Earth."

"Are there any guarantees or safeguards against corruption?"

"The safeguard is the fact that no single person or entity controls it. Contrary to popular belief, humans are inherently good. Selfishness, austerity, individualism, these are learned traits. Think about it. If you were stranded on an island with a handful of people, would you work together to survive? Or would one person hoard all the coconuts?"

"On a tiny scale, sure, you would work together for the common good. But doesn't the history of humanity suggest otherwise? I'm pretty sure humans have been at war with each other for, like, ever."

"But in the same vein; one person, or a small handful of people, are corruptible. Every human as a collective isn't. Aren't there trillionaires in your world? While poor people starve? Do you think it's normal for one person to hoard more money than they can spend in thousands of lifetimes? They're sociopaths. There's something broken in their brains. That behavior is not normal at all, and the vast majority of humans don't operate in that way. Most people would give a man dying of thirst a drink. Your trillionaires are constantly making the decision not to, every minute of every day, for the entirety of their lives."

Chloe is sounding a bit like my mom, or more likely my dad. Which is not surprising, considering she had probably spent more time with my dad than I ever did. I agree with her, though. It makes sense. I've always thought that the average person is compassionate. It's just the brutal individualist societies that have existed for far too long that corrupt them. I've heard the 'human nature' argument being used against collectivism often, but it just doesn't hold water.

Nearly every aspect of modern society is designed to encourage selfishness. There's a point where schoolchildren go from learning that sharing is important to being taught that your worth as a human is determined solely by what you can personally contribute to society. When a kid is asked what they want to be when they grow up, they answer based on what they're passionate about. They don't say; 'I want to be a doctor because they make a lot of money,' they say, 'I want to be a doctor to help sick people'.

But little by little, those hopes and dreams are quashed. Especially if you're from a poor family. You can't decide to just go out and help homeless people, there's no money in that. 'Charity' shouldn't need to exist in a developed country, anyway. Charity is proof of capitalism's failure to care for the most vulnerable in society. Marginalized people have to hope that some rich asshole decides to try to distract from their exploitation of the working class by throwing what essentially amounts to a few pennies at the needy. When crowdfunding became the most preeminent healthcare provider in the US, that was a clear sign that the country, and capitalism overall, had utterly failed.

When I answer 'Yes' to a cashier asking to round up my order total to the nearest dollar for charity, it means I've donated a higher percentage of my wealth to people in need than the CEO of Idolon has. A trillionaire donating a million dollars is equivalent to me donating a penny. The disparity doesn't end there, not even close. If my mom donated ninety-nine percent of her wealth, we would both become homeless and destitute. But if the Idolon CEO donated ninety-nine percent of his wealth, he would still be left with more money than he and the next ten generations of his family could ever spend.

I snap back to reality and say, "So I'll concede that, overall, humans are inherently good. But I still don't quite understand why everyone decided to get the Implant and also agreed to abandon their cities and countries and come live here."

"People were literally lining up to get the Implant once it was developed." Chloe looks around the table to see if anyone else is within earshot, then whispers, "After the Event, everyone was desperate to get it."

"Why are you whispering? What's the Event?" I say at a normal volume.

"Shh! Take a hint, bro. People don't like to talk or even think about that. You'll find out later, during your history lesson. It's too hard to explain right here and now. As for why everyone agreed to live in one place, that's because of Hivemind. Just think, Hivemind contains the collective knowledge of every climate scientist—and scientist in general—in existence. Everyone with the Implant knew that the current way of living was completely unsustainable."

"But what about, like, all the governments of the world? They all sang 'kumbaya' and came to live in harmony?"

"The people did. It wouldn't matter if the politicians and the world leaders agreed. They are vastly outnumbered by the people."

Wow, it's like a leftist's wet dream. "So there's no authority in Utopia, other than Hivemind? No police?"

"There's no need. I wouldn't even call Hivemind an 'authority'. People listen to Hivemind because it's rational and always works for the betterment of mankind. Not because they're forced to or anything."

"No one ever gets violent? No one ever hurts anyone else?"

"Think about the factors that lead to violence in your world. There's several." Chloe starts counting on her fingers. "Monetary gain? There's no money in Utopia and everything is free. To exert power over someone? Everyone is equal here, there's no power dynamic. Mental illness, or addiction? The med pods take care of that. Cycles of abuse? There's no abuse to begin with."

"I'm sorry, but I refuse to believe there's zero violence here. That just can't be true."

"Sure, there are extreme cases. Mostly familial disagreements that escalate. But Hivemind can step in and put the aggressor in time out before anything bad happens."

"Time out?"

"It's like an involuntary nap."

—-

Chloe and I both decide to put the history lesson off until the next day. We need to have some fun after the intense discussion we just had. Chloe is also desperate to get back into her fantasy game to try to grind out that special quest. Instead of playing in the Rec Room again, Chloe and I head to separate demo rooms. We can sync up together from our individual rooms and communicate in real time through Hivemind.

We become completely immersed in the game for the next several hours. Playing Chloe's game in the demo room is an entirely different beast, as I thought. The game becomes a living, breathing world that I step into, losing myself in its depths as I navigate with the moving floor and get engulfed in the expansive, immersive view. The physical demands are even more intense than in the Rec Room, but it only adds to the thrill of the experience.

It takes five tries to beat Chloe's quest, but we manage eventually. By the end of the session, my Warrior has a crossbow that is much stronger and more accurate than the shortbow I was using before, a new short sword infused with the power of a dragon, and an entirely new set of much more defensive armor. Chloe's long-awaited staff is so powerful she can vaporize dozens of enemies at once, with barely any loss of mana. We can take on some of the hardest quests now.

Once we're tired and hungry enough, we end the gaming session and head to a cafeteria for dinner. We excitedly decompress from the last few hours of intense questing while eating our meals. We have a few more hours to kill before bed, so I ask Chloe if we can watch a movie. I'm not even sure if Utopia has movies, but of course, they do. Chloe gives me the rundown.

In Utopia, there are various options for consuming non-interactive media. If you're an adult with the Implant, you can summon a floating screen to appear in front of you wherever you are. Alternatively, you can simulate the experience of watching a movie in a theater. The family and couple's suites also have large Hivemind screens that provide access to entertainment content. Even the sleep pods, like the ones Chloe and I slept in, have Hivemind screens built in to the walls. With a simple command, they can transform from their usual plain white state into displays that show whatever content you desire.

Portable Hivemind tablets are popular among children and teenagers who don't have the Implant. These devices provide a range of entertainment options, like watching media, playing games, or reading books. You can even use the demo rooms, and fully immerse yourself in a story by using the moving floor to change your perspective and feel like you're part of the scene unfolding around you.

Perhaps the most interesting method is by using the entire ceiling of the cafeteria we're sitting in or even the Rec Room's ceiling. I didn't even know that the Rec Room ceiling doubles as a screen, like in the cafeteria. There's screens everywhere in this place. Even though the ceiling here and in the Rec Room is flat and horizontal, you can have your media display perpendicular to you through the use of depth and distortion correction. Chloe shows me an example on the ceiling above us. It looks like a giant rectangle is hovering in the air, perfectly angled to match my line of sight.

I don't think it would be comfortable to sit here for hours and watch something. I want to recline and relax. The cafeteria chairs aren't the most ideal for long-term stays. My back is already a bit sore from sitting here for the last hour or so, so we settle on using a gaming station in the Rec Room. Supposedly seats can pop out of the floor.

We make our way over there and find a secluded station to use. Sure enough, as we walk towards the screen, two seats slowly rise out of the previously flat and seamless-looking floor. I take the one on the left. The seat is comfortable, just soft enough for me to relax and unwind. I lean back a bit and the rear part of the seat moves with me.

"What kind of movie do you want to watch?" Chloe asks after she sits down.

I like all kinds of movies, I don't have a favorite genre. "I don't know. Is there a catalog or something?"

"No. It's not like your world. You tell Hivemind what you want to watch and a movie will be generated for you. You can even specify an exact length if you want. Or you can tell Hivemind to surprise you. Endless possibilities."

"Are they all animated or CGI?"

"Not all. It can be live action, black and white, claymation, anything."

I'm confused. "Who would the actors be?"

"No one. Just made-up, non-existent people."

"Weird. Are there no aspiring actors in this world?"

"Sure there are. They can live out those fantasies in a Hivemind simulation. Aren't you getting with the program by now? Celebrity culture and Hollywood are extremely problematic capitalist constructs. Do you ever wonder why the biggest celebrities are all super rich? Because the hero worship culture means they can't live a normal life. Famous people can't take public transit, or go to the grocery store. They need to have bodyguards, drivers, and personal chefs, and live in mansions away from the riff-raff. They're always at risk of being attacked by someone suffering from parasocial psychosis."

"I know celebrity culture is bad. I just didn't think there was a viable alternative. Entertainment is important. People need an escape from their world."

"There could potentially be ways to do it more ethically, but I doubt it could ever happen under capitalism. Tabloids have a profit motive that derives from creating Gods out of mere mortals. And I don't mean to make celebrities out to be victims here. Pretty much all of them fully embrace the capitalist bullshit. Imagine making more money than you'll ever need from acting in one movie and *still continuing to work*. Wouldn't you retire? Or act solely out of passion, instead of for a big paycheck?"

"Money has always felt like a useless barrier to survival to me. I don't ever want to have to think about it, and I don't want to be rich. I just want a stable life."

"Exactly, bro. That's how most people would feel without all the capitalist propaganda. And when you put otherwise regular people on these pedestals, nothing good comes from it. Why does a celebrity or rich CEO get national coverage when they share their uneducated take on geopolitics, but the people who dedicate their lives to studying those fields are ignored?"

I keep my mouth shut. I don't have an answer. The question seems rhetorical anyway. It's one of the main reasons I mostly stay away from social media and even mainstream media. I've never cared about which celebrity married or divorced which other celebrity. I have favorite actors and actresses, sure, but I try my hardest not to learn anything about their personal lives. Anything I've learned about them has been entirely against my will.

Chloe shifts gears. "So, what's your favorite genre?"

We settle on a crime drama. I found it a bit weird because Hivemind must have based the movie on the conversation we just had. I'm used to my phone listening in on my conversations and feeding me targeted ads based on what was said, but this movie took that concept to a completely new level. At least Hivemind isn't doing it for a profit motive, though.

The movie was about an obsessed stalker fan who killed a popular female celebrity. They left a trail of evidence that a pair of investigators had to follow. As they pieced everything together, the investigators realized that the celebrity was in an abusive relationship and was forced to keep working and making more money by her spouse. The twist was that there was no killer. She had committed suicide and had planted the trail of evidence by herself to both expose her spouse and make it look like she didn't kill herself so that her pristine image was preserved.

It was by far one of the best movies I have ever seen. It was a scathing critique of capitalism and celebrity culture. The pacing was perfect, I didn't have any inkling of the twist before it was revealed, and the acting was sublime. It's strange to think that the people in the movie didn't exist and were a figment of Hivemind's imagination, though.

Me and Chloe are both emotionally wiped by the end, so we're ready for bed. We hop onto a travel pod, make our way to our individual sleep pods, and say our goodnights to each other.

Chapter 15

I wake up after a few hours of sleep; my bladder is about to burst. I roll out of bed, put my clothes and slippers back on, and make my way out of the sleep pod and across the hall to the public restroom. When I'm standing at the sink washing my hands, I notice an older woman behind me, carrying a stack of light gray clothes. I watch through the mirror as she walks over to the cabinets and starts carefully and slowly distributing the folded clothes onto various shelves.

When she's done, she turns towards the mirror I'm looking through and we make eye contact for a second. I say 'Hello' but get no response. She almost seems like she's sleepwalking, or on autopilot. I shrug it off and head back to my pod to sleep.

—-

When I meet up with Chloe in the morning, that situation is still on my mind. I had a weird dream about it. It was sort of like the other one I had with the faceless Utopia denizens. This time I was in an assembly line of faceless automatons, being assembled limb-by-limb by robot arms.

I decide to bring it up to Chloe. "Hey, so I think I saw someone doing their 'chores' last night." I use the term Chloe had used earlier.

"Oh, yeah?" she responds.

"A lady was stocking the cabinet with clothes. It was really weird though. She seemed to be in a trance, or sleepwalking or something. She was completely unresponsive when I tried to interact with her."

"Yep, that's normal. She was in a long-term Hivemind simulation."

"What? How was she doing both at the same time?"

"I guess maybe it's more accurate to say that Hivemind was doing the chores while she was immersed in her simulation."

"Uh, so you're saying that Hivemind can control her body? Why didn't you tell me that before?" I'm a bit annoyed to only be learning that pertinent bit of information now.

"When you asked about jobs the other day I hadn't yet told you about the Implant and how it worked. I'm trying not to overwhelm you with too much information at once, you know?"

"I think that's a pretty important detail, isn't it? Especially if you're trying to convince me to get the Implant?"

"I guess? I mean, it's not that weird. Let me explain. When you go into a long-term simulation, your body has to be in motion every once in a while to protect your muscles from atrophy. It's a fully consensual thing. That woman would have agreed for her body to do some work every once in a while she's in her simulation."

"Does anyone not agree with it?"

"I don't know. But why wouldn't they? Your body has to be walking around every few days anyway, plus it's your responsibility as a Utopia citizen to help out with simple duties, so why not kill two birds with one stone?"

"Sure, that makes sense, but it's kind of worrying that Hivemind can just take control of your body."

"In your world, maybe. Here, though, it's not done for nefarious reasons and it never would be. The only time Hivemind would take control without your explicit consent is if you were about to hurt someone, or yourself. If you haven't learned by now, Hivemind is a tool to make your life easier and better. You can trust it. I would never let you get the Implant without you knowing every detail. Neither would Hivemind, honestly. But I think the history lesson today will clear things up."

—-

I finish eating my breakfast in quiet contemplation. It's difficult for me to completely trust something like Hivemind, especially after being disillusioned by the rampant corruption in my world. Every time I voice a concern, there's always a seemingly convenient solution, but I can't decide if that's a red flag or if I've just been conditioned for my entire life to anticipate the worst in every scenario.

Chloe asks if I want a private session to get the history of Utopia or if she should join. I want her there because I often feel more comfortable talking to an actual person as opposed to a disembodied angelic voice in my head. The lesson will take place in a demo room since we need somewhere private.

As the door of the demo room closes behind us, we're surrounded by pristine, almost blinding white walls, which gives me a flashback to my little adventure in frustration here the other day. The room is empty, save for the two of us standing in the center. Chloe turns to me and asks, "You ready?" I nod in approval, then she looks forward and directs the next part to Hivemind. "Hivemind, start from the beginning, please."

The room is suddenly no longer white. I'm gazing at a man who appears to be in his thirties or forties. I remember seeing him in old family pictures; it's my grandfather. As the image widens, it reveals that he has his arm draped over his wife's shoulder. Me and Chloe's grandmother.

Hivemind's voice appears, seemingly emanating from the walls. *"Maximus Karlson the First was an American scholar and engineer who had been contracted by the American military to work on defense systems during the Cold War. He became disillusioned by capitalism and the military-industrial complex in America and defected to the Soviet Union after the death of his wife. He worked closely with other Soviet engineers and scientists on advanced technological systems while attempting to find a way to expand the capabilities of the human mind through technology. He believed that the Soviets, under a collectivist system, would be more responsible with this type of technology."*

The scene in front of us changes to a Soviet spacecraft flying through space. It has a large sphere at the front, with a white strip with the initialism 'CCCP' repeating around the circumference. A hammer and sickle symbol is sitting in between each set of letters, with a red Soviet flag smack dab in the middle of the strip. Attached to that is a conical body, with various pipes and satellite dishes and other mechanisms protruding from all sides. Two arms are stretching out from the body, which hold solar panels outwards, like the wings of an eagle.

"In 1975, the Soviets launched an orbiter and lander to Venus to relay photographs from the surface of the planet. It was known as the Venera 9. A photo taken of the surface of the planet was shown to the public. However, the lander also accidentally found evidence of an anomaly outside of the planet. The Soviets later sent several more Venera orbiters to collect more information about this anomaly."

On the screen, a funnel-shaped opening in space comes into view. Beyond it, distant stars can be seen, their image warped and twisted by the funnel's distortion. As the camera angle changes, a white and beige planet with swirling patterns is shown next to the funnel. Venus.

"The anomaly was determined to be a wormhole. The Soviets kept this as a closely guarded secret. Only a small handful of engineers, scientists, and top officials knew about it."

I chime in, "Wait, so the Soviets made a discovery that huge and kept it a secret?"

"Apparently," Chloe says. "The funny thing is, they probably would have been considered the winners of the space race had they released that info to the public."

When I learned about the space race in school, it had been unbelievably biased toward the US. The Soviets were made out to be bumbling failures. My mom set the record straight on that when I told her what I was taught, though. She explained the many innovations and records set by the Soviets in space exploration. They were the first to launch a satellite. The first to put an animal into space, the first man and woman into space. The first spacewalk was a Soviet astronaut. They launched the first space station.

The US did more than just put a man on the moon, though, that wasn't their only claim to fame in the space race. But aside from that, the Soviet achievements at the very least matched what the US was able to do. If anything, it seems like the space race was more of a tie, but the US was able to capitalize on the impact of having men walking on the moon and physically planting the American flag there. The footage they obtained captured the attention of the entire world. The fact that the Soviets kept this discovery a secret was interesting, though. They seemingly thought it was more important to keep this information from getting into the wrong hands than it was to win the space race.

Hivemind continues, *"Years later, the Soviet Union dissolved, and the US declared victory in the cold war. But Maximus continued to work in secret, as he was on the verge of a breakthrough."*

The setting shifts to a rundown laboratory, where our grandfather is hunched over a complicated device. He's sitting at a wooden desk cluttered with wires, electronic parts, and tools. He's staring through a mounted magnifying glass as he fuses wires together with a soldering iron.

"Maximus no longer had funding for his work, and it became more difficult for him. However, he managed to finish the prototype of his device a few years after the fall of the Soviet Union. It could be considered as version one point zero of the Hivemind Implant. With the help of a former Soviet surgeon, he had probes inserted into his brain which connected to the device."

Now Hivemind is showing a close-up of the device on Maximus' head. It's a series of wires wrapped around his head like a hat, with a small box sitting neatly on top. Two of the wires are protruding directly from incisions in small bald spots on the back of his head.

"With the device, Maximus was able to control a computer with his brain. He could also obtain detailed readings about his brain and the electrical impulses that sent commands to the rest of his body."

The device on Maximus' head is now shown to be connected directly to an old-fashioned computer via a colorful bundle of wires. The computer has an ancient-looking CRT monitor that has lines of green text flowing down the screen, almost like in the *Matrix* movies. It's perched on top of an off-white case that must contain the brains of the computer.

"Maximus couldn't progress any further in his research without funding. However, he had connections to some former engineers who worked on Soviet spacecraft. They were planning to do one final secret manned space mission to explore the wormhole near Venus. Maximus convinced them to let him be the sole astronaut aboard the rocket. He wanted to pass through the wormhole while connected to his device to measure what would happen to his brain."

A rocket appears on the screen on a launchpad, ready to take off. It's thin and tall and mostly white, with a few red stripes around the body. The bottom of the rocket has four large propulsion units, protruding outwards at a slight angle to form a larger base.

"The Soyuz-X launched in secret with Maximus on board and headed towards the wormhole near Venus. His brain was connected to a computer for the duration of the mission. The spacecraft was set to slingshot around Venus, pass through the wormhole, and then continue back to Earth, if possible."

The spacecraft is shown heading straight for the wormhole. Most of the rocket is no longer attached, as it would have separated after launching. Only the nose portion remains, and solar panels are now protruding from the sides of the vaguely peanut-shaped vehicle.

"The Soyuz-X passed through the wormhole and set off a chain of events. First, Maximus' brain became so overloaded that he instantly died. Second, a new reality split off from the main one, creating a completely new timeline. This is referred to as the Split. Third, every human with a myelinated brain in the new reality became cursed with knowledge."

"Cursed with knowledge? Myelinated? What does this mean?" I ask Chloe.

"It means they instantly gained the collective knowledge of everyone else on Earth," she answers. "Hivemind will need to answer the second question. I can't remember."

"Myelination is the process under which an adolescent body produces layers of myelin to wrap around the neuronal axons of the brain. It is an important stage of brain development."

"Is that what you were talking about before with the Implant? You need to have undergone a certain stage of brain development?" I ask Chloe again.

"Yep. Couldn't remember the term for it."

"But why would gaining knowledge be referred to as a curse?"

"Gaining knowledge is good. But too much of a good thing can become a bad thing. Imagine knowing exactly what, I don't know, four or five billion other adults know. Every thought they've ever had. Every horrible—or good—thing they've ever done. The collective life experience and knowledge of all those people being condensed into each of their individual brains was too much to handle. It was definitely a curse."

"I guess... I don't think I would want to know about even one person's deepest thoughts, let alone everyone's. And I definitely wouldn't want anyone to know mine."

"Same here. Luckily, we were born way after the Event."

"So this is what the Event was? The 'curse of knowledge'?"

"That's what started it. Think about it. Every serial killer was instantly revealed. Every child molester. Every crooked politician. Infidelity between partners. A concerning amount of people fit into all of those categories. It was complete mayhem. The world came to a standstill. People stopped going to work; there were murders, lynchings, suicides, lots of violence."

"How many people died?"

Chloe looks uneasy. "Hivemind, give us a breakdown?"

"Fifty-four million suicides. Thirty-five million murders. Three million other deaths can be directly attributed. Ninety-two million total deaths, rounded down."

"Oh wow. That's a lot. Why so many suicides?" I ask Chloe.

"Some of them were out of shame from their secrets being revealed, but most were from people driven crazy by the sheer amount of information swirling through their heads. It would have been completely overwhelming. You would have trouble sleeping at night. If you weren't completely mentally stable before the curse, you didn't have a good time after."

"I'm having trouble comprehending that number and the implications of it. But anyway, what happened next?"

Hivemind continues with the lesson. The screen surrounding us begins showing scenes of mass unrest. Hordes of people are protesting outside of parliamentary buildings. Businesses, cars, and infrastructure are burning, and looters are smashing windows. Mass graves are shown, with unmarked piles of dirt scattered through fields of green grass. Military battleships are shooting at each other in the open ocean.

"For several months, the entire world was in turmoil. The Soyuz-X returned to Earth in both realities, carrying the corpse of Maximus Karlson the First. Both versions of his son inherited their father's watch, which he had been wearing when he passed through the wormhole. The watch had been imbued with the ability to transport the wearer between realities, which both versions of Maximus Karlson the Second quickly discovered."

Now the screen is showing two identical people working together in that same Soviet lab. It's me and Chloe's dads. It's similar to the scene of our grandfather tinkering alone, but the device they're working on is much smaller, and the equipment they're using is much more modern.

"Both Maximus' worked together to develop Hivemind two point zero. They had access to the readings from the device their

father had been wearing, the prototype device itself, plus the collective knowledge of every scientist in the world. They were quickly able to produce the new Hivemind Implant, which is the very same one still used today."

A close-up of the two men appears on the screen. Both have small white lights coming from their temples. They look identical to each other, with the same shaggy brown hair which was not unlike mine, the same bushy eyebrows, and the same scar under their right eye.

"The Implant was tested on both versions of Maximus. One had been cursed with knowledge, the other had not. For the Maximus who was cursed with knowledge, it allowed him to forget everything he had learned and only access the information that was necessary to him. For the other Maximus, it granted him access at will to that same information."

A med pod is now visible on the demo room's screen. It looks identical to the one I used, which corrected my eyesight. The pod is open, and a Russian-looking man is lying inside.

"The pair were able to produce several Implants that were given out to a selection of people. The newly implanted team began work on mass-producing Implants as well as med pods that could perform the surgery automatically. Med pods and Implants were distributed around the world, and eventually, every person cursed with knowledge was freed from their burdens."

Me and Chloe are now looking at a massive lineup of people waiting to get Implants at the med pods. The line stretches as far as the screen can show. There's a grouping of dozens of med pods at the front of the line, which people are continuously entering and exiting.

"*Once all the Implants were installed, the humans of Earth experienced peace for the first time. Hivemind had taken control, instructing and guiding each individual-*"

"Is it talking about itself in the third person?" I whisper to Chloe. She elbows me in the ribs.

"*-on what their duties were to prepare to build Utopia. The process was done half a decade later, and the rest of the Earth was left to the animals and nature.*"

Chapter 16

"So my dad worked with your dad to create the Implant?" I ask Chloe. We're sitting in chairs in one of Utopia's lounge areas, decompressing from the Hivemind history lesson.

"Yeah. Like I said when we met, the Maximus Karlson name holds a lot of weight around here. We're not much for hero worship, but everyone knows your name here, bro."

Great, people here know my name too. "Then do the people of Utopia know about the other reality? Since there were two versions of our dad making the Implant? Do they know that I exist?"

"No. I don't think very many other people, if any, know about your world, or that their hero sort of has another child. They think my dad created the Implant alone."

That's a relief, at least. I can be incognito here. "But I thought the curse of knowledge meant everyone knew everything?"

"Before the Implant, yes. But Hivemind erased that knowledge from everyone with the Implant, including most of the other knowledge that was gained."

"And our grandfather is a hero here too? Even though what he did technically lead to, what, almost a hundred million people dying?"

"Utopia couldn't exist without what he did. Most people's lives are much better now than they were before," she lowers her voice, "even if they lost loved ones in the Event."

"That's still a hard pill to swallow. That's like over one quarter of the current population of the US."

"You're thinking about it the wrong way. How many people needlessly die every year in your world?"

I actually have an exact answer to that. My dad had constantly brought it up in TV interviews and debates when he was still alive. "At least twenty million people die every year because of capitalism. Eight million from a lack of food, another eight million from a lack of clean water, and four million from vaccine-preventable illnesses. That doesn't include deaths in capitalist wars."

Chloe looks surprised. "You sound exactly like your dad."

"Well, that's where I got it from. My dad was known for disparaging capitalism in my world." Most people would get very mad when my dad would talk about that, but it's true. There are stats to back it up from non-governmental agencies and humanitarian groups.

"So twenty million per year. That's more than the death toll of the Event in just five years. Those deaths don't happen here in Utopia. Every single human in this version of Earth has free food, free water, and free medical aid."

"If you had a button in front of you that would kill ninety-two million people but also create Utopia, would you be able to push it?" I ask her.

She deflects. "You've heard of the 'trolley problem', right?"

It's a classic philosophical thought experiment that I studied in school. "Of course."

"Let's simplify it a bit. On one side of the trolley tracks, you have ninety-two people tied down. The other side has only twenty people, but there are another twenty people every kilometer for hundreds of kilometers of track. You're at the switching lever. The trolley is approaching. Which side do you choose?"

"I think that's too simple. There are more factors at play."

"Your button analogy is also too simple, and I think you're looking at it the wrong way, anyway. The button's label shouldn't say 'kill ninety-two million people'. It should say 'force humanity to work together by any means necessary for the greater good'. Would you push that one?"

I don't want to admit it, but Chloe is right. This world is better. I've learned enough about it that I can say that with confidence. Since it's been this way for decades, humanity has almost certainly gained more from Hivemind to counter the number of people who died in the Event. My world is nearing full-on collapse from human-caused climate change. I've read plenty of studies about the risk of human extinction coming up in just the next twenty or thirty years. We'll probably have a full scale climate war before that point. We need our own version of the Implant, badly.

I suddenly realize something else. "Wait, my dad had the Implant? Even before I was born?"

"Yes..."

"Did my mom know about it? If she did, she would have to know about Utopia, right?"

"I'm not sure."

Could my dad have kept that a secret for the entire time? "Why didn't he have white lights coming from his temples?"

"Oh, you can turn those off. When they're off, it's impossible to tell if someone has the Implant just by looking at them."

I still wonder if my mom does know, but now I'm thinking about if she *should* know. Should I tell her about Utopia and what the watch can do? I usually don't hide anything major like this from her, but then again, I haven't ever had a secret this big before. My mom hates capitalism more than I do. She would probably love this place if she could ever somehow come here.

Now that ridiculous conspiracy article I read a few days ago pops into my head, the one that said he died as a result of interdimensional travel. "I know you seemed uncomfortable talking about this before, but I have to ask. My dad died of a brain aneurysm. I now know that he spent a lot of time here, and he also had the Implant. Did that have anything to do with his death? How does your dad fit into this? He died, what, a year before mine? Am I supposed to think that's just a coincidence? Am I in danger, now that I've spent some time here?"

Chloe goes silent for a few seconds. She seems to be trying to form her words carefully. "My dad also died of an aneurysm. But you're not in danger. I promise."

I'm not that shocked. I assumed their deaths were somehow related. "How am I not in danger if two other, uh, reality-shifters both died of a brain aneurysm? You've used your watch too, right? Aren't you scared?"

"They didn't die simply because they went to a different reality. They died because they were carbon copies of the same person, and they spent too much time together in the same reality. It did irreparable neurological damage to their brains."

Well now I'm shocked. I didn't see that coming at all. But it seems like it could be true. "So they knew they were gonna die?"

"Yes. Hivemind couldn't help. They knew for a long time before it happened. They stopped being in the same reality at the same time, but it only delayed their deaths by a bit."

"So that's why they swapped between realities? To avoid an earlier death? I guess that makes sense." I feel a familiar tingling sensation coming from my wrist. It catches me by surprise, even though we've been talking about the watches. I pop out the crown and give it about a half turn. "I need to go back soon. I have to go to work in, like, seven or eight hours."

Chloe has a sad look on her face. "Oh, okay."

I check the watch, which is still showing my timezone, back at home in my world. It's four AM there. "My mom will be getting up for work soon. I want to check in with her before she leaves for her job."

"You guys just work, work, work, huh?" Chloe jokes.

I grin at her. "Well, unlike you spoiled Utopia kids, we have to earn the right to live in my world. No handouts."

"Listen, this might be a weird question, and feel free to say no, but... can I come with you? You'll have some time to kill before work, right? Do you want to show me around your world a bit?"

I think about it for a second. "I guess since you've been gracious enough to give me a tour of your world, I should return the favor."

"Awesome! Let's get ready to go then."

On the way to the nearest private area; another demo room, where we can disappear without arousing any suspicion, Chloe grabs a few to-go bars from a Hivemind terminal since she won't touch the food in my world.

"How will you find me in my world?" I ask Chloe.

"I'm pretty sure the watch can take me right to you. Where are you going, your bedroom?" she responds.

"Yeah. My mom will be home, so you'll have to hide there and be quiet until she leaves for work." I know that if my mom finds me with a girl in my room, she would assume it's a secret girlfriend or something, which could make things quite awkward for me and my alt-sibling.

"Okay. I'll wait for you to disappear, then I'll use my watch and follow right behind. Is it gonna stop soon?"

"It's just starting to tingle again now."

I'm thinking about my bedroom as the tingling intensity grows, and a minute later, I'm there. Noticing how messy it is, I try to frantically shove dirty clothes into a corner, but Chloe materializes a few seconds after me, putting an end to my frenzied cleaning attempt. It's my first time seeing it happen myself. She just appears in an instant, with no fade-in, and no particles swirling around like in the movies. The space in the middle of my room was empty, and then a nano-second later, it isn't.

I hold a finger to my lips, preemptively shushing Chloe before she even opens her mouth. "I think I can hear my mom downstairs," I whisper.

"I won't make a peep," she whispers back.

"I have to change out of these clothes. Turn around and close your eyes." I'm still wearing the matching light gray set from Utopia, which would confuse my mom.

Chloe turns around and quietly jokes, "I've already seen you in your boxers, remember?"

I flashback to when I first traveled to Utopia wearing only my boxers. It seems like a lifetime ago already, but it's only been a few days. As I strip out of my Utopia get-up and into some clean-ish clothes that were sitting on the floor, I whisper to Chloe, "What's up with the clothes situation in Utopia by the way? Why do the younger people like you wear unique clothes but the adults all dress the same?" Chloe is currently wearing a plain yellow shirt and a pair of light blue shorts.

"You can customize your clothes with the Implant to whatever you want, which other Implant users can see as well. So all the adults wear the same physical clothes for logistical reasons, they're easier to mass produce. But you can also change your hairstyle and makeup, virtually."

"So what, you get a character creation screen like in video games?"

"I know you're kidding, but yes, essentially."

I finish getting dressed. "I'll be back in a bit, just, uh, make yourself comfortable, I guess. Silently, though."

I leave my bedroom, gently shutting the door behind me. At the bottom of the stairs, I see my mother sitting in the kitchen, eating breakfast. It all feels strangely familiar, just like the last time I saw her. But at least this time I didn't scare her.

"My son! You're home! When did you get in?" she says excitedly when she spots me entering the kitchen.

"Pretty late last night. It was really cold, we bailed on the last night. We all work today anyway." I'm surprised that I managed to come up with that lie on the spot.

"Well? Did you have fun? What did you get up to out there?"

"You know, the usual. Campfire, roasting marshmallows and hotdogs. There was a hiking trail around the lake. Charlie brought inflatable boats, so we floated on the water."

"Sounds great! Maybe we should take a trip sometime?"

"If you want, sure. Sometime." I'm fiddling with my watch, debating whether to ask my mom about everything I have learned about my dad.

"Still wearing the watch, huh? It's nice to see, I'll admit. Your dad wore that thing every day, same with his dad."

"Yeah, about that... did Dad ever talk to you about this watch?"

She looks slightly uncomfortable. "Uh... what do you mean? Not really..."

"Oh, nothing. I was just wondering if there was anything special about it. I couldn't find anything about the brand online." Another quick lie. "Wearing this made me think about Dad, and how he used to disappear all the time. Do you know where he was going?"

She looks even more uncomfortable now. She's squirming in her seat a bit. "That's... kind of a major discussion, son. We can talk about it later if you want, I guess. I'm gonna be late for work."

I watch as she grabs her half-eaten piece of toast, puts it in her mouth to free up her hands, and hurries toward the door. I say, "Okay, see you later. Love you."

She muffles something through the piece of toast in her mouth as she slips on her shoes, grabs her coat, and quickly heads out the door.

I trudge back up to my room to check on Chloe. She's still standing in the same place, right in the middle of the room. "I told you to make yourself comfortable. You could have sat down at least."

"Sorry. I didn't want to mess up any of your... things." She glances around the room.

"It's already messed up," I laugh. "I'm not a very tidy person. This is probably a bit unsettling for you, considering Utopia is spotless everywhere."

"Not really. My sleep pod is a bit messy." Chloe looks over at the computer on my desk. "What's this beast of a thing?"

"Well, you do your gaming on giant screens, and I do mine from a few inches away from a normal-sized screen."

"This is a computer? I thought they were smaller than this."

"Most are. Desktops are typically better for gaming. They used to be popular before laptops and tablets took over."

"It's so... flashy." Chloe's eyes widen as she stares at the colorful RGB lights emanating from the desktop computer, her gaze fixated on the pulsating hues of every color in the rainbow.

"Yeah... I didn't choose for it to be like that. Gaming components tend to be a bit gaudy. They assume every PC gamer wants it to look like a disco club on their desk."

"Want to show me your favorite game? We played mine a few times, after all..."

"It's single-player only. They don't make many two-player games anymore."

"That's fine. How about I watch you play? I don't know how to use your keyboard thing, anyway."

I boot into my FPS game and play a few rounds with Chloe watching over my shoulder. I feel a bit of pressure with her watching, but I manage to play pretty well. In the first game, I get five kills before dying. In the second game, though, I make it all the way to the end, with only one other person left. I just narrowly lose the one-on-one and blame it on the other person being a whale, of course. I have to explain what that is to Chloe, who has no idea.

"So this game costs money?" she asks after learning about the whales.

"Technically no, it's free to play. But you can pay to get better gear."

"So the people who have more money have an advantage?"

I can't help but laugh. What she said sums up just about everything in my world. After the gaming session is done, I give Chloe a tour of the house. She seems surprised by the most mundane things. The washer and dryer. The garage.

"I thought only the richest people could afford houses here? Is your family rich?" she asks me.

"We're definitely not rich. Most major cities, including this one, have completely unaffordable housing. I would never be able to buy my own house unless something drastically changed. Most people my age will never own a house. My parents bought this place decades ago before the prices became out of control."

"Where do poor people live if they can't get a house?"

"They rent apartments or basement suites. Or they just become homeless and stay in shelters or out on the street."

Chloe's eyes narrow to thin slits, her eyebrows furrowed in frustration. "I can't believe you guys just take that bullshit. Where are the riots?"

"The governments and the corporations and the richest of the rich have perfected the art of brainwashing people into thinking they have no choice but to accept it. They designed the work week to be just long enough so that people have no time or energy for collective action."

"Do you think that will ever change?"

"I've heard that the one thing that would get the average person to take to the streets is hunger, and that point seems to be rapidly approaching. Inflation is making food way more expensive while wages are staying the same. Climate change is impacting more and more farming areas. It will be an interesting decade, that's for sure."

"How do you think it will play out?"

"Right now, the elites are doing a balancing act on keeping people poor and destitute, but not so poor and destitute that they take action. If someone is hungry today, there are soup kitchens and food banks. But if the global food supply starts to dwindle, nothing can be done. There will be climate wars between major countries. They're brewing already. Most people my age will be drafted into them and we'll die fighting other poor people at the behest of the rich."

"Wow. Bleak. Can't say I disagree though, from what I've seen and heard of this world."

—-

The pair of us leave my house to explore the outside world. Chloe wants to see what trains are like, so we head toward the nearest station, which is only a few blocks away. It's a nice, overcast day, not too warm and not too hot. The sky is a pale shade of gray, with fluffy clouds floating lazily across the horizon. The sun peeks through occasionally, casting a warm glow over everything. When we reach the station, I walk over to the ticket machine to buy a day pass for Chloe. I have a monthly pass for myself, of course.

I show Chloe how to scan her pass at the turnstiles, then we make our way to the platform to wait for the next train. I decide I want to show her a wonderful shrine to consumerism; the local shopping mall. Malls have always felt like a combination of amazing and horrifying to me. When I tell Chloe where we're going, she seems concerned because she has no money. I tell her not to worry about it. I have some money in my bank account that we can use. We don't necessarily need to spend much, because window shopping is an interesting enough pastime.

The train arrives, slowly rumbling down the tracks towards us. It makes a loud screeching noise as the brakes slow it to a complete stop. Both the train and the platform are full of people, which is normal for rush hour on a weekday morning. Most of them are heading to work or school. When the doors of the nearest train car open, me and Chloe shove onto it and find a place to stand a few feet away from the doors. Every seat is full, and Chloe seems to be very overwhelmed by the situation. She takes in the scene, scanning the crowded train car with its colorful, intrusive advertisements plastered near the doors and lining the walls, the majority of passengers buried in their electronic devices, likely being served more ads while they browse their favorite apps.

I try to comfort her. "Are the pods ever this packed in your world?"

"Not like this, no. Hivemind can manage the travel system quite well to avoid congestion."

I wonder if anyone around us is listening and getting confused by what we're saying, but everyone seems completely engrossed in their own busy lives, as usual. The remainder of the ride is spent in silence. It's not a long journey, only about fifteen minutes and five stops down the line. The train arrives at the station connected to the shopping center, and I motion towards the exit. We navigate through the crowded train car and finally make our way onto the slightly more spacious platform outside.

"This way," I say as I point to the left.

We follow the horde of mall workers and shoppers to the end of the train platform where a bank of escalators takes us down a floor to the mall. It's still early; the mall doesn't officially open for another half hour, but you can walk through it to get breakfast in the food court or to go to the grocery store that's open twenty-four hours a day. There's a chain coffee shop right near the mall entrance we had come through, so I suggest we grab a table to kill some time until the mall opens. As she sits down I say to Chloe, "I'm getting a coffee. Do you want anything? Have you ever tried coffee?"

"I haven't. I don't know, I'm kind of scared to try anything from this world," she replies.

"I get mine with oat milk and stevia. It's a natural sweetener. And the milk doesn't come from a cow."

"Okay, I'll give it a try, I guess." She still looks unsure.

I get in line and wait for my turn to order. I ask for two medium coffees from the barista and make sure to get my rewards card scanned before paying because I'm close to getting a free one. I bring the drinks back to the table and put one in front of Chloe.

"It's hot. Don't worry if you don't like it. You don't have to finish the whole thing," I say as I take a sip from my cup.

"I don't want to waste it." Chloe carefully brings the cup to her lips and takes a tiny sip. She smacks her lips together a few times, then takes a bigger sip. That one makes her shudder. "It's... bitter."

"Yeah, you get used to it, though. You can put in more sweeteners, but then it tastes like candy. I'm surprised there's no coffee in Utopia. Why is that?"

"I think it's too hard to grow the beans." Chloe is looking out in the mall, watching people go by as she takes careful sips. She remarks, "Everyone seems to be in a hurry here."

"Yep. That's the thing I noticed about your world. No one was rushing anywhere. It's a lot more mellow there. It's nice."

The sound of metal-on-metal suddenly reverberates through the mall, echoing off the walls. It's a symphony of steel and hinges, a mechanical chorus signaling the start of a new day of consumerism as the stores in the mall open their security gates in unison. Chloe is looking around in confusion. I say, "Malls open, should we do a lap?"

"Sure, is that what you do here? Just wander around?"

Half-full coffee cups in hand, we walk side-by-side into the massive mall hallway. "I guess, yeah. You walk until you see something you want to buy. Some older people come here just for exercise. They're called 'mall-walkers'. They don't like to walk outside."

We pass by a few clothing stores. Chloe seems interested in them and I tell her to let me know if she wants to go inside any. Just ahead is a shop that sells Christmas decorations all year round, for some unknown reason. "I thought Christmas was in the middle of winter?" Chloe asks, confused.

"It is. Apparently, enough people buy Christmas knick-knacks year-round for this store to stay in business. Do you guys celebrate Christmas in Utopia? Or any holidays?"

"Some people do. I think it's nice that they keep traditions like that alive. I've never celebrated anything, though. Well, my birthday I guess."

"That's just a few days away, right? Any plans? Other than getting the Implant?"

"Not really. My dad used to do something special for me every year. After he died, your dad stepped in last year." A look of concern shows on her face. "Sorry, does it make you mad when I talk about your dad spending time with me?"

"It's fine. I stopped caring about him a long time ago. It's not your fault that he abandoned me. Don't worry about it." I'm lying. It annoys me.

Chloe seems to know I'm not completely telling the truth, and she changes the subject. "What did you do for your eighteenth birthday?"

"Not much. I've never been very sociable. Some kids from my school would head up to Canada on their eighteenth so they can legally drink, but I don't care about that."

"Interesting. We don't have alcohol in Utopia. But the Implant can simulate the effect of any drink or drug."

I haven't thought about how alcohol and drugs would work in Utopia. Simulating drugs using Hivemind is probably a decent alternative, though. You would never have a bad trip with hallucinogens, at least. And it would be impossible to overdose on anything.

The center of the mall is an impressive sight with its large open atrium and glass roof, allowing natural light to filter in and illuminate the area. The space is filled with plants, trees, and an artificial pond, all strategically placed to create a serene and inviting atmosphere. "Not quite like the Park, hey?" I say to Chloe.

"No, but it's nice. It's good to see some nature in this place." She notices the koi fish swimming in the pond next to us. "Whoa, are those real?"

I look at the colorful fish she's pointing at. "Yep. We don't have the technology to simulate them here." I laugh.

"I've never seen a real fish. We have fake ones in the ponds in the Taiga Biome. These are so pretty, though!"

"You know what? I know what to show you. Follow me."

—-

We continue walking for a few minutes until we reach the spot I had in mind. As we get within range, I point down the hallway. Chloe is in awe; she can hardly contain her excitement. In this mall, they have a petting zoo set up in one of the hallways year round. It's a small enclosure with some sheep, goats, pigs, rabbits, and even a llama. I grab a few coins out of my pocket and feed them into a machine that dispenses food for the animals. I give a handful to Chloe, telling her that the animals will eat right out of her hand if she wants.

We step through the gate onto the straw-covered floor. A few kids are laughing and having fun while petting and feeding the goats. Their parents are standing outside of the fence, drinking coffee and keeping an eye on their kin. Chloe nervously steps towards a fluffy sheep. She has the food enclosed in her left hand, and she carefully and tentatively reaches out her other hand to pat it lightly on the head. She seems too nervous to let it eat out of her hand, so she drops a few bits of food on the ground in front of the sheep, who happily nibbles at it.

I'm crouched down, letting one of the small pigs eat out of my hand. I beckon Chloe over, showing her that it's safe to do so. Another pig runs up to her when she bends down next to me, so she opens up her hand to let it lap up some of the food. Her face is beaming the entire time. Once we had made the rounds to all the different animals and had both run out of food, we exit the petting zoo, getting some hand sanitizer out of the dispenser to get cleaned up, and then resume our walk through the mall.

"Where did those animals come from? Are they someone's pets?" Chloe asks me, after taking one more glance behind us at the petting zoo.

"There's a company that loans them out to places like this for petting zoos. They're probably farm animals or something. I wouldn't call them pets." I answer. It seems ironic, considering we were in a 'petting' zoo.

"What's the difference between a pet and a farm animal?"

"Pets are like part of a family. People take care of them and get a fun, cute thing to interact with in exchange. Farm animals are meant more for making money. If farms aren't using their animals for something like a petting zoo, then they're raising them to a certain age and then selling them to a slaughterhouse to become food. Then there are zoos, which have a variety of animals for people to pay to see in person. I could take you to one here sometime if you want."

"That's kind of weird, though, isn't it? Aren't they slaves?"

"Oh, absolutely. It's not okay, but people have been doing it since, like, forever, so they just keep exploiting them. Some zoos only have animals that they've rescued on display, which is slightly better, but it's always annoyed me that they rescue these animals just to put them in a cage for the rest of their lives, with people gawking at them all day."

"Why do you think they do that?"

"It's all about profit, unfortunately. It's not enough just to save an animal's life, you have to find some way to make money out of it. The money might go towards saving more animals, but it would be nice to live in a society that doesn't need to exploit animals in order to save them. It's not a problem in Utopia, with your simulations."

"Definitely not."

I know I'm a hypocrite since I still eat animals sometimes and enjoy going to the zoo every once in a while. But everyone is a hypocrite. It's impossible not to be in the modern world unless you go live off the land somewhere and farm all of your own vegetables. Even to do that, though, you need to buy land with money that would almost certainly be gained through unethical means, unless you want to live in fear of being arrested for trespassing for your entire life. There is no ethical consumption under capitalism, the entire system needs to change. Even though Chloe grew up in a society that is completely free of exploitation, she's still excited to interact with the exploited animals in the petting zoo. Capitalism always succeeds in distracting from exploitation and enticing people to consume unethically.

I need to eat something before work, so we head to the food court. "I know a decent vegan place here if you want to try some food," I offer.

"I think I'm good with my to-go bar. I'm not too hungry yet anyway."

Well, at least she tried the coffee. I grab some orange juice and a vegan breakfast wrap from my favorite fast food place while Chloe finds a table for us to sit at. When I sit down and go to take a bite of my wrap, Chloe looks confused.

"What's up?" I ask her.

"I thought you were getting vegan food. That looks like meat and eggs."

"It's vegan. There's fake sausage, fake eggs, and fake cheese in it. It's all made from plants."

"Why do they make fake versions of animal products? Why not just eat plants as they are?"

"I don't know. It's probably easier to get people to eat plant-based food if it's similar to what they've always eaten. I don't mind, this is delicious. It's not very healthy though, it's all processed crap."

While I eat my wrap and drink my orange juice, Chloe is looking around at all the different vendors in the food court. She says, "I can't believe how many options there are. It's overwhelming. How do you choose?"

"You just give everything a try, over time. You'll find your favorites, eventually. I bet Utopia has the same amount of food options, they just aren't laid out like this, so you don't realize."

"I guess. Oh, right, did I tell you how food works with the Implant?"

"Uh, no, is it different?"

"The Implant can trick your mind into thinking you're eating whatever you want to. You could think you were eating a steak, but it would just be a slab of vegetables. It would even look like steak, with the juices flowing out and everything. The taste could be made identical to what you're used to in this world."

"Isn't that kind of the same as my fake meat?"

She puts a finger to her chin in quiet contemplation. "I didn't think about that. I guess so."

"But kids can't do that, since they don't have the Implant?"

"No, that's why the food comes in different colors and shapes and flavors. It's normal if you grow up eating that like I did."

"Will you simulate eating a steak when you get the Implant?"

"Hm, I don't know. Good question. Maybe once, just to see what all the fuss is about."

—-

We have time for one last activity before I have to leave the mall and head to work. I know exactly what we should do. There's still one place in this world where you can go to play two-player video games. An arcade.

Even though arcades have been steadily dying off over the last few decades, this mall still has a massive one. It's more than just an arcade, though. They have pool tables, ping pong tables, virtual reality games, golf simulators, and even axe throwing. It's a multi-level complex with a restaurant and a few take out counters integrated within. When Chloe first walks into the 'arcade', she says it reminds her of the Rec Room in Utopia, just a lot more flashy. I agree, other than the fact that it isn't free like in her world. Everything costs money here. I load up a couple of wristbands at a kiosk with twenty dollars on each so we can try out a variety of games.

We start with a few multiplayer stations. One is an alien shooter. It has large, mounted plastic guns to shoot at the enemies on-screen, which Chloe seems to enjoy. The next is a racing game that has a steering wheel and pedals to control the virtual cars. It takes her a few minutes to get the hang of it, but she eventually manages to complete an entire lap without crashing into anything.

We move over to the ticket games, where you can play to earn tickets to get little plastic knick-knacks from the prize redemption booth. Chloe is enamored with these simple games; she's going from station to station, trying them all out. There are games where you have to stop a wheel and try to hit the spot with the jackpot, ones where you press a button to drop a ball and it falls into holes with different ticket values, and ones where you throw a ball to try to knock something over. When I was younger, these games would dispense physical tickets. Now, the tickets are virtually added to your wristband. It isn't quite as exciting as it used to be when you won a jackpot and the tickets started shooting out, but it's easier now since you don't have to carry stacks of tickets to each game.

Chloe eventually runs out of credits to play with, but I offer her my wristband. She doesn't want to take it at first, but I tell her that I'm having more fun just watching her play. Once the second wristband is depleted, we head to the prize redemption spot to see how many tickets she won. I didn't realize that this arcade actually has some useful prizes to use your tickets on. They have various electronics and gadgets, stuffed animals, board games, all kinds of interesting things, in addition to the cheap plastic crap of course. I scan the two wristbands and add the tickets from both together. We don't have enough to get any of the cool prizes. Not even close.

I ask Chloe if there's anything she wants that we can afford with our small ticket total. She isn't interested in any of it, so I get a couple of candy bars that I'll snack on later. As much as I want to stay in the arcade and mall with Chloe, it's time for me to catch the train and head to work.

The train is way less busy this time since rush hour had ended a few hours earlier. Me and Chloe easily found a pair of seats to sit down on. "So, what did you think of the mall?" I ask Chloe once we settle into our spot.

"Honestly, pretty overwhelming. It was fun, though. I just couldn't help thinking about how much money everything cost you, especially the arcade. How much was it?"

"Forty bucks. It's no big deal. Don't worry about it."

"How long did you have to work to make that?"

I do some quick mental math. I'm subtracting the taxes I have to pay from my hourly wage. "About three hours, I think."

"So you had to work for three hours just for us to have one hour of fun? The math doesn't add up there, bro."

"Yeah, I know. Gotta splurge every once in a while, though, or else you'll go crazy or get depressed. There's nothing I can do about it."

Chloe purses her lips, her expression one of skepticism and concern. "You don't believe that, do you?"

"What, that I can do something about it? What do you mean, like get a higher paying job?"

"You still don't understand, after everything you've learned the past few days? Do you honestly think you're powerless? You don't think you're destined for something other than being a wage slave your entire life?"

"Like... what? I'm nobody."

"You're not nobody. Look who you're descended from. Your father and grandfather literally changed the world. Give yourself a bit of credit, please. You have more power than you think. Keep that in mind, okay?"

The conversation between Chloe and me has become heated, causing a noticeable tension in the air. The rest of the train ride is spent in silence between us. When we reach the station near my place of work, we exit the train and make our way down the escalators to the street below.

"My warehouse is about five minutes away. How long until your watch stops?" I ask Chloe.

She looks at the watch on her wrist. "Less than an hour, I think."

"Are you gonna be alright? My shift starts in fifteen minutes. What are you gonna do?"

"I want to see where you work, so I'll walk with you. I'll be able to find something to do until I'm sent back. Don't worry."

"You can walk me to work, but you can only go as far as the parking lot. They're pretty strict about security there." We start walking down the street in the direction of the Idolon warehouse. It's so big that we can see it from several blocks away. Now that I've been in Utopia, though, it doesn't seem quite as impressive as it once did.

Chloe notices the massive, black, nondescript building and says, "Wow, is that it? It looks a bit like a much smaller version of Utopia. In the winter, when it turns black."

"Yep, that's my warehouse. Idolon has a bunch of them in most major cities around the world."

"Oh, you work for Idolon? I always see and hear that name everywhere when I'm in this world. They're pretty big, huh?"

"Yep. They kind of came out of nowhere a few decades ago, but they got so big and became worth so much money that they just started buying out all their competitors. They've expanded into most industries now."

"Isn't that bad? I thought people liked to say that capitalism was good because of competition."

"People say a lot of things about capitalism that are completely untrue. Even if there were multiple major companies in each industry, they would just work together to screw over poor people instead of competing with each other."

"What's it like working for them? Are you in a union? Those are good for workers, right?"

I laugh. Idolon Corporate does everything they possibly can to deter workers from unionizing. One of the reasons they design the warehouses to have a high worker turnover rate is so that no one is there long enough to start organizing labor. I was bombarded by anti-union propaganda during my orientation. "Definitely not in a union, no. But yes, despite what the rich assholes try to brainwash people into thinking, unions are great for workers. I heard a saying once that stuck with me; 'divided we beg, united we bargain'. And you're always begging for scraps when you aren't in one."

At the edge of the parking lot, Chloe and I come to a stop. She opens her arms for a hug, and I reciprocate, pulling her close.

"Reach out next time you come to Utopia. Don't be a stranger." Chloe walks a few steps away before turning around to say one last thing. "And remember what I said on the train. Think about it. That's all I ask."

I watch her turn back around and walk away, without giving me a chance to respond. I sigh, then walk across the vast parking lot to the warehouse entrance, and step inside to start my ten-hour shift.

Chapter 17

It's a good thing that I can do my job on autopilot mode because my mind is somewhere else completely for my entire shift. I've been recounting the events of the last few days.

I still don't know how to feel about my late father. When I found out that he died a couple of weeks ago, I didn't care. He wasn't part of my life anyway, so why would I? I didn't want anything from him, especially not the watch that has now been firmly attached to my wrist for the past few days. But something about the watch had drawn me in. It was a feeling I'd never felt before. Something otherworldly.

The note that came with it seems typical of my late father. Emotionless, concise, and to the point. Enough ambiguity to leave me questioning the purpose behind it. What were his motives, exactly? Why send me to Utopia? Did he want me to get the Implant like he did? Did he want me to see what humanity could become? Is this what Chloe is hinting at?

I still don't understand how exactly I fit into this story. I'm not a genius engineer like my father or grandfather. But would I even need to be if I get the Implant? I could have access to the collective knowledge of every engineer on Earth. Every scientist, every scholar, every single person who has dedicated their life to the pursuit of knowledge. Where would I go from there, though? Keep living my life in this world, suffering along with all the other exploited working-class people? Or spend most of my time in Utopia where everything is free, and no one suffers? What would I tell my mom? And does she know more than she's letting on? Some of her reactions have been a bit suspicious.

Then there's Chloe, my new alt-sister. I've been an only child for my entire life. I didn't necessarily want a sibling, either. I had been okay growing up without one. But it is nice to have someone my age to talk to since I lost touch with most of my former friends after graduating high school. She's been really fun to hang out with. Playing games together with her gives me a joyful feeling that I'm not sure I've experienced for a long time. Maybe ever.

Many siblings have strained relationships after growing up together, but the fact that Chloe and I have no history could work in our favor. There are no lingering resentments from arguments during our teenage years. We have a clean slate to build a relationship on.

I've enjoyed my time in Utopia, it's an interesting place. I haven't felt stressed at all while in that world. When I'm there it seems like I have no obligations and can just enjoy myself, until I have to come back to my own world, at least. Never thinking about money and knowing that I can visit a med pod without going into life-altering medical debt is a game changer.

—-

The buzzer sounds for my meal break. I shuffle away from my station with my fellow workers and head to the cafeteria to grab something to eat. I manage to get my meal and get outside without attracting any unwanted attention this time.

Fatigue is starting to set in. I'm jet-lagged without even having taken a flight because of the time zone difference in Utopia. I've been awake for over sixteen hours at this point, and I still have at least another four hours to go before I can go sleep in my bed.

Which makes me think about the 'housing' situation in Utopia and the sleep pod I had used for the last few nights. It was free, like everything else there. But the system intrigues me. There is much less of an emphasis on personal belongings in Utopia, which is refreshing. You can switch pods every few days if you want to. You don't need to worry about furniture or decorations or even utility bills.

Everything feels a bit too clinical there, aside from the Park, but apparently the Implant would change that. From what I understand about it, I'm pretty sure it enables you to change the wall colors to whatever you want, make the bedding look different, have virtual art hang on the walls, anything you can imagine. It would be like you're in a life simulation game, cycling through different designs until you find the one you like.

I could probably do something like that in the sleep pods now, though. The walls are all Hivemind screens. I keep forgetting to test that out, since every time I had settled into my pod I had been wiped from the day's activities and ended up going straight to sleep.

—-

The buzzer sounds again, right after I finish my meal. I throw the container in the garbage and head back to my workstation to complete my shift. I quickly fall back into my trance-like automaton state. I'm thinking back to what Chloe said about me not being powerless, and what she might possibly mean by that.

I know that there's a certain subset of people that worship either my dad or my grandpa. Or both. Even after death, they have a cult following in far-left, anti-American, anti-capitalist circles. But I've stayed completely out of the limelight. I never speak publicly about anything. I don't know if any of those people even know I exist. So what power do I have? The watch? That could be what she's talking about. After all, with the spin of a knob, I can warp to a new dimension. But what would that accomplish in this world? Maybe Chloe knows something that I don't about the watch. She has one too, although hers works the opposite of mine; it brings her from Utopia to here.

It's not like anyone else can use the watches but me and Chloe. She told me that since it had been passed down to us when our fathers died; we gained the sole ability to use each respective watch. But can the power be harnessed into something else that other people can use? I don't even know where to begin with figuring that out. Maybe Hivemind knows; maybe I would learn more if I decide to get the Implant.

I would be in such a unique position if I did decide to get the Implant. I would be the only person in this world to have access to the collective knowledge of every human, except for Chloe, when she would come to visit. But would I have the combined knowledge of everyone in my world or just Utopia? I'll have to ask Chloe or Hivemind that question.

She said it doesn't work the same way in this world, and I still don't know exactly what she meant by that.

What could I do with that kind of knowledge? Blackmail trillionaires into giving up their wealth? Maybe. That's a fast way to get a major target on your back, though. After all, laws only really apply to poor people in this world. The rich can get away with literal murder, and they often do. It greatly annoys me that any crime punishable by a fine is only illegal for the poor. A speeding ticket to someone rich enough to drive a car worth hundreds of thousands of dollars is nothing. It can ruin a poor person, though.

Could I use the knowledge to become rich somehow and then start buying off politicians like the other rich people did? Maybe. That could take a long time, though. I would most likely have to become a trillionaire anyway, since that's who I would be competing against. You can't amass that kind of money without exploiting thousands of people, which I could never bring myself to do, simply because I'm not a sociopath.

—-

There goes the final buzzer of the day, signaling the end of my shift. I'm free, until tomorrow at least. Luckily, the day had flown by since I was lost in my thoughts for the whole shift. I do have to be careful about that, though. If my productivity falls too low I'll be reprimanded by my bosses. On the other hand, if I complete my tasks too quickly, it may create higher expectations for me and put pressure on both myself and my colleagues to maintain an unsustainable pace.

It's a tightrope balancing act. There's an unspoken agreement between us workers to never push ourselves too hard in hopes of avoiding an increase in our target metrics.

I make my way through my workstation area to the lockers to grab my belongings, pick my phone up from the security desk, and then exit the building into the cool night air. I'm planning to walk home today. No train this time; it's only one stop, anyway. I walk through the parking lot slowly, watching my coworkers load into their cars one by one. But then I see something I'm not expecting at all.

Chloe. She's standing at the edge of the parking lot, exactly where we had parted ways ten hours earlier. When I'm close enough for her to hear, I say, "Uh, hey, you're still here? Or did you come back?"

"Hi. Sorry, I had some things to do, so I stuck around."

What could she possibly have to do in this world? "Oh, okay. So, what are you up to now?"

"Well, I was hoping to show you something, if that's okay with you. I know you're probably super tired after your shift and everything else we did, but it would mean a lot to me."

How can I say no to that? "Of course, no problem. What is it? Where?"

"You'll see. Follow me."

She takes me down a side street, in the opposite direction of the route that would take me home to my safe, comfortable bed. We walk in silence for about ten minutes. Chloe is keeping a very steady pace; I'm struggling to keep up with her. We emerge onto a familiar road lined with shops at street level and apartments above them. Another few minutes walking down this street and we're at our destination.

It's a communist bookstore that I've walked past a few times but have never been in. I like the vibe though, it seems like a cool place. A banner above the entrance has the name *The Iron Curtain* on it and a hammer and sickle emblem. Chloe walks up to the door and presses a buzzer next to it. After a few seconds, the door makes an unlocking sound, and she pulls it open, beckoning me inside.

"It's late, isn't this place closed? What are we doing here?" I whisper to Chloe.

"Don't worry, I know the owners," is all she says in response.

We snake our way through the aisles stacked with leftist books and apparel to the back of the shop. As we pass shirts with Karl Marx's face on them and books from Vladimir Lenin, I don't see anyone else in the store, so I'm wondering who buzzed us in. Chloe walks straight towards a bookshelf on the back wall. It's stacked head to toe with the same book: a biography of our late grandfather, Maximus Karlson the First. I've never bothered to read it. When I'm standing next to Chloe in front of the shelf, she says, "Hivemind, open up, please."

Like a secret doorway to a world unknown, the bookshelf parts with a soft whisper, exposing a pristine white staircase leading into the unknown depths of the building. A single light flickers on from within, casting an eerie glow that beckons us forward. What the hell is going on? What is this? Once the bookshelf is open wide enough for her to pass through, Chloe moves past it and looks behind her to make sure I'm following. I'm not gonna miss this. It feels like I'm in a spy movie. I'm right on her heels.

The stairs descend for what seems like forever. We finally approach a small landing with a tall blank screen that looks exactly like the ones lining the halls in Utopia. What the...? I'm now noticing that all surfaces in this hallway are white, just like Utopia.

When we reach the landing, Chloe pivots around the corner. The stairs continue downward, and we descend for a few dozen more steps until we finally reach level ground. There's a door-sized cutout in an otherwise all-white wall. As we approach, the cutout slides open to the side, similar to the doors in Utopia.

We enter a spacious room that resembles a science lab. Nearly every inch of this room is covered in white, from the walls and floor to the ceiling. Several Hivemind screens are mounted on the walls, similar to the one we saw on the staircase landing. The tables are cluttered with electronic parts and tangled wires. There's about a dozen people in the room, some focused on tinkering with the components, others engaged in conversation, and a few spaced out in their own thoughts.

As we enter the room, all eyes turn to us and the people scattered around the lab tables start to gather in the center. Their movements are coordinated, like a well-oiled machine, as they form a group and seem to anticipate our arrival. A tall, muscular black woman is standing front and center, smiling in my direction. She looks familiar to me. I think I've seen her somewhere before, but I can't place where. Then, to my surprise, my friend Joe pushes his way through the group to stand in front, right beside the tall black woman, who seems to be the leader. His face is clean and his clothes look new, or at least freshly laundered; I almost didn't recognize him at first, but it's definitely him. He gives me a slight smirk, which is all the confirmation I need. Compounding my surprise and disbelief, I see another familiar face as I scan the group standing in front of me.

It's my mother.

I can see her face sticking out between the shoulders of a few strangers in front of her. When I make eye contact with her, she navigates her way from the back of the small group to stand up front.

At once, a white light illuminates on the temples of every member of the group that stands facing Chloe and me, including both Joe and my mother. The light is like a beacon, casting a halo of illumination around the group of people gathered before us. Their faces are bathed in an otherworldly glow, each one conveying a different emotion - curiosity, joy, hope. My mother's expression is the most haunting, a mixture of regret and longing that seems to speak volumes without a single word.

As the leader speaks, her voice is like thunder, echoing off the walls and reverberating through the room. The silence around us is shattered, replaced by the intensity and power of her words. "Welcome to the revolution, comrade."

II

Chloe

Chapter 18

"I need to warn you about a few things before we take this trip," my father says to me.

I finish swallowing my last bite of food and place my fork on the tray in front of me. "You've told me all about Dystopia, Dad. I know what to expect," I respond, tilting my head back to reach the last drops of water in my cup. My father has always called the alternate reality version of our earth 'Dystopia', because in nearly every way and by nearly every metric it's the opposite of our world. The name fits quite well.

"We haven't even scratched the surface. Honestly. Dystopia is nothing like what you've grown up with, here in this world. It will be a massive culture shock to you. You need to be ready for that." He looks concerned. "I know, you're sixteen now, you're old enough to get the Hivemind Patch and start to become more independent. But Dystopia is not the place to test that out."

"Okay, okay. I'll take it seriously, I promise. Can I please go get the Patch now? You said I could after breakfast."

"In a minute, I'm not done yet. As you know, we waited until your birthday for this trip, because with your new Patch and my Implant, we can communicate from anywhere on the planet. Hivemind's capabilities are greatly limited in Dystopia, but we can at least talk to each other through it. If you get lost, if we get separated, we can reconnect easily." He stares at me with a look of great concern, while I quite literally vibrate with excitement. "Don't you want to hang out with your friend on your birthday? We don't have to do this right now, you know," he says, knowing the answer.

"Come on Dad, finish your last bite so we can get going, *please*?" I plead with him. I stand up and stack my dishes on my tray. As soon as my dad picks up his last bite of food, I swipe his tray out from under his arms and combine the contents of it with my own. After the table is automatically sprayed down I give it a quick wipe and bring the tray to the counter to deposit it. Dad has to speedwalk after me as I beeline towards the nearest Hivemind screen.

I abruptly come to a halt in front of the large black screen on the cafeteria wall and say, "Hivemind, I'm sixteen now. One set of Patches, please." I make sure I'm polite to Hivemind, as always, even though I'm anxious to get my hands on the Patch and get permanently connected to the all-knowing mastermind of Utopia.

A tray pops out of the wall next to the screen without any acknowledgment from Hivemind, and I hurriedly grab the first Patch and instantly plop it behind my ear, using the Hivemind screen as a virtual mirror. After securing the second Patch behind my other ear, I say aloud, "Testing, is this thing working?"

A familiar voice appears from inside my ear, or maybe my head, I don't know how to categorize the source of it. *"Hello Chloe, congratulations on receiving the Patch. Happy birthday."* I'm used to hearing the angelic sound projecting from various areas around Utopia, but this is a completely new sensation for me.

"Thanks, Hivemind! I'm so excited!" I turn to face my dad, who has been silently watching me from a few feet away.

He has a look on his face I haven't seen very often. It seems to be a mixture of concern and pride.

"All set?" my father asks me. "Do you know how to use it?"

"*Da-ad.* Obviously. I know how Hivemind works. Can we go now?"

"Fine, fine. Let's find the nearest private room. Hive-"

"I got this. Hivemind, show us to the nearest private room please," I interrupt him, eager to use my Patch for the first time. The screen comes to life, displaying a map view of the nearest safe space for us to teleport away, just down the hallway.

Once we're secure in the designated room, my dad puts one hand on each of my shoulders, leans in, then says in a low, firm voice, "Follow my lead. Do not try to go off on your own, stay by my side the entire time. Do not even make eye contact with anyone unless it's someone I know. Do you understand me?"

I shyly nod in agreement. My father releases me from his grip and moves to my side. He says, "Wrap your arm around my shoulder. You might feel a bit of nausea, but it should subside quickly."

I do as I'm told, while my father reaches over to his watch-adorned wrist and fiddles with the dial. "Don't let go. I'm setting it for about two hours. We can extend if necessary. Here we go."

He clicks the crown of the watch inwards, and the two of us vanish from the room instantly.

—-

We materialize together in a small room. He's right, the wave of nausea that flows through me subsides quite quickly. I blink and survey my new surroundings. It's very dim in this unfamiliar room, which I'm not used to. Utopia is quite well-lit, to say the least. The walls themselves emit a clean white light.

I feel my dad pull away from my grasp and walk over to the nearest wall. He flicks a switch, bathing the room in warm light from a fixture on the ceiling. The sparsely furnished room is now fully revealed to me, and I take it all in. I notice a small counter with a sink and an unfamiliar white box with buttons and a window on it in one corner. The opposite corner has a pile of blankets lying haphazardly on a metal frame with a small brown cabinet next to it, the surface empty.

"Is that your bed, do you sleep here?" I ask my father.

"It's a cot. Sometimes, not often. The other me sleeps here more than I do," Maximus says.

"Alt-Dad? Oh, cool. Are we meeting up with him today?"

"Not today." He doesn't elaborate any further.

I walk over to the sink and stand in front, inspecting it. It's a lot... dirtier than I'm used to seeing. The sinks in Utopia are all self-cleaning. I examine the strange electronic device next to it. "What is this?" I ask my father, pointing at it.

"That's a microwave. It heats up food."

"Hm. Interesting." I head towards the door on the nearby wall and lift myself up onto my tiptoes to peer through the peephole. The hallway on the other side is empty, nothing catches my attention.

"I need to change out of these gray clothes. I have to blend in here," my dad says from across the small room. "Wait right there, and don't open that door." He pulls a duffle bag from under the cot and grabs a shirt and pants out of it, then walks over to the only other door in this tiny apartment. I see a quick glimpse of a toilet on the other side of it before he closes the door behind him. Soon after I hear incomprehensible muttering coming from the bathroom. Is he talking to himself, or Hivemind?

"Looking good, Dad," I say as he emerges from the bathroom a minute later. He's wearing brown shorts and a patterned, collared shirt. "Do I need to change?"

"No, your clothes are fine. You won't draw any suspicion. The Utopia-issue shoes look kind of like slippers and might be weird to wear outside, but I don't have anything that will fit you here. Don't worry about it."

I look down at the gray slippers peeking out from under the hem of my beige pants. I pull on my pink tee shirt. "So teenagers here dress like this?"

"Yes, many do. Others don't. You'll be fine."

—-

We have to ride a rickety old elevator down 3 floors to leave the apartment, it shocks and scares me a bit. It's nothing like the travel pods in Utopia. That unnerving feeling wears off pretty quickly once I step outside, though. The street is a blur of colorful cars, swerving and honking as they speed by. Pedestrians walk quickly on the sidewalk, some talking on their phones or carrying bags of groceries. The road and sidewalk are littered with trash, bits of paper, and plastic bottles scattered among the gray concrete.

The smell here overwhelms me. Utopia doesn't have any lingering scents. This new, unfamiliar place though? The air is thick with the scent of exhaust fumes from the cars and the mild stench of rotting garbage. A hint of perfume clings to some of the pedestrians as they pass by.

"Where are we?" I ask my dad, clutching his hand tightly.

"New York City. Probably not the best place to take you on your first trip, most of this world isn't as hectic as it is here. But there are only so many safe areas to travel to. We can't reveal our little secret, or give anyone a heart attack by appearing in front of them."

A woman walks past us, pushing a stroller with one hand and holding onto a leash with the other. "Is that a real dog?" I excitedly whisper in my dad's ear.

"Remember what I told you about pets in this world? They're all real. Nothing like our holograms. I think that's a beagle," he whispers back.

I've only seen virtual holograms of dogs in Hivemind demo rooms and in the Park in Utopia. The Desert Biome has African wild dogs roaming around. They look quite a bit different than this one.

Dad lets go of my hand and steps down from the apartment stoop. He walks across the sidewalk and stands right on the edge of the curb, stretching his hand out above his head. I look on, puzzled, until a yellow car comes to a stop right in front of him. He opens the rear door and motions for me to climb inside. After he enters the opposite door and takes his seat, I watch him pull a belt around his chest and buckle it in, so I follow suit, fumbling to grab mine from behind my shoulder and having to use two hands to secure the buckle.

The cab driver is a friendly-looking man who seems amused by me staring out of the window in awe as we drive down various New York streets. My jaw hasn't shut since we pulled away from the curb. "First time in the big city?" the cab driver asks me, looking in my direction through the mirror attached to the windshield.

I'm not sure whether I should answer this stranger's question until I feel a nudge in the arm from my dad. "Yes sir, never been anywhere so... busy. There's so much going on."

"I would say you'll get used to it eventually, but even I haven't after driving these streets for a decade now," the driver replies.

I'm not sure if I could ever get used to this world, even if most of it isn't like this. Everything is different. Everyone is different. They walk differently, they talk differently, they all have various types of gadgets grasped in their hands or hanging out of their ears. Everything is so... colorful, but also quite drab at the same time. There seems to be a layer of dirt on nearly every surface. Black bags are overflowing with trash, lining many of the streets we drive past.

The buildings are all different shapes, sizes, and patterns. Some are run down and look like they're about to collapse any minute now, and others are brand new, shining, and sparkling in the sun, covered bottom to top in glass windows and panels. They seem to have a constant, never-ending flow of people entering and exiting them. Where are they all going? Everyone is in such a hurry.

The cab comes to a stop next to a small grassy park with a few trees in it after about twenty minutes. I watch my dad hand a plastic rectangle to the driver, who holds it near a black gadget until a beep sounds. It spits out a small white piece of paper that he hands to my father. I notice the driver has a weird expression on his face as he watches me examine this process, my face giving away my utter confusion. Realizing I'm beginning to arouse suspicion, I look away. I'll try to maintain as neutral an expression as possible from now on.

My dad pockets the slip of paper, thanks the driver, then reaches over me to pull a silver handle on the door and push it open. I take this as a cue and try to exit the cab, but I'm trapped by my buckled seatbelt. Dad quickly unbuckles it for me, releasing me from another awkward moment. I mutter, "Thanks," and scurry out of the cab to get away from the prying eyes of the driver.

"Are you okay? A bit overwhelmed?" my father asks when he catches up to me.

I reply, staring at my shoes, "He was gawking at me, it was embarrassing."

My dad places his hand on my shoulder to try to comfort me. "Sorry, I should have prepped you better for this. It's hard to imagine what minor things you'd have to learn. Honestly, I'm worried that the driver thought I had you locked up in a basement for your entire life or something."

The pair of us walk slowly through this small park, me following my father's lead. We come up to an empty bench, and after checking our surroundings to make sure no one is in earshot, Dad ushers me to sit down. He turns to me and says, "You're about to meet a few friends of mine, and I want you to be prepared."

"Okay..." I say, intrigued.

"You don't have to pretend around these people, they... know everything. They've been to Utopia. A few times."

"Oh? Uh, how, exactly? Do they have their own watches?"

"No. There are only two. His, and mine."

I know exactly who he means by 'his'. "So how have they been there? Alt-Dad has been taking them?"

"Yes, exactly. He can take people from here to there, and I can do the opposite."

"But, why?"

"Well, you see, we're trying to build up a, um," Dad pauses for a second. "I don't like this wording. But, for lack of a better term, 'army'."

"What kind of army? Who are you fighting against?"

"It's not an offensive thing, well not yet at least. It's more of a defensive thing. There are very powerful entities in this world that almost certainly know about us outsiders. We don't know for sure, but with the level of surveillance and the firm grip the authorities here have, especially in this country, it would be silly to assume they don't know."

"What do you think they would do to us?" I ask nervously.

"Nothing good. You've studied Dystopia politics. I'm sure you know what this government will do to anyone who is a threat to it, or capitalism itself. Did you learn about Fred Hampton, like I told you to?"

"Yes, Dad. Are we—I mean—are you a threat?"

"Hopefully. The people in this world need liberation. With the help of Hivemind, we can almost certainly make that happen. Which is why we're building an army."

Chapter 19

"Hivemind, tell them we're here."

I look up at the worn brick walls of this ordinary apartment complex we're standing in front of. Well, ordinary compared to the rest of this world, at least. It looks similar to all the other apartment buildings on this street. I wonder if we're at the right place; I thought a secret hideout for an interdimensional army would stand out. Or, maybe it shouldn't. To avoid suspicion.

The door my father is staring at cracks open, and a high-pitched voice emerges from inside. "Who goes there?" the voice inquires. I hear a muffled giggle before my father can answer.

"You know who it is, Jackie. Come on, we're trying to be subtle here, remember?" Dad replies, annoyed.

The door opens wider, and my father quickly enters, with me right on his heels. We're in a long hallway, carpeted with a red patterned runner, and nothing adorning the light beige walls. I jump a bit as the door loudly shuts behind me, and turn to see the young-looking woman who had just closed it. She's smiling so wide, so infectiously, that I can't help but crack a smile myself, even though I'm trembling with nerves.

"It's so good to meet you, Chloe! I've been waiting so long!" the woman practically shrieks, extending her arms wide open to indicate she wants a hug.

I lean in to accept the embrace from this total stranger. Quite a beautiful stranger, I can't help but think. Her blonde hair is cut in a bob, falling just above her shoulders in soft curls. Her face is delicate and youthful, with a small, upturned nose and round cheeks. Her blue eyes sparkle with excitement and curiosity. She wears a light layer of makeup, enhancing her natural beauty. As I hug her, I am enveloped in the sweet and refreshing scent of flowers. It's as if Jackie has just rolled around in a flower patch - the fragrance of different blooms mingled together. It's a pleasant and calming scent that instantly puts me at ease.

"Chloe, this is Jackie. I've known her for many years," Dad says once Jackie releases her grip on me. "You can trust her with anything."

"Aww, that's so nice of you to say, Maximus! Welcome to the SECRET LAIR!" Jackie giggles, forcing me to follow suit. Then she puts on a super serious face. "I'm kidding, this is my apartment."

I move out of Jackie's way as she skirts between me and my dad, walks quickly down the hall, and makes a left turn at the end of it. She moves with the grace of a ballerina, almost floating above the ground. I look at my dad, who nods in the direction of Jackie's disappearance.

The hallway takes us into a room that looks similar to the ones I've studied in preparation for my first foray into Dystopia. Which is to say, nothing like any of the rooms I'm accustomed to in Utopia. This is what Dystopians call a 'living room', if I remember correctly. There's seating off to the left; a couple of couches surrounding a large, low table. There's a brick outcropping on the wall, which must be a fireplace. The opposite end of the room would be the kitchen, I think, based on the cabinets, counters, and tall white fridge. There's a large table separating the kitchen and living room, with a dozen chairs surrounding it. The dining area.

I notice Jackie quietly watching me take it all in. "Bit of a culture shock, right hon?" Jackie asks.

"Yeah, I've studied this world a lot in Hivemind simulations, but actually being here, and knowing it's not a simulation is different for some reason," I reply.

Jackie gestures for me to follow her to the seating area and she takes a seat herself. I look around to see what my father is doing. A man had entered the room, previously unnoticed by me, most likely from a door near the dining area. Dad walks over to greet the man, and then the pair take a seat at the dining table, as far away from me and Jackie as they can be. They lean in close and speak to each other in a hushed tone, which I have no chance of making out.

"Don't worry, that's just Christoph. He's a friend," Jackie reassures me.

"What are they talking about?" I ask.

"You know, I've learned to not worry about it. If it's important enough for me to know, they'll tell me. Compartmentalization can be a blessing in circumstances like these," she smiles at me. "But what about you? Anything special you want to do on your first trip to capitalist hell? Happy birthday, by the way! Any plans?"

"Well, not really. Dad said the first trip should be quick, so I'm not overwhelmed. I guess I agree, this has already been like nothing I've ever experienced before, outside of a simulation, of course."

"That's fine, if that's what you want, as well. I know you think you have to listen to everything your dad says, but you're sixteen now. You just got the Patch, right? This is the time when you can let your independence flourish!"

"I guess," I blush. "I'm basically at his will and command in this world, though. I can only get here with him, and he controls when I leave with the watch."

"Hey, same goes for me, when I go to Utopia. I would love to stay there longer, even forever if I could, but I can only go when your, uh, other dad brings me."

"Do you know my alt-dad well?" I ask, quickly realizing it's a silly question.

"Of course! I hang out with one, or both of them all the time!"

"Me too. I don't see them together anymore, though. Usually when one disappears, the other shows up soon after." I look over at my dad. Christoph is holding tightly to my father's wrist, his eyes fixed to a watch on his own wrist. He seems to be counting seconds.

Jackie must have noticed the confusion on my face. "Christoph is a doctor. Nothing to worry about, he checks in on me often, too."

"But what exactly is he doing?"

"Oh, just checking his pulse. We have no med pods here, remember?"

"Is something wrong with him? Why would he have to check on him when he can just use the pods?"

"It's just Christoph, he's not a fan of Hivemind's style of medical care. 'Too impersonal', he says." Jackie's forced smile betrays her.

Chapter 20

"You can't repeat anything I just told you, okay?"

"Why tell me at all? I kind of wish you didn't."

I've been babbling nonstop about my adventure in Dystopia from earlier today, but I suddenly feel dejected. My closest friend and confidant, Hanna, has been sitting there looking bored while I recall the events of the day. I've been too excited to notice. I stare directly at Hanna now, trying to get a read on her current feelings. Her obsidian hair frames her heart-shaped face with enigmatic hazel eyes. She always wears black and gray clothes, a stark contrast to the rest of the Utopia teenagers, including me, who mostly want to distance ourselves from the plain-gray-adorned adults by choosing only the most vivid-colored attire.

Hanna's face always holds a near-permanent, somehow-endearing scowl, which I've always been quite fond of. Now, however, the scowl plastered across Hanna's face makes me feel uncomfortable. I'm never uncomfortable around Hanna.

"What's going on? Are you jealous of Jackie? That I called her pretty?" I know I'm reaching, but I don't know how to broach the subject.

Hanna exaggeratedly rolls her eyes. "Can we just talk about something else? It's your birthday, don't you want to do something interesting?"

"I thought we were..."

After an uncomfortable, too-long silence, we decide to head to the nearest cafeteria to get a birthday treat for me, then play a Hivemind game together before bed. Most of my other friends have a big get-together for their birthdays, especially one as important as the sixteenth, but I'm content with winding down the rest of the day with my closest friend, despite the tension.

We scarf down the sweet, delicious birthday treat that Hivemind dispenses for us, then head to the nearest gaming station. "Sooooo, what are we playing?" I ask slyly, knowing the answer.

"It's obvious, isn't it? Fire it up for the birthday girl, Hivemind," Hanna responds, giving a sideways smirk to me.

We rarely play my favorite fantasy, Orc-slaying game together, because Hanna much prefers games that aren't so physically involved. This session is no exception. Me and Hanna's characters are highly experienced, with extremely powerful gear, but so are our enemies. Despite Hanna using an archer class and mostly staying out of the fray in favor of lobbing arrows from afar, I can tell she's wiped after a couple of hours of rigorous play, so she finally initiates a stoppage.

"I think I'm ready for bed, how about you?" I ask Hanna, who's doubled over panting after our besiege of an entire Orc hideout.

"Definitely. Walk me to my sleep pod?" Hanna asks.

"Oh, um, I was thinking that since I'm sixteen now, and uh, so are you,"—I cringe at my awkwardness—"we could bunk together tonight? I don't have to stay in the family suite with my dad anymore."

"Ah, right. I completely forgot. I remember how excited I was months ago when I finally got to be on my own. Is your dad okay with it? You should still ask even though it's your choice now."

"Already cleared it with him. Well, sleeping in my own pod, I guess. Not, uh, bunking with someone else." My face must be bright red. "We could get a couple's suite..."

Now it's Hanna's turn to go crimson. "I don't know... I just switched to a new pod yesterday. I- uh, we... should use it for a few more days at least. The bed is big enough for both of us."

I'm staring at nothing on the floor, trying to suppress my overwhelming emotions. "Your pod it is. Lead the way."

—-

The pair of us take a quick shower—separately—then after performing our nightly skincare and teeth-brushing routines next to each other at the bank of sinks in the expansive communal washroom, we retreat to Hanna's sleep pod. We've slept in the same bed together many times before, having relatively frequent sleepovers for years now. We had always been in the same suite as our parents, however.

I crawl into bed after Hanna, settling in next to her, under the covers. There is technically enough space for the pair of us on the sleep pod bed, but only when we're pressed up next to each other. Neither of us seem to mind; I certainly don't. I take the Big Spoon position behind Hanna, wrapping my arm around my best friend's stomach. Hanna's still slightly moist hair is right in front of my face. I try to subtly inhale her freshly clean scent.

"What are you up to tomorrow?" Hanna slurs, half asleep already.

"I think I'm going back to Dystopia with my dad," I reply.

"Oh.... Okay..." Hanna trails off.

"Is that okay with you? Did you have other plans? ... Hanna?"

She's fast asleep. I'm also quite tired from the long, adventurous day, but I'm not ready for sleep quite yet. Too many thoughts swirling around my head. I clutch tighter onto Hanna's torso, taking hold of my closest friend while letting my mind wander.

I think about how I had actually traveled to another dimension today, and back to this one after a few hours. How I had finally met some of my dad's acquaintances, some of the people actively plotting to liberate an entire class of people in a different world. I think about how enamored I was by Jackie, and how I desperately want to hang out with her again. I would love for Hanna to meet my new friend, but I'm not sure if I should even try to ask based on Hanna's reaction to hearing about the alternate world.

Most of all, I worry about what my father was whispering to that mysterious doctor, Christoph. I hadn't even been formally introduced to him, he took off in a hurry after he was done talking to my dad, only giving a quick, curt nod in my direction.

Now my thoughts turn to my night with Hanna. I've been attracted to Hanna for years now, and I'm quite sure that the feeling is mutual. Both of us are much too awkward to take things further, or even discuss our feelings, though.

We've been content with spending most of our free time together, playing games, holding hands... now snuggling in bed in a private room together. I figure this will become our new normal. It just feels... right.

Despite the awkwardness between us earlier, this has definitely been my best birthday ever. No contest.

Chapter 21

I immediately fell into a 'new normal' routine of splitting my time between Utopia and Dystopia. Over the past several weeks I had accompanied my dad on trips to the alternate dimension nearly every day. I had done a couple of overnight, multi-day trips as well. But I spend most of my time in Dystopia without my dad, without either version of my dad, even. As soon as me and my father arrive in the new dimension and meet up with Jackie, he takes off to do his own thing, leaving me to hang out with her. I don't mind this at all, I want to spend more time with Jackie. She's helping me experience all of the sights and sounds of the new world. Her energy is electric, and I'm quickly becoming addicted to it.

I've learned more about Dystopia just by spending the last few weeks with Jackie than I have in the preceding several years I've been studying it with Hivemind. We've visited war memorials and museums together and attended a few Alcoholics Anonymous meetings, we went to an imperialism documentary screening held by the local communist group, it's like a guided tour of all the horrors that come with living in a capitalist dystopia. For some strange reason it doesn't depress me; it motivates me. Jackie has a type of vicious optimism that makes me more and more excited for what is hopefully to come if my dads' ragtag group of freedom fighters succeed.

The only thing I haven't learned in my time in Dystopia is... basically anything about the plan that is being hatched.

I still haven't met any of my dad's acquaintances, aside from Jackie. I've briefly seen Christoph a few times, but he and my dad always immediately take off to do whatever it is they're doing.

—-

I ask my dad about it once, after we materialize in Jackie's apartment. "I'm sorry sweetie, you're just not ready for that yet. Stay with Jackie, learn more about this world. Get used to it. I can't just throw you straight into the deep end."

I scowl. "Don't be so vague. Where do you always disappear to? You can tell me that at least."

"In due time, I promise. Listen, I have to go, Christoph is waiting. Jackie?" my dad calls out as she enters the room. "Keep her safe, okay?"

"Yes sir!" Jackie says, standing with her back straight and saluting Maximus, who's already making his way to the outside door. She giggles, then loosens up and walks over to stand next to me, placing her arm over my shoulder.

I blush at the unexpected physical contact. "How long do I have to wait until he stops treating me like a kid? I'm sixteen."

"Believe me, I get it. I was in your position, oh, five years ago? I was just as frustrated as you. To be honest, I'm still not fully in the loop. Your dads, both of them, really know how to keep a secret."

"I wish I was your age. I just want to skip through these awkward teenage years and be an adult already."

"Again, I thought the same thing at your age. If you want my advice, cherish it. Being an adult can be just as frustrating." Jackie smiles at me. "You ready to head out? I have a surprise for you!"

—-

I'm not sure what I initially expected with Jackie's 'surprise', but it isn't the situation we find ourselves in now. We took a bus to a nondescript beige warehouse, and now I'm stationed next to Jackie at a huge table while the two of us put various items into a backpack. We're assembling kits of essential goods to hand out to the homeless population. Socks, underwear, hygiene products, snacks, water bottles, and more.

I ask Jackie, "Do you do this often?"

"I try to help out as much as I can. It's easy to forget that while I'm nowhere near as well off as the billionaires and trillionaires of this world, I'm still able to live much more comfortably than the unhoused."

"What else do you do to help?"

"I take a few shifts a week at a mental health support center. There are a lot of suffering people out there who just need someone to talk to. There's a phone number they can call and chat about, well... anything."

I wonder, "Don't you need some sort of education for that?"

"Not for my position, no. I'm just the first level, if I get someone who needs serious help, I can hand them off to an expert with the skills and experience to help them."

I can't help but feel even more enamored by Jackie. Her bubbly, intoxicating personality, her striking good looks, the fact that she goes out of her way to help the less fortunate; I'm becoming more and more obsessed each day I spend with her. I also can't help but feel a pang of guilt for my other crush, Hanna, who I keep abandoning in Utopia.

Once we finish assembling the backpacks, we load them all up in a large panel van and hop in the cab with a driver from the aid organization we're working with. We drive out to a few different areas with a high concentration of homeless people to hand out the backpacks. I notice that there is a huge variety of people coming up to receive care packages. All different age ranges and ethnicities patiently line up to grab a bag. Jackie and I greet each one with a smile, and despite some being clearly strung out on some type of drug, they're all very grateful for the support.

The stock of assembled bags runs dry halfway through the third location, but luckily we have a stack of grocery store gift cards for the people at the back of the line who don't get a backpack. After returning to the warehouse, Jackie and I wait outside for a bus to bring us back to her apartment.

"You know, I've heard all about the homeless situation and the factors that lead to it in my Hivemind studies, but seeing all of those people in person puts it into perspective. I can't believe they all live in shelters or on the street," I say.

"That's one of the reasons I do what I do. It keeps me motivated to try to change things. It shouldn't be this way, every rational person knows that. We've all just been completely browbeaten by capitalism and the status quo; most people feel completely powerless," Jackie replies.

"Why can't we recruit them all to join our cause?"

"Hopefully we can, over time. But in these early stages, we have to be extra judicious with who we enlist. The powers that be are always watching, and they'll pounce on any bit of weakness."

I grow nervous. "Do they know about us, and the watches?"

"As far as we know, we've been undetected so far. We always take extra precautions with even the most mundane things. But just between you and me, I think it would be crazy to think that the most advanced surveillance system in the world, operated by those pesky three-letter agencies, hasn't gotten a whiff of our organization."

The bus pulls up and we hop on.

—-

"Thanks," I say to the driver, and Jackie and I hop off the bus and head into her apartment.

"So as I was saying, I think next time you're here we should-"

As Jackie stops talking and freezes in her tracks, I notice her previously bright and determined expression morph into one of terror and dread. Her eyes widen in fear and her mouth hangs open in shock. I turn to follow her gaze, my heart suddenly hammering in my chest.

Christoph is crouched on the ground, his strong arms wrapped firmly around my father's head, trying to control the violent convulsions taking hold of him. The soles of my dad's shoes leave jagged black streaks as they slide back and forth on the white tile floor, his legs trapped in an uncontrollable spasm.

Chapter 22

It's been a week since I've seen my father. Consequently, it's been a week since I've been to Dystopia. I've spent the last seven days angry and confused, left completely out of the loop. One-hundred-and-sixty-eight hours ago me and Jackie had walked in on my father having a violent seizure, and the only news I've heard since is simply that he's alive and doing okay. It came via Hivemind, he didn't even tell me himself.

Hanna's been invaluable during this time. She seems to know exactly what to say and do to calm my nerves and get me to relax. We moved to a couple's suite instead of a cramped pod designed for one, which has given me some much-needed private time, away from the rest of the Utopia denizens. I haven't left the suite since returning from Dystopia, dazed, confused, and clutching onto my exhausted, almost lifeless father.

Two large men whom I didn't know approached us immediately after we materialized in Utopia. The strangers, a bit like my father, had lifeless eyes, staring intently at nothing in particular. They must have been locked away in long-term simulations with Hivemind controlling them. One of the men carefully and softly grabbed my arm to separate me from my father and took my place under his arm. The other man grabbed onto my dad from the other side and they started half-carrying, half-dragging him away from me.

Hivemind piped in through a voice inside my head to inform me that they were taking Maximus to the nearest medical pod and that I needn't worry. It didn't ease the emotions coursing through me one bit. Nor did the next Hivemind message that I received three days later. I had been asking Hivemind to speak to my father every hour or so each day, and after being denied over and over again, Hivemind finally relayed a message that was supposedly from my father. It said:

> "Hi sweetie, it's your dad. Don't worry about me, I'm fine. I'm working with both Hivemind and Christoph to make sure I'm okay and that this won't happen again. I hope to see you soon."

It felt wrong being relayed to me through the androgynous voice of Hivemind, yet I didn't take up Hivemind's offer of emulating his voice. That also seemed wrong to me. I just wanted to see him, to see with my own eyes that he was fine.

Hanna agrees.

"I don't want to disparage Hivemind or your father, but it is really weird that after witnessing him writhing on the floor like that you haven't been able to see him or even talk to him for a week," she says to me, cradling my head in her lap.

"It makes me feel so helpless, and worthless," I reply, wiping a tear from my cheek. "I don't even know if he's in this world. He could be anywhere."

As if on command, Hivemind's voice pipes up from the walls of the suite. *"Maximus Karlson is trying to reach you, Chloe, I assume you'd like me to connect you to him?"*

"YES," I shout as I sit straight up, startling Hanna. "Put him through."

The disembodied head of someone who likes exactly like my father appears on the wall of the suite. "Hey, kiddo. Sorry, it's not your actual father. It's your Dystopia Dad."

"Oh, hi alt-Dad." I feel a mix of emotions wash over me, I'm a bit let down from the unintentional bait-and-switch, but still excited to hear from my alt-dad, who I haven't seen in months.

"I'm here in Utopia, but you must know that. Want to meet up?" my alt-dad carefully asks, clearly seeing the disappointment showing through on my face.

I muster up a smile. "Of course!"

—-

I run into my alt-dad's open arms, happy to at least be embraced by an alternate version of the man I've been stressing about for the past week. We decided to meet up in the Park to continue our tradition of going for a walk through the Tropical Forest Biome.

We hug in silence for several minutes, until I finally break the embrace to wipe my eyes. "I haven't seen you in so long," I tell him, unable to look him in the eyes.

"I know, sweetie. Me and your dad hate keeping secrets from you, which is why I'm here. To tell you everything." He pulls my chin towards him to look me in the eyes, seemingly a way to prove that he's finally being completely sincere.

I believe him. "The only thing I want to hear right now is whether or not my dad is okay. Nothing else matters right now."

"Honestly, that's a tough question to answer. Yes, he's okay, right now. He is more or less back to how he was before the seizure. But as for long term, that's a different story."

A sense of dread creeps up on me, "...what do you mean, 'long term'?"

"Well, this seizure didn't come out of nowhere. It isn't even the first one he's had, it's just the worst one by far. This is something we've both been dealing with for quite a while now."

"Both of you? I don't understand."

"I've been having seizures too, kiddo."

I don't know how to process that information. I stop dead in my tracks, right in the middle of the forest path we've been walking down. "But you both have Hivemind implanted into your brain, right? You have access to the best medical care in the pods. How can this be possible?"

My alt-dad, noticing I stopped, turns around to face me. "From all the work we've done, it seems like this is a problem that Hivemind can't fix. It's something that no human has seemingly ever experienced."

"What does that mean?"

"Well, the hypothesis is that this is happening to both of us because we've spent so many years together in the same dimension. Our bodies are identical; our brains: identical. Not like twins, though. We're the exact same person, just... duplicated. It seems that our brains can't handle being in the same dimension, and over time they've become... damaged. Irreparably."

"What do you mean, *irreparably*?" That word hits me like a punch in the gut. "Are you sure there's nothing Hivemind can do?"

"The problem is that Hivemind's knowledge comes from that of humanity. This is not something that any other human has ever dealt with. There's never been any research about it, and no existing remedy has had any effect. We're in undiscovered territory, here."

"You said something about long-term effects. What are they?"

He pauses, then lets out a sigh. "I hate to drop it on you like this, kiddo, but all signs point to it being terminal. For both of us."

——-

My legs are too shaky to stand or walk, I had to be helped by my alt-dad to the nearest seat. We've been sitting here for several minutes now, the silence only occasionally pierced by a whimper or sniffle that I can't suppress. I don't even bother trying to wipe away my tears now, I let them flow, some landing on the shoulder of my alt-dad, who I'm leaning against. His arm is draped around my neck, his hand clutched firmly onto my opposite arm, holding me close to him.

Neither of us seems to know what to say next. I'm fine with just sitting here, crying and listening to the sounds of fake birds chirping, but since I know my alt-dad won't break the silence, I do. "How long do you have?"

He doesn't answer for a few seconds. "Hivemind thinks, and Christoph agrees, that it's advancing quickly. The seizures are becoming more frequent, and worse. It could happen anytime in the next couple of years, months, or even days. We don't know."

I know exactly what he means by 'it'. A new surge of tears flows down my cheeks.

He continues, "I want to make sure you know that this is the reason I haven't visited you in months. It's not because I didn't want to. It's because I physically couldn't. As soon as me and your father started to understand the gravity of the situation, we immediately stayed in our separate worlds. We've been coordinating with each other to change dimensions at the same time. When he comes to my world, I come to yours."

That makes complete sense to me, and I believe my alt-dad. If them being in the same dimension together had caused this, continuing along that path would just make things worse. I feel a bit of relief at this realization but quickly push it aside. It doesn't change the fact that both versions of my dad will die at some point.

—-

We eventually make our way to the eating area in the Park, but there's no way I can eat anything. I stare at my bowl of colorful food which has sat untouched since my alt-dad brought it to me. I'm trying to understand how the next part of my life will play out, and what I'll do when my dad—when both versions of my dad—are gone forever.

A thought pops into my head. "What happens with the watches when you guys are...gone?"

"We've thought about that. You'll inherit your father's, and my son, Max, will inherit mine. Unfortunately, the watches only seem to work for me and your dad."

"Yea... I may have 'borrowed' my dad's once when he was sleeping. Nothing happened when I wound it up."

"Trust me, we've had plenty of people from both worlds test them out. It only works for us. We've even tried out each other's, and still nothing, which was the most perplexing. But this is another reason why I haven't seen you in so long. Ever since we began to understand our fate, we've been working tirelessly towards our goal of liberating Dystopia. Without knowing if the watches will work after we're gone, without knowing if anyone will be able to travel between worlds, we need to get as much done before that time as we can."

I pipe in, "What specifically have you been doing? Are you gonna clue me in yet? It seems like the time to do that."

"We will, both of us. I promise. There's no point hiding anything from you anymore. You, along with your... uh, alt-brother will need to take the reins soon."

"What? Really? You mean I'm gonna meet him? Does he even know about this place?"

"It all depends on if the watches continue to work. If they do, you'll meet him. We've discussed this strategically. The plan is for you to, for lack of a better word, train him."

Chapter 23

I'm almost too tired to function. I trudge back to me and Hanna's suite after parting ways with my alt-dad. He told me that he had to get back to work, and I didn't mind at all, since I'm still overwhelmed, trying to process the events of the day, and week.

I stumble into the suite and straight to the bed where Hanna is lying, reading something on a Hivemind tablet.

"Uh, hello?" Hanna says to my back as I slide under the covers. "Are you okay? What's happening?"

"Oh, not much," I slur, half asleep. "My dads are gonna die. Goodnight."

I don't hear her response. I fall asleep as soon as my head hits the pillow.

—-

I eventually clued Hanna into my discussion with my alt-dad this morning, at breakfast. I apologized for what I said to her last night, I know it was rude to leave her in the dark, especially after what I've been through this week. We're seated at the small two-person table next to our bed in the couple's suite. Aside from my outing with my alt-dad the previous day, we've been eating every meal in our private room. Food conveniently dispenses from the Hivemind terminal in the corner. The suites are fully equipped for a couple of shut-ins; with the bathroom and shower attached, we don't have to leave for anything.

Hanna's been listening intently to my recap of everything I learned last night. I ramble non-stop, relaying my thoughts and experiences in a stream of verbal diarrhea. That's one of the things I admire most about Hanna, she knows when to stay quiet and let me babble. Finally, I stop to catch my breath.

Hanna breaks her silence and chimes in. "So, what's your plan? Spend as much time with them before they... you know..."

"I guess," I reply. "I think I'm gonna be put to work though. I have a lot to learn, now that they'll let me."

"Okay... I understand. But, if you'll allow me to be selfish for a second, what does that mean for us? Will I still see you? What about after they're gone? Will you be spending your time over... there?"

I realize I haven't thought much about what this means for me and Hanna's relationship. I've been too distracted to think about it. Hanna doesn't seem to want to have anything to do with Dystopia, she likely won't be willing to help out. I respond, "I guess we'll have to play it by ear if you're okay with that. But I won't willingly abandon you, Hanna, and I think you know that. You've been such a great... friend to me throughout this, and for the entire time we've known each other."

Hanna smiles. "You too, Chloe. I hope you understand that. You've helped me out more times than I can count."

Hivemind interjects, *"Chloe, I have a message from your father. He would like you to meet him. Should I direct you to his location?"*

"Yes, of course, thanks." I look over at Hanna. "Bad timing, huh? This isn't a sign of things to come, I promise. I'll see you soon."

—-

"Is it actually you this time?" I ask the man who looks like my father, except maybe a few years older. Turns out violent seizures age you a bit.

"Yes, it's me." He pauses while I squeeze the air out of his lungs with a tight hug. "I'm really, truly sorry for what you've gone through this week. I know it's been hard."

I sit down in a chair in one of Utopia's many lounge areas, following my dad's lead. I say, "That's an understatement. I doubt it's been a walk in the park for you, though."

"I'm happy you understand that. I hope the other me did a decent job clueing you into the situation at hand. There's a lot of work to be done, and we can't waste any time."

"I know, Dad. Tell me what I need to do. I'm up for anything."

"Hopefully that's true, because I have an... interesting proposal."

"Shoot." I'm intrigued.

"I know it can be a very touchy subject, but we need to talk about your mother. Well, the other version of her."

I raise my eyebrows. I certainly didn't expect to hear that.

My father continues, "I know you've heard that we need to bring her son, er... your... alt-brother, into the mix. Which means you'll need to coordinate with her. You need to meet her, in person, I think. Would you be okay with that?"

I think for a second. "I know she isn't technically the same person who abandoned us, but, well, she sort of is, isn't she? It's the exact duplicate of her. Wouldn't she have done the same thing if she ended up in this world instead of Dystopia?"

"For what it's worth, she hates what your mother did to us. She can't believe she did that. That's what she says to me every time I talk to her. Also, I know that I forked off into two identical people after the Split, but I can tell you that we've become different from each other over the years. The environment you live in shapes you, in a way. Your mother lived in this world, in Utopia, for two decades before she abandoned us. That's a long time."

Hearing that the other version of my mom condemns her actions makes me reconsider my initial apprehension. I will never forgive my mother for what she did to me and my father. She abandoned us when I was only a child, leaving my fathers, both versions, to raise me. She is somewhere here in Utopia, but I've never seen her. I'm assuming she went into a long-term Hivemind simulation and created her own world to live in. Maybe she replaced me and my father, virtually.

"I will meet her, on one condition," I say. "You have to tell me the real reason mom left. No more avoiding it. Right here, right now. Tell me."

My father sighs and picks at the hem of his shirt. He seems to understand that I have a point. "Okay, you're right, you deserve to know. When the Split happened, when me and your mother survived the Event, and when we helped to create Hivemind, our relationship couldn't have been stronger. After Utopia was built and we moved in here, everything was fine. We had you, which she was ecstatic about since she always wanted a child, and life was perfect."

I interrupt him, "Yea yea, I've heard this part, get to the point."

"Give me some time here. I had always felt some extreme guilt that your mother and I were the ones that ended up in the 'good place', so to say. We were the lucky ones. The other version of us was stuck in the same old capitalist, brutal world. It didn't seem fair. Having this watch that let me directly compare the happiness of the people here in Utopia to the doom and gloom over there in Dystopia just made these feelings worse."

He pauses, seemingly to collect his thoughts. I patiently wait for him to continue.

"This is when I proposed a plan. **The** plan, the same one we're working on now. Liberate Dystopia, with the help of Hivemind. The Dystopia versions of me and your mother were fully on board. Your actual mom, though, wasn't so sure about it. Still, she went along with the plan, as long as she didn't have to do anything. She refused to even step foot in the other world. She had never been there, after the Split, even though I could easily bring her with me. She thought this place was perfect and wanted to live here in peace, without thinking about those in Dystopia.

"Over time, she began to see less and less of me, since I was spending so much time in Dystopia with my double, working tirelessly to recruit and vet comrades. When I was here in Utopia, I spent a lot of time helping to get the candidates Implanted and trained in Hivemind demo rooms. You would have been too young to understand how this strained our relationship. But, to get to the point, she eventually reached her breaking point, I guess, and took off. She didn't even say goodbye, she relayed a message to me through Hivemind. I haven't heard a word from her or seen her since."

"Wow." It's all I can think to say. In a way, hearing that makes me slightly less angry at what my mother did, but I still bitterly hate her. At least there was an actual reason behind her actions. Not a valid one, but a reason all the same.

"I'm sorry it's taken so long to tell you that," alt-Dad says. "I just wasn't sure you were ready for the real reason. Until now, of course."

I declare firmly, "Okay. I've decided. I'll meet her. In fact, I'll be happy to meet her, to see how mom could have turned out. When will we arrange it? This week?"

"About that... she lives in Seattle, on the other side of the US from where Jackie and Christoph are. I need to go to Seattle for something today... so how about right now?"

Chapter 24

I'm standing alone, in a random Seattle neighborhood, staring at a nondescript house on the opposite side of the street. My father brought me to this exact spot fifteen minutes ago before hopping into a taxi to go wherever he needed to go. I haven't moved an inch since. I haven't worked up the courage yet.

I'm imagining what it would have been like for me to be born to this world's version of my mother and father, and live in this house that I'm staring at. As I understand it, my alt-dad had also 'abandoned' his family, so to say. My alt-brother grew up with only one parent, just like me. Well, he hasn't had access to two different versions of the same parent, so I have that on him. Not that it's a contest.

I think about how angry I am with my mother, who abandoned me, and how my alt-brother must feel about his father, who abandoned him. It's weird that I have such a close relationship with him, but his actual son doesn't. It feels wrong. I wonder if I'll have to admit that to him eventually.

My feet are starting to fall asleep from standing in the same position. It's time to go. I take a few tentative steps towards the curb and make sure to look both ways before stepping out onto the street. I made that mistake once, culminating in a near miss from a speeding taxi in New York. I reach the front steps of the house, carefully placing one foot after another to elevate myself to the level of the front door. I step towards the door, and hold out my hand to knock, but I pause; my arm hanging limply in the air.

Before I can bring my knuckles to make contact with the door, it slowly opens. The woman standing before me has delicate features, almost like a mirror image of my own. Her hair is auburn, cascading in soft waves around her shoulders. Her eyes are a deep, piercing blue, with wrinkles starting to form at the corners. She is wearing a flowy black dress, a stark contrast to her fair skin and bright red lipstick. This stranger looks exactly like my estranged mom, just a bit older than I remember.

—-

After an awkward introduction, the two of us walk to a nearby park to talk. Even though her son is at work, we don't want to risk him coming home early and finding me there, so we don't linger at the house. On the way to the park, we tried to decide how I should refer to her. We settled on using her actual name, Joanne, since it seems wrong to call her 'Mom', or 'alt-Mom'.

As soon as we find an empty bench to sit at Joanne pulls out a few photographs of Max to show me, so I can finally see what my alt-brother looks like. I rifle through the glossy 4x6s, noting the similarities between me and him. He looks exactly like a masculine version of me, which makes sense; our genes are nearly identical.

The entire concept of physical photographs is foreign to me. I know that most people in Dystopia view memories digitally, on their phones. However, none of the Freedom Fighters I've met use their phones while discussing official business, because, as I've been told, the powers that be can listen in through the microphones, even if the device is turned off. But, like, Utopia doesn't even have any cameras. Memories can be conjured at will by Hivemind, and experienced either statically like Dystopia photos, on the walls or on a tablet, or dynamically with full immersion in a Hivemind simulation or demo room.

"He looks like... a great son." I feel awkward saying it, but I'm not sure what else to say.

"He is," Joanne replies. "From everything I've heard, you're a great daughter. You've handled this week extremely well. I'm surprised at how mature you are since, like Max, you're still a kid. Well, a teenager, I guess."

"Thanks. Listen, I don't want to talk about my mom at all, and I doubt you do either. I've put it behind me. It feels a bit weird talking to you, but we don't need to rehash anything from the past, and you don't need to apologize for what she's done."

"Don't worry, I won't mention her. I'm focused purely on what's to come, anyway. I've only known about the, uh, medical situation with my husband and your father for a few weeks, they neglected to tell me until recently. It's really important that we stick to the mission. This is a crucial time."

"I'm still waiting for instructions. I don't know what I can do, or what needs to be done. I assume that's why I'm here, right?" I ask.

"In a way, yes. I know my son better than anyone else, and I agree that the best way to bring him on board is through you. He will relate to you more than anyone. You two are similar in many ways, and you can learn a lot from each other about your respective worlds. This, of course, completely hinges on whether or not the watches will continue to be usable."

"When will I meet him? It should probably happen while we know the watches still work, right?"

"We've discussed this with some key people, and we think my son should figure out some things on his own. Ideally, he will inherit a working watch from his dad after he passes. We don't want it to seem like he's being forced into becoming a Freedom Fighter. He needs to find out about Utopia naturally."

"But without knowing if the watch will work for him..."

"As morbid as it sounds, we will know once one of the Maximus' dies. That's the plan. If your father goes first and the watch works for you, then we can wait until Max inherits his naturally, if you know what I mean."

Chapter 25

I return to Utopia with a fire in my belly. I finally have a goal to dedicate myself towards, which will also keep my mind off of the impending doom of my dad and alt-dad. When I'm not in Dystopia learning about the capitalist world, I'll be studying it with Hivemind and planning out how best to train my alt-brother and prepare him to take the reins from our fathers.

I spent a few more hours talking to Joanne, learning as much as I could about my future trainee. We discussed which parts of Utopia he would connect with most and how to make him understand and comprehend the differences between worlds. I have to have a firm grasp of Dystopia to be able to point out the differences and why it's so important to liberate the exploited people there. We think it's best if I don't let on how much I actually know about his world, so he can more easily come to some conclusions on his own.

Right now though, I have a choice to make. I'm desperate to hop into a demo room and study Dystopia some more, but I sort of ditched Hanna earlier when my dad reached out to me. I didn't even tell Hanna I was going to another dimension, I had been too distracted. Even though I know going to see Hanna is the nicer thing to do, I've made up my mind.

"Hivemind, can I talk to Hanna please?" I ask aloud while walking toward the nearest demo room.

"*Uh, hello?*" A familiar voice appears inside my head.

"Hi Hanna. Sorry about earlier, I got caught up with my dad and completely lost track of time. What are you doing?"

"Oh, not much, just laying in bed. Is everything okay?" Hanna replies.

"As okay as it can be, I guess. Listen, I have some work to do, I finally have an assignment and I just *have* to get started on it now. Are you okay with that?"

"Oh... uh, it's pretty late, I was about to go to sleep."

I can sense a hint of annoyance in Hanna's voice. "That's fine, don't wait up. I'll try to be quiet when I get back so I don't wake you."

—-

I've now spent nearly every hour of the last few weeks working on my new mission. I've been trying, and ultimately failing, to balance my time between going to Dystopia, studying Dystopia in Utopia, and hanging out with Hanna. I'm seeing my best friend less and less, often only right around bedtime, and sometimes not even then. Hanna never stays up late, and I often get back to our suite when she's already sleeping.

I ask Hanna many times if she wants to accompany me to a study session in a demo room, but she steadfastly refuses. I don't even think about asking my dad if Hanna can tag along on a trip to Dystopia because I know what her answer will be. I can't shake the feeling of guilt, considering I'm spending way more time with Jackie in Dystopia than with my closest friend, who I have strong romantic feelings for.

I manage to push those guilty feelings aside with the justification that my time with Jackie is part of a mission; it's not a social thing, it's *work*. I know deep down it isn't that simple but it helps me feel better about myself at least. I know I'm getting closer and closer to Jackie while moving further and further from Hanna, though. The problem is, I don't necessarily think that's the wrong move. I'm fully on board with the mission, it's the only thing that really, truly matters to me.

—-

I tear my eyes away from the book I've been studying in a public library in Dystopia. I've been having trouble concentrating, as I have Hanna stuck on my mind. I relay my concerns to Jackie, who's sitting across from me.

"If you're asking me if personal relationships are more important than our mission, I don't think I can answer that question, Chloe," Jackie says. "The only thing that matters is what's important to you."

I reply, "I get it, I'm just scared of letting people down."

"From what you've been telling me, it seems like someone will be let down either way. Your friend, or your comrades. Which isn't the end of the world, you can't please everyone. The sooner you stop trying to, the sooner you can push those nagging thoughts aside and just live your life."

Jackie really does know exactly what to say; I feel a little more at ease hearing her take. I turn back to the book I've been reading. It's about 21st-century anti-capitalist media, and one title catches my eye. I ask Jackie, "Have you ever seen *Watchmen*?"

"The show or the movie? I mean, I've seen both. Oh, and I've read the graphic novel it was based on a few times. I would start with the movie."

"It seems pretty interesting, I'd like to see it sometime."

"How about we watch it later today when we get back to my apartment? Unless you want to see it by yourself."

"No, that sounds great! I'd love to watch it with you."

Jackie smiles wide. "It's a date!"

I blush.

Chapter 26

I wake with a start. An intense feeling of dread is washing over me, unlike anything I've felt before. It's like a heavy fog, thick and suffocating, seeping into every pore and making my limbs heavy and leaden. I look over at Hanna, who is still fast asleep, facing away from me. I will my legs to move as I carefully crawl out of bed, put on my slippers, and exit the suite.

"Hivemind, can I speak to my father please?" I ask.

After a few seconds, I get a reply back. *"Maximus Karlson is unreachable."*

That's unnerving, but this isn't exactly an uncommon occurrence. My father is often too wrapped up in his work to reply. Maybe he's sleeping?

To distract myself, I decide to take a walk to the nearest cafeteria and get some breakfast. I pick up my favorite meal from the counter and find a table away from anyone else to eat at. Unfortunately, I quickly realize I don't have much of an appetite. I can't shake this intense feeling of concern, and the bowl of food in front of me is doing absolutely nothing to distract me.

After a few minutes of staring at the bowl and pushing around the food inside with a fork, I notice a familiar face approaching from a ways away.

"Jackie?" I say to myself, standing up from the table and rushing over to her.

"Hey Chloe," Jackie says when I'm within earshot, reaching out to accept a hug from me.

I break away from Jackie's hug and look at her face. Her usually bright and happy expression is replaced with a blank, emotionless stare. The lines on her face are tense and her eyes lack their usual sparkle. It's as if all the color has drained from her, leaving behind a pale and lifeless facade. This further cements my dread.

"Which one is it?" I ask.

"I'm so sorry, honey. It's your dad. He... he had an aneurysm this morning. He's gone."

—-

The rest of the day flies by in a whirlwind. The news of my father's passing wasn't a surprise for me, but that doesn't lessen the impact at all. I'm happy that Jackie was the one to break the news to me, at least, I thought that having my dad's double do it would have been weird.

Jackie stays by my side the entire day, helping me with a few tasks, like gathering the belongings my father had in his sleeping pod and getting it ready for a new occupant. Utopia denizens are all cremated after they pass, and no time is wasted. Only a few hours after I learned of his fate, I find myself at a small ceremony to see my father's body off.

It takes place in a small room that I've luckily never seen before. A white table is positioned in the middle, without any other embellishments in the room. My father's lifeless body lays on top of it. It feels unnecessary and uncomfortable for me; I want to remember him alive, not dead on a table. I work up the courage to kiss him on the forehead and whisper goodbye before retreating to Jackie's side and clutching her hand.

There are only four people aside from me and Jackie at this ceremony. My mother is, of course, not one of them. I recognize three, they're close family friends that I had grown up with but haven't seen in years. I don't say a word to any of them, I'm too busy staring at the floor and willing this awkward experience to end already. I glance at the one I don't recognize, the stranger, only for a second. It's a man who looks to be in his thirties. He's staring back at me curiously.

Jackie's presence in Utopia means that my alt-dad is here as well, he would have had to bring Jackie with him. Yet, I don't see him until much later in the day; once I'm physically, mentally, and emotionally wiped and ready for sleep. Me and Jackie are sitting together in a lounge, chatting about nothing in particular, trying to keep our minds off of the stressful events of the day, when I start to get an uneasy feeling deep in my chest. A few moments later, Maximus walks into the room.

"Hey, kiddo. Jackie, do you mind giving us some privacy?' he says to the two of us.

"No problem, boss."

She stands up, gives me a slight smile, and squeezes my alt-dad's arm before walking away from the seating area. My late father's double takes her seat.

"Sorry I haven't been around, there's a lot to do. I couldn't show my face at the ceremony, not everyone there knows about the, uh, situation. It would probably give them quite the shock." He taps his watch. "Speaking of, I have something for you."

He pulls a small item out of his pocket, wrapped in a light gray towel. As he hands it to me, I can feel its weight and energy pulsing against my fingertips, drawing me in like a moth to a flame.

"Is this what I think it is?" I ask my alt-dad, knowing the answer.

"It's yours now, kiddo. How do you feel about that?"

I'm not sure how to feel. My body does, though, my chest has been tightening with impatience since I grabbed the watch. I'm itching to put it on my wrist. After carefully unwrapping it from the towel, I examine the worn face closely. This is the first time I've seen it up close, in the light, and it looks entirely unremarkable. It's weird how such a mundane object holds so much power.

"I promise I won't lose it," I finally mutter.

"I'm certain you won't. I don't think now is the right time, but I- well, we, will need you to test it out sometime soon. Maybe tomorrow? A lot hinges on the watch working for you. I had a trusted acquaintance give it a try earlier, just to see if anything happened. Nothing did, obviously."

"I'll test it out tomorrow, I would tonight but I'm way too tired. I'm pretty certain it will work for me though, I can feel it deep down inside. It's almost calling out to me."

He exhales. "That is a relief to hear, kiddo. I felt the same thing when I first received it from my late father, your grandpa. It was almost urging me to use it."

"I'll let you know what happens tomorrow, either way. Are you and Jackie sticking around for the night?"

He checks his watch. "No, we're due back in a few minutes here. Let's find Jackie and say our goodbyes, then you should head off to bed."

Chapter 27

It's the anniversary of the day I first stepped foot in Dystopia. Which means, of course, it's also my birthday. I have a feeling my seventeenth birthday won't be quite as enjoyable as my sixteenth, though. I can't believe my dad had the *audacity* to die a few weeks before my birthday. At least my sense of humor didn't die along with him.

Deciding where to spend my day this year is a difficult choice: should I stay here in Utopia with Hanna or head over to Dystopia to be with my alt-dad and Jackie? Since I inherited the dimension-hopping ability of my late father's watch, I can decide for myself. It would be great if Hanna wanted to join me in Dystopia, but I know she isn't interested, so I won't even bother asking. Then a thought hits me - why not bring alt-Dad and Jackie over here instead?

I wind the watch for about half an hour and zip over to the other world, popping up in Jackie's living room. Or, at least I thought that was where I was heading, it's what I was thinking about when I pushed in the crown. Truth is, I have no clue where I am, it's pitch black. As I frantically look around, my eyes strain to see anything in the complete and utter darkness. No traces of light or shadows can be seen, I'm engulfed in a void of blackness. I can't even see my hand when I hold it an inch in front of my face.

"Christoph, *she's here!*"

As the room is suddenly flooded with light, I have to squeeze my eyes shut to shield them from the blinding brightness. When I finally open them again, I'm met with a completely unexpected scene. A surprise party. I'm definitely that: surprised.

"Happy birthday!" My alt-dad and Jackie say in unison after popping up from behind the kitchen counter. They shoot off a couple of confetti poppers that make two loud bangs in quick succession.

As the colorful bits of plastic rain down around me, I take in the scene. The entire room is decorated in a variety of colorful balloons, streamers, and a banner with 'Happy Birthday Chloe' written on it. There's a tray of what looks like Utopia to-go bars on the kitchen counter, a candle sticking out of each. Christoph is standing off on his own by the side of the room, near the light switch. It's clear that the three of them put a lot of effort into making this a special day for me, which is all the more awkward considering that I came here simply to invite them over to Utopia.

"Wow, thank you! This is amazing!" I finally say. "But, how did you know when I was coming here?"

Jackie steps out from behind the counter, gives me a hug, then says, "We've been sitting in the dark for over an hour. We wanted to surprise you!" She giggles.

"Well, you did it. Thanks a lot, I really mean it."

My alt-dad interjects, "So, is this what you wanted to do for your birthday?"

"Um, about that..."

—-

Jackie doesn't need any persuasion, she's fully on board with coming to Utopia, since she doesn't get the chance to all that often. Christoph, as I guessed, bows out, leaving just my alt-dad to try to convince. He agrees to do it on one condition, he will take a few new recruits with him to get implanted and familiarize themselves with Hivemind while we have our little get-together. He's always one to multitask.

I spend the few minutes left on my watch helping Jackie sweep up the confetti littering the ground. She's chattering away to me, but I barely hear anything she's saying. Now, I do love my alt-dad, but I really wish my real father was here to celebrate with me. This is the first birthday of mine he's missed.

The first of many.

The realization stings.

When my wrist starts to tingle, I say a temporary goodbye to my alt-dad, Jackie, and Christoph, and appear back in me and Hanna's couple's suite in Utopia. She's still tucked into bed, snoring away.

"Hey, sleepy-head," I say as I give her a gentle shake.

She yawns and wipes the sleep away from her eyes. "Hey, birthday girl! How long have you been up? Why didn't you wake me earlier? Aren't we spending the day together?"

"Um, about that..."

—-

If I thought my alt-dad was hard to convince, it's nothing compared to Hanna. I know that she only agrees to come to the impromptu get-together that I concocted because it's my birthday, and she can't say no to me on my birthday. I figured as much, but I'll take what I can get. I really want her to meet

Jackie. I don't even feel bad about abusing my birthday girl privilege to arrange it.

As we're speeding away towards the Park on a travel pod, I can tell that Hanna is feeling anxious; her usual habit of picking at her fingernails gives it away. It's a clear sign that she's worried about something. I try to comfort her, telling her that there's nothing to worry about and it's just a simple gathering. There's no expectations of her.

We make it to the Lake Biome in the middle of the Park. We have perfect timing, I can see Jackie and my alt-dad from a distance, making their way through the sandy beach over to our meeting place.

"Hello again, birthday girl!" Jackie says once we link up. She pulls me in for a big bearhug, hanging on to me a little longer than usual. "Wow, Chloe, you told me Hanna was pretty but you didn't say she was this gorgeous!"

Hanna's face turns bright red as Jackie pulls her in for a big hug as well. "N-Nice to meet you," she stammers out.

"I've heard so, so much about you, I'm so happy to put such a beautiful face to your fabulous name! Maximus, have you met Hanna?" Jackie asks my alt-dad.

He responds, "Of course, I've known Hanna here since she was oh, about yea high." He holds his hand out in front of his waist as an indication.

"Alright, alright, let's not embarrass her," I come to Hanna's aid, knowing how uncomfortable she must be right now. I ask my alt-dad, "What's going on with the recruits?"

"They've been implanted already, and Hivemind can take it from here. I'm all yours," he says.

"Okay, there's an empty picnic table over there, why don't we all take a seat?"

—-

We spend the next hour or so chatting away. Well, three of us do, at least. Hanna is quiet most of the time, only speaking up when a question is directed at her. Jackie dominates the conversation, as usual. Unfortunately Jackie only seems to want to talk, or more accurately, complain, about Dystopia, a topic which doesn't interest Hanna in the slightest.

Jackie seems even more flirtatious than normal. Every time she grabs onto my arm or brushes my shoulder, I glance over at Hanna to gauge her reaction. She looks uncomfortable in her own skin. When Jackie finishes a tale about her run-in with the cops while at a climate protest, Hanna taps my arm and asks if she can talk to me alone for a second.

We excuse ourselves from the table and once we're out of earshot of Jackie and my alt-dad, I say, "Sorry, Hanna. She can be a bit much."

"It's fine. I need to go lie down in our room. Come find me later if you want to hang out alone." She gives me a hug and a quick 'happy birthday', and starts walking to the nearest pod station.

"She's leaving so soon? No goodbyes?" Jackie says when I sit back down at the table.

"Hanna's, uh, feeling a bit sick. She needs to lie down."

"Well, her loss. Should we go for a swim?"

Chapter 28

I look past the line of people separating me and the person I'm stalking. When he glances in my direction, I avert my eyes and pretend to be looking at the bus stop sign he's standing under. My alt-brother Max still has no idea I even exist, let alone that I'm following him. This isn't the first time either, definitely not. I've taken to following my secret brother around on a fairly regular basis. I justify the admittedly creepy actions as a form of preparation. I need to learn as much as I can about him, and I don't want to wait until the day we formally meet.

Having exclusive access to my late father's watch has given me the ability to go to Dystopia whenever I want and stay here as long as I want. I take advantage of this as much as possible. There's a big time difference between the US and the former China, where Utopia is, so I adjusted my schedule to match that of US time. This has caused further strain in my relationship with Hanna, but I've found ways to mitigate it, making sure to take at least one day off a week to spend exclusively with my best friend.

The consequences of spending more of my time on the west coast of the US, across the country from Jackie, means I also see my Dystopia friend less and less. Similarly, I make sure to visit New York at least once a week to catch up with Jackie. In the year since my dad passed, I've found a way to balance my time to keep all three of the most important people in my life, including my alt-dad, appeased.

I often compare my relationship with Jackie to my relationship with Hanna, but I subconsciously know that it isn't equivalent at all. Jackie doesn't need me, I need Jackie. Conversely, Hanna and I need each other, equally. Jackie has an entire group of Freedom Fighters to lean on for support, but Hanna has no one but me. Hanna isn't a social person, she latched tightly onto me after we both turned sixteen and gained independence.

The bus pulls up to the stop. I slowly move towards the open doors, making sure to see where Max sits so I can find a seat out of his view to watch him without being detected. He picks a seat near the middle of the bus, right next to the exit door, as always. If there are no seats available in that area, he will stand in front of the exit door. I board the bus and sneak past him quickly to take my usual seat, at the very back corner.

Watching him for as long as I have has made me realize that my alt-brother is a creature of habit. He rarely strays from his norm. He walks to work every shift but takes the bus home after. This has been consistent since his very first shift at the Idolon warehouse, which I bore witness to.

Before he started working, I stalked him to and from high school every day. I even trespassed in his school a few times, trying to blend in as a student so I could figure out which classes he was taking and study the syllabus. I stopped that immediately after the time I was questioned by an administrator and asked to produce a school ID. After making a hasty excuse, I left the building as fast as possible and never tried to enter it again. I still watched him when he had gym classes outdoors, though, from a safe distance. With a pair of binoculars.

When the bus is one stop away from my alt-brother's destination, I signal the driver to stop. I always get off one stop early to avoid suspicion. I jog along the bus' path to take my usual place behind a particularly thick bush, which provides good cover and a safe distance for me to watch Max depart the bus, cross the street, and head home for the night.

Once he gets home after a shift at work, he never leaves. I used to watch his bedroom window from outside until the light went off after every workday, but I gave that up after, oh, the hundredth or so time. Instead, I go visit some of my new Seattle comrades to check in once Max is in for the night.

The Seattle operation is quite a bit different from the New York operation, or at least, what I've seen of it. The Seattle HQ is very secretive. It's in the basement of a leftist bookstore, and you can't even get access to it without having a Hivemind Patch or Implant. From what I've come to learn about the New York operation, it has more of a focus on recruitment. Seattle is focused on technology. We have a few extremely talented engineers on board here in Seattle, working tirelessly to bring Utopia technology to Dystopia. The main focus is on med pods, or at least some way to be able to install Implants in this world, without having to take people to Utopia a handful at a time.

It makes sense that the Seattle HQ focuses on technology since Seattle is where the Idolon headquarters stand. This is crucial, as the neural technology that Idolon is developing is similar in many ways to the Hivemind Implant.

Idolon is in the late testing phase of a brain implant that will connect the end user directly to the internet. The Hivemind Implant does the same thing, except it connects people's brains directly to Hivemind instead.

I'm still not fully in the loop on the Freedom Fighters' operations, but from the few whispers I've eavesdropped on in the Seattle HQ, I know that we have a few infiltrators in the upper echelons of Idolon corporate. This is all very hush-hush, though, and I never dare to repeat what I've heard, to anyone. There's a lot of compartmentalization with the operation, and I completely understand why. You never know who could be a mole.

After finishing the twenty-minute trek to *The Iron Curtain*, I pass through both security checks and enter the white lab, made to look exactly like a room from Utopia. I always feel an extra level of comfort entering this room; it really, truly feels like home, even in an unfamiliar world. They even have mock Hivemind screens, with very limited functionality of course.

No one goes out of their way to greet me. A few of my engineer comrades seem to be busy working on something that is way above my technical skill, or lack thereof. But, out of the corner of my eye, I notice a familiar face in the kitchen. "Xara?"

"Chloe! Hey girl."

Xara's towering frame stands at over six feet tall, making her an imposing figure. Her dark, black skin is a striking contrast to the white walls of the lab. Her braided hair cascades down her shoulders, framing her strong features. Her arms are bulging with muscle, a testament to her physical strength. She wouldn't hurt anyone, unless they were fascist scum, at least.

I have to stand on my tiptoes to properly hug Xara. "I haven't seen you around in a while, I had no idea you were coming here!" I say.

"I wasn't planning on it, but it's not often that I find a way to shake my fed shadow, so I had to take advantage of that," Xara replies, with an air of arrogance.

Xara has become known worldwide as an anti-capitalist, anti-cop champion of marginalized people everywhere. Her brother was slaughtered, or, as Xara prefers to say, 'martyred' by racist cops when he did nothing wrong at all. Not that committing crime is any justification for cops acting like judge, jury, and executioner, however. Her late brother Jak had been walking home from school one day, listening to music and supposedly making shooting gestures with his hands. This was enough for a pair of white nationalist thug cops to open fire on him, moments after he didn't respond to their request to put his hands up. He couldn't hear them over his music.

In the wake of her brother's tragedy, Xara became outspoken about police brutality and the societal conditions that lead to it. She had amassed a following of millions of left-leaning people, which the Freedom Fighters have taken full advantage of as part of our recruitment initiatives. But her fame came with increased scrutiny from the powers that be, which Xara has to be unrelentingly aware of. People in her position often find themselves dead in a car crash after their brakes were cut, or hanging by the neck from a tree, the rope rigged in a manner no single person could execute.

This is why it's so rare for me to see Xara, although I follow her social media closely while in Dystopia. This is only the third time I've seen her in person. We chat for a few minutes, catching up on what each of us has been up to for the weeks since we last saw each other.

"Chloe, sweetie, it was great to catch up with you but I have to head out. I need to be in LA early tomorrow morning."

"No worries, Xara. Do you need me to make sure it's clear?"

"Please, girl, if you don't mind." She glances around the room. "Seems everyone else here is too busy."

After leaving the basement hideout and emerging back into the bookstore above, I call out to the tattoo-covered comrade who serves as both a cashier for the bookstore and a lookout for the hidden operations.

"Anything on the cams, Rach?" I ask.

"All clear. Check the shadows," Rachel replies.

"Will do."

I exit the building through the back, into the alley behind the store. It's usually empty back here, but I notice a pair of feet protruding from around a corner, which wouldn't have shown up on the security cams. I approach the owner of the feet, who is someone who looks to be homeless.

"You hungry?" I ask. I hear an affirmative grunt and pull a twenty-dollar bill out of my pocket. "Here. Why don't you go grab yourself a hot meal?"

I know it's weird and inappropriate to bribe him to leave, but you never know who could be a spook or a glowie. I've learned to never put anything past those alphabet agencies.

Once the homeless gentleman lumbers away, I shine a flashlight at the corner he was sitting on, making sure he didn't leave a listening device or camera behind. There's nothing there but cigarette butts and food wrappers.

I head around to the storefront to check the cars parked on the street. If there are any with suspiciously dark tint or window coverings, I'll have to notify Xara. After peeking in the windows of the several cars parked nearby and seeing nothing fishy, I send an 'all clear' message to Xara through Hivemind.

I walk back around to the alley just in time to see Xara emerge from the back door. I ask, "Did Rachel call you a cab?"

"Yep. Should be here in a few minutes. Want to wait with me?"

Me and Xara slowly wander down the street to her pickup spot, which we always make sure is far enough away from *The Iron Curtain*. A thought suddenly pops into my head.

"Hey, how many times have you been to Utopia?" I ask Xara.

"Oh, at least a dozen. I was there to get the Implant. But I've also had to escape there a few times. I've gotten in some hot water before with some of the activism I do. Luckily, I can call your, uh, I can call Maximus with Hivemind and get him to bring me to safety."

"Wow, I hadn't thought of that. No one can find you in another dimension, huh? What will you do after he's gone?"

"I was wondering the same thing about you," Xara says. "Is the plan for his son to take up his mantle still in the works? How is that going?"

"Well, it's okay. I still find it weird that I have to wait for my alt-dad to die before I can meet my alt-brother. But I've come to realize that this plan we've hatched is probably the best option, after studying Max for as long as I have."

"Studying him? How? Like, his socials?" Xara looks confused.

"No, he doesn't have much of an online presence at all. I talk to his mom a lot, have you met her?" I continue after Xara nods her head to indicate 'yes'. "You can only learn so much about a teenager through their parents. So I've been... stalking him. A lot."

"Really? Wow, that sounds exciting. Have you found anything interesting?"

"Not really. His life is kind of mundane. His mom let me search his room once, but there was nothing unusual there."

"What, no dirty mags under the mattress?"

Me and Xara both burst out laughing. "No, I think the boys in this world keep their porn on their phones."

Xara's cab pulls up, and after a nice, long hug between the two of us, we say our goodbyes and the cab takes off into the night.

Chapter 29

After I spend the last thirty or so minutes left on my watch wandering around random Seattle streets, I materialize directly into the couple's suite I share with Hanna. I'm expecting to see her laid up in bed reading, as per usual. But this time the bed is empty.

"Hivemind, where is Hanna?" I say aloud.

Immediately a reply comes to me. *"She does not wish to be disturbed at this time."*

This is unusual. Hanna has never put a block on me. Not even when we have our occasional fights. This is supposed to be our day together, Hanna knows that for sure. We had planned to play her favorite Hivemind game together in a Rec Room.

I feel lost, and confused. I check the nearest lounge, where Hanna and I sometimes sit to talk when we need to get out of our suite. I check the cafeteria and find the table that we always sit at empty. I search the Rec Room, where we're supposed to play together later. I walk our favorite route through the Park. Hanna is nowhere to be found.

I'm exhausted from searching all over our quadrant of Utopia for my best friend. I'm drained from pinging Hivemind every few minutes, waiting for the block to be taken off. I resign myself to returning to our suite to try to get some rest.

I had checked our suite every hour or so throughout the day to see if Hanna had returned, finding it empty every time. This time, however, is different. I see Hanna fast asleep in our bed when I enter.

"Hanna!" I run over to the bed, shaking my friend awake. "What's going on? I've been searching for you!"

Hanna rolls over and mumbles, "We'll talk about it tomorrow. I'm tired. Get some sleep."

I slip into the bed. It's soft and inviting, the covers plush against my skin. My thoughts, however, are chaotic and restless, causing me to toss and turn. The silence in the room is deafening, only broken by the sound of my own uneven breathing. I won't get much sleep tonight.

—-

I must have fallen asleep at some point, because I wake up to an empty bed, just as it was when I materialized here yesterday. I instantly panic and flip over to face the rest of the suite, then notice Hanna sitting silently at the dining table, with two bowls of food and two cups of warm liquid in front of her.

"Hi Chloe, ready for breakfast?" Hanna is smiling, but it seems forced.

I saunter out of bed and over to the table, taking the seat opposite her. I raise the cup to my mouth and take a small sip of the lukewarm beverage. "What happened yesterday? Why did you block me on Hivemind?" I ask after placing my cup down in front of me.

Hanna is silent for a few seconds too long. When she speaks, it's a little too blunt for my liking. "I was with a friend."

"You don't have any friends." I snap back.

"I guess I won't beat around the bush then. This isn't working. Whatever this is." She makes a circular gesture with her hand between the two of us.

It feels like my stomach has dropped to the floor. "Oh."

"I get that you have a mission, or whatever, some noble goal you're working towards, but I can't tolerate it anymore. I barely ever get to see you. When I do, you won't stop talking about the other place."

I sputter, "Why don't you just come over there with me sometime, see it for yourself? You might understand?"

"What is the point, Chloe? We live **here**. You were born **here**. It's great **here**. You can simulate that shithole of a world all you want with Hivemind. Why can't we just live here in peace, together?"

I would never expect Hanna to act this selfishly. This is a side of her I've never seen before. "There are real people there, Hanna. Suffering. Billions of them."

"You think you can save them all? Or any of them? Come on. It's a pipe dream. Every time you head over there, I half expect you to never return. I picture you dead on a street somewhere. Every single time. I can't handle that anymore. It's safe here. Stay here, with me."

"You know I can't do that. People there are counting on me. I'm part of something big, and important, Hanna. Haven't you listened to anything I've said before?"

"Honestly, no. I tune out every time."

Her cold tone makes tears flow down my face. I realize now that this relationship is over. There's no saving it. "So that's it then, Hanna? You're done? If I don't stay here permanently, it's over?"

"Yes."

"You sound exactly like my mom before she abandoned me and my dad. At least you have the guts to say this in person, I'll give you that much. She was saying the exact same things, Hanna. Word for word, to my dad. How could you do this to me?" My face is hot and red, my cheeks tinged with a deep shade of crimson. I can feel the wetness on my skin from my tears.

"That's why your mom left?" She pauses while I wipe away a tear. "You've never told me that."

I snap my head towards her, unleashing a surge of emotions without constraint now. "Does it change anything?"

After an uncomfortable silence and a fierce stare from me, Hanna says, "No. It doesn't. I'm sorry. I have to go."

Just like that, she's gone.

—-

I spend the next three days holed up in the couple's suite. I'm supposed to vacate it and switch to a sleep pod now that I'm single, but I hope Hivemind will give me some leniency. I'm correct.

I rotate between crying and sleeping, on and off, for these three days. I haven't eaten a single bite of food. I have to force myself to drink some water so I won't die of thirst. I keep replaying my conversation, my fight, with Hanna, over and over. I know from her tone that Hanna was truly done. I don't even want to try to reach out. Deep down, I've known that something has been boiling over in Hanna for quite a while now.

I can't help but wonder if the mission is truly worth this sacrifice. Hanna was someone who I wanted to spend all of my time with. I could imagine us being together for a long time; maybe forever, becoming much more than just friends. But not anymore. I've avoided the writing on the wall for too long. I didn't do what I would have needed to do to save our relationship. I wish I could have mustered up the courage to break the stupid watch wrapped around my wrist, but there's no chance of that ever happening.

After it seems like every tear has been drained from my body, I finally decide that it's time to leave my cave. I step into the bathroom for a much-needed shower, put on a fresh pair of clothes, and head out into the blank white hallway of Utopia.

I ask, "Hivemind, is my alt-dad around?"

"*Maximus Karlson is not in Utopia at the moment.*" Hivemind's response comes from inside my head.

I've been AWOL for three days, I know I need to check in with the Freedom Fighters. It's time to head over to Dystopia. I grab a snack for later from a Hivemind terminal, carefully stash it in my pocket, and head to the nearest private space; a restroom. I set the watch to New York time, wind it enough to give myself a few hours in the other world, and then press the crown inwards, disappearing instantly.

I pop into Jackie's apartment, as usual. There's no one in the living room or kitchen. Hivemind startles me.

"Chloe, Jackie would like to talk to you. Should I connect you?"

That's troubling. Jackie must have set Hivemind to notify her as soon as I appeared in Dystopia, since the message came through so fast. "Yes, Hivemind. Let me talk to her."

Jackie's voice appears in my head. *"Chloe, you're here? Are you okay?"*

"I'm fine Jackie, what's going on?"

"We'll be there in ten minutes, sit tight."

After exactly ten minutes, Jackie rushes into the living room of her apartment, with Christoph following close behind. She runs over to me and pulls me up and out of the chair I've been sitting in, squeezing me a little too hard with a bear hug. After we separate, even Christoph comes over for a hug, which he's never done before. I examine his aging face as he leans towards me. There's a look of concern plastered across it.

"I'm sorry I've been gone for a few days, I've been dealing with a few things," I admit to Jackie and Christoph. I sit back down, and the other two take their seats as well.

Jackie speaks up, "We've had zero communication with Utopia for the last couple of days, we had no idea what was going on. I'm just glad you're okay!"

Christoph speaks up, "You haven't looked at the news, have you Chloe?" He looks at the TV in the corner, which is turned off.

"No... why? And why didn't you have any contact with Utopia? Couldn't my alt-dad just... oh." I know what happened now.

"I'm so sorry, sweetie. Maximus passed away two days ago."

Chapter 30

"You're it!"

"No, you didn't tag me!"

Me and Max's mom, Joanne, are watching a group of children play in the grass in front of us. Joanne's eyes are welling up with tears. She's trying her hardest to hold them back.

"It'll be alright, Joanne. We knew this was coming. At least it wasn't a blindside. When my dad died last year, it hurt a lot, but it was much easier to deal with since I knew it would happen, eventually."

Joanne wipes her eyes with the sleeve of her blouse. "I know, I just wish I could have spent one last day with him before he died. I hadn't seen him for weeks."

"How is Max handling it?"

"Oh, he doesn't even care. At least he's not showing it if he does. I don't blame him. As far as he knows, his dad abandoned him when he was a young child."

"Well, he technically did, didn't he? Even though he had a good reason for it? That doesn't change what Max thinks about him."

"I hate how much I've had to lie to him all these years. I know we all decided that this would be the best way to get him on board with the movement, but I can't stand lying to my son."

A pair of women pushing strollers pass in front of me and Joanne. It's a warm afternoon in early autumn, and the park is busy with people enjoying the weather. A large group has gathered at the other end of the park. They seem to be celebrating someone's birthday.

"The watch is safe, right? It didn't fall into the wrong hands?" I ask.

Joanne turns to face me. "The lawyers have it. There's a ton of paperwork that has to be done before it can be passed on to Max. I still don't know if he'll even accept it, though, especially after his attitude around his father's death."

"If it's anything like my experience, he won't be able to avoid it. I felt instantly drawn to my dad's watch when he died. It felt like it was pulling me in. Just get Max in the same room with it. The watch will do the rest. I'm sure of that."

"It has to work for him, right? If it doesn't, the entire movement will grind to a halt. A setback like that could kill all momentum. We're still nowhere near close enough to being ready to deploy Implants in this world."

"I don't see why it wouldn't. We had those same doubts before my dad died. But the watch works the same for me. I can still bring people from Utopia to here, so Max should be able to bring people from here to Utopia."

"I'm just worried I won't be able to go back there. I miss it already. It's so much nicer than this world. I feel trapped."

"Hopefully soon enough you'll feel more comfortable in your own world. If the mission succeeds, of course."

A black crow perches itself on the garbage can on the opposite side of the path from where Joanne and I are sitting and starts pecking at a discarded potato chip bag. The garbage can is overflowing with candy wrappers, plastic to-go containers, and single-use coffee cups; there's a pile around the base. A grizzled man in tattered clothes is sleeping in the shade of a tree a few feet to our right, with a shopping cart full of blankets, clothes, and trinkets next to him. I look at Joanne, who is squinting at something in the distance. Following her gaze, I see a digital billboard that's shining so bright through the midday sun that I have to narrow my eyes to see at it as well. It's displaying an advertisement for bulletproof backpack inserts for schoolchildren.

Joanne sighs.

Chapter 31

"How are you holding up, cutie?"

I snap out of my daze and look over at Jackie. I've been distracted, I hadn't even noticed that the movie we were watching has ended. "Oh, you know. Holding it together."

I've been hanging out with Jackie a lot this week, considering I don't have Hanna or my alt-dad to spend time with anymore. I feel safe, and most of all, comfortable, in Jackie's presence. I just received word from Joanne that Max now has the watch in his possession, so I've been growing increasingly anxious, waiting for him to figure out how it works.

"Are you spending the night here again? Should I get the pillows and blankets and set up the couch for you?" Jackie asks.

"No, not tonight. My watch is gonna stop in a few minutes and then I'm out of here, I'll sleep in Utopia tonight."

"No worries. I hope you know that you're welcome to stay here anytime, and not just because of what happened a few weeks ago. It's not a pity thing, I quite like having you around."

Jackie seems to be staring at me differently. Has she always looked at me this way? Or am I just noticing it now that Hanna is out of my life? "I like being around you too. It makes me feel safe, and comfortable." I can feel my cheeks turning red.

Jackie continues to stare at me. She places her hand on my thigh, right above my knee. She asks me, "How much time do you have left?"

I nervously check my watch. "Only a couple minutes, I think." She leans in closer, her hand gripping my thigh tightly. Her face draws nearer to mine, so I tilt my head toward hers and close my eyes, ready for a kiss.

"Oh my god, Chloe, no!" I open my eyes to see Jackie shooting up out of her seat.

"I'm sorry, I'm sorry, I'm sorry, I thought you were trying to kiss me." Shame envelops me like a thick fog, blurring my vision and making my cheeks burn with humiliation. I long to disappear into the earth, to escape the weight of my mortifying mistake.

"I was just slowly standing up. My feet fell asleep from sitting this way, I was leaning on you for support. Why did you try to kiss me back if that's what you thought?"

"I guess I mis-, uh, misjudged things. Won't happen again, I promise." I can't look Jackie in the eyes.

"This is a problem, Chloe. We're like co-workers. Also, you're a kid, and I'm an adult!"

She's never belittled me like this before. "I'm not a kid, I turn eighteen in a week."

"You know what I mean. This is wildly inappropriate. I'm sorry if I lead you on somehow, but you're like a little sister to me! This is the last thing I thought would happen!"

I'm at a complete loss for words. I can't think of a single thing to say.

Jackie turns her back to me. "I think we need some time apart. I could get in a lot of trouble for this. This kind of drama can kill the momentum of a movement like ours completely."

"Wow, that seems like an overreaction." Now I'm just straight-up pissed, and I rise up from the couch, staring Jackie right in the eyes when she turns her head to look at me. "It was a schoolgirl crush, get over yourself."

"How long have you had these feelings? I've known you since you were sixteen!"

"Don't worry about it. You're the adult in the room, you've made that quite clear, so act like one. We can forget this ever happened, and get back to work. Okay?"

"Listen, I'm serious, I think we need some time apart. I know you're still broken up about Maximus-"

I interrupt her. "You don't know the half of it."

"What? What else is going on?"

"Everyone in my life that I've grown close to has abandoned me. At least my dads had a valid reason, they fucking died." My wrist is starting to tingle, like tiny needles pricking my skin.

"Who else has abandoned you? Hanna? Is that why you disappeared for three days?"

I say nothing, but my silence is enough of an answer for Jackie.

"I'm sorry, I had no idea. Fuck, this is bad timing. What should we do?"

My wrist now feels like it's on fire, throbbing with a burning sensation, like my face was a moment ago. It's almost time for me to leave. "You've made it quite clear Jackie. We'll go our separate ways. I'm gone."

And with that, I disappear from the room.

—-

Tears stream down my face, blurring my vision as I materialize in the private restroom. I walk over to the mirror and see my red, puffy eyes and tear-stained cheeks. I look defeated and broken. I'm not sure if I can take any more humiliation. It's eating me up inside.

Hivemind's angelic voice appears in my head. *"It's time."*

I reach for the towel on the counter and use it to dab away the tears streaming down my face. I force myself to stop crying; now is not the time. Once I feel like I'm presentable enough, I stuff the towel in my pocket and put on a fake smile, staring at myself in the mirror. "I can do this."

I exit the restroom and check Hivemind's guide markers on the nearest screen. Around the next corner, a short way down the hallway, I can see a lanky-looking boy about my age, wearing nothing but his boxer briefs, sitting stunned on the floor.

Max has arrived in Utopia.

Epilogue

Chloe found herself in a familiar place; a dense bush, with a pair of binoculars clutched in her hands. She lifted them to her face and peered through. In the window of the building across the parking lot from where Chloe lurked, she could see a pretty, blonde-haired, blue-eyed girl sitting at a desk, with a headset strapped to one ear, talking animatedly to someone on the phone. That someone she was talking to, was Chloe.

"Those feelings are completely normal, Jess. I've had them before. Plenty of times!" Chloe heard through the speaker on her phone. She had given out a fake name and had been talking at a lower pitch to avoid detection. Chloe had made sure to memorize the blonde woman's volunteer schedule, just in case. She was a bit worried that her stalking habit was becoming a problem, but she didn't care enough to stop.

Hivemind sounded off in her head. *"His Patch is no longer connected. He is not in this world anymore."*

Chloe pulled the phone away from her mouth and whispered to herself, "Shit." She wound her watch a bit too much; she was stuck here for another hour. He would have to wait.

She put the phone up to her face again and spoke into the mouthpiece, "Sorry about that, Jackie. Where were we?"

Don't miss out!

Visit the website below and you can sign up to receive emails whenever Mackenzie Spenrath publishes a new book. There's no charge and no obligation.

https://books2read.com/r/B-A-PTWV-QEQRC

BOOKS 2 READ

Connecting independent readers to independent writers.

9 7 9 8 2 2 3 7 8 3 5 0 3